Kingsley Amis, the celebrated novelist, critic and essayist, was born in London in 1922. He was educated at the City of London School and St John's College, Oxford. During the Second World War he served in the Royal Corps of Signals at the rank of lieutenant. In addition to his exceptionally successful and versatile talents as a writer, Mr Amis has also had a distinguished academic career. He has been Lecturer in English at the University College of Swansea in Wales, Visiting Fellow in Creative Writing at Princeton University and Director of Studies in English at Peterhouse, Cambridge, where he was also a Fellow of the College. He resigned his Cambridge post in 1963, but visited Vanderbilt University, Nashville, Tennessee, as a professor for a semester in 1967–8. His interests outside his writing include the 'white' jazz of the Thirties, classical music of the eighteenth and nineteenth centuries and the study of detective fiction and science fiction, on which he is a considerable authority.

Kingsley Amis is married to the novelist Elizabeth Jane Howard.

The Alteration:

'Mr Amis is attempting a work far outside his previous range and it is exhilarating to watch him ... The castration theme is kept clear of comic or prurient suggestion, but it does prompt some entertaining exposition of the importance, delightfulness and absurdity of copulation'
Michael Irwin, *Times Literary Supplement*

'It is very funny ... Mr Amis d............
than anyone'
Robert Nye, *The Guardian*

Also by Kingsley Amis

Fiction

Lucky Jim
That Uncertain Feeling
I Like It Here
Take a Girl Like You
One Fat Englishman
The Anti-Death League
I Want It Now
The Green Man
Girl, 20
The Riverside Villas Murder
Ending Up

Short Stories

My Enemy's Enemy

Poetry

A Case of Samples (Poems 1946–56)
A Look Round the Estate (Poems 1957–67)

Non-Fiction

New Maps of Hell: A Survey of Science Fiction
The James Bond Dossier
What Became of Jane Austen? And Other Questions
On Drink
Rudyard Kipling and His World

With Robert Conquest

Spectrum I, II, III, IV, V (science fiction)
The Egyptologists

Kingsley Amis

The Alteration

TRIAD PANTHER

Published in 1978 by Triad/Panther Books
Frogmore, St Albans, Herts AL2 2NF
Reprinted 1978 (twice)

ISBN 0 586 04496 5

Triad Paperbacks Ltd is an imprint of
Chatto, Bodley Head & Jonathan Cape Ltd and
Granada Publishing Ltd

First published in Great Britain by Jonathan Cape Ltd 1976
Copyright © Kingsley Amis 1976

Made and printed in Great Britain by
Richard Clay (The Chaucer Press) Ltd
Bungay, Suffolk
Set in Linotype Granjon

To Joanna and Terry Kilmartin

CHAPTER ONE

Hubert Anvil's voice rose above the sound of the choir and full orchestra, reaching the vertex of the loftiest dome in the Old World and the western doors of the longest nave in Christendom. For this was the Cathedral Basilica of St George at Coverley, the mother church of all England and of the English Empire overseas. That bright May afternoon it was as full as it had ever been in the three centuries since its consecration, and it would scarcely have held a more distinguished assembly at any time: the young King William V himself; the kings of Portugal, of Naples, of Sweden, of Lithuania and a dozen other realms; the Crown Prince of Muscovy and the Dauphin; the brother of the Emperor of Almaigne; the viceroys of India, New Spain and Brazil; the High Christian Delegate of the Sultan-Calif of Turkey; the Vicar-General of the Emperor Patriarch of Candia; the incumbent Archbishop of Canterbury, Primate of United England; no fewer than twelve cardinals, together with less preeminent clergy from all over the Catholic world – these and thousands besides had congregated for the laying-to-rest of His Most Devout Majesty, King Stephen III of England and her empire.

He had been a good king, worthy of his distinction in matters of faith and observances, enjoying mutually-respectful relations with both Convocation and the Papal Cure, held in tender affection by the people. A large number of those attending his Requiem Mass would have been moved as much by a sense of personal loss as by simple duty or the desire to assist at a great occasion. Just as many, perhaps, were put in awe by the size and richness of the setting. Apart from Wren's magnificent dome, the most renowned of the sights to be seen was the vast Turner ceiling in commemoration of the Holy Victory, the fruit of four and a half years' virtually uninterrupted work; there was nothing like it anywhere. The western window by Gainsborough, beginning to blaze now as the sun first caught it, showed the birth of St Helena, mother of Constantine the Great, at Colchester. Along the south wall ran Blake's still-brilliant frescoes depicting St Augustine's progress through England. Holman Hunt's oil-painting of the martyrdom of St George was less celebrated for its merits than for the tale of the artist's journey to Palestine in the hope of securing authenticity for his setting; and one of the latest additions, the Ecce Homo mosaic by David Hockney, had attracted downright adverse criticism for its excessively traditionalist, almost archaizing style. But only admiration had ever attended – to take a diverse selection – the William Morris spandrels on the transept arches, the unique chryselephantine pyx, the gift of an archbishop of Zululand, above the high altar, and Epstone's massive marble Pietà.

To few but the tone-deaf, the music must have been far more immediate than any or all of these objects: Mozart's Second Requiem (K.878), the crown of his middle age and perhaps of all his choral work. Singers and musicians had just entered upon the Agnus Dei. There was a story about this too, that it had been written out of the composer's grief at the untimely death of an esteemed and beloved younger contemporary, but its celestial plangency needed no such eking-out. From its home key of D minor the piece moved through the relative major into the G minor section for solo voice and orchestra. With its long runs and jagged melodic line it made great demands on the singer, but Hubert Anvil was more than equal to them, hitting every note in the middle, moving from top to bottom of the wide tessitura with no loss of tone or power. Throughout the huge congregation all were motionless, and remained so when the section came to a close and the choir was heard again.

Some stayed still because they felt they should rather than from artistic or pious feeling. Two such were the aged representatives of the Holy Office in their black vestments symbolically piped in scarlet: Monsignor Henricus and Monsignor Lavrentius, or to give them the familiar names by which they were known in their native Almaigne and Muscovy, Himmler and Beria. Not far from them, a third man held himself rigid out of a desire not to give the smallest grounds for offence to those many of his neighbours who made no attempt to conceal from him their often hostile curiosity. The Archpresbyter of Arnoldstown was the first holder of his office ever to have crossed the threshold of St George's and there was some resentment at the admission of a Schismatic eminence – in plainer terms, a surpliced heretic – to today's ceremony. At his side, Cornelius van den Haag, New Englander Ambassador to the Court of St Giles, had become too far immersed in the music to stir.

For Federicus Mirabilis and Lupigradus Viaventosa, what they were now listening to was a significant part of their entire reason for attendance. Mirabilis's eyes were open, though they saw nothing; Viaventosa's were lightly shut, with a tear showing at the corner of each. Both men knew Mozart's masterpiece by heart and had the skill to remove from consciousness the wood-wind decorations, the solemn brass chords, the throb of the kettledrums, the surge of the strings. All that the two heeded was Hubert Anvil's performance. Neither relaxed or moved until it was complete, until the supremely difficult solo flourish in the coda had been accomplished, until indeed the final bar had been passed and, at the end of some seconds of total silence, a great rustle and clearing of throats filled the nave. Then Mirabilis turned and looked questioningly at his companion. After wiping away his tears, Viaventosa nodded his head slightly several times.

Outside the basilica, thousands of the people waited in the extensive paved square formed by its western face, the archiepiscopal palace opposite and, to the north and south, the Chapter-House and the offices and residences of the Archdeacon, the Dean, the Vicar-Choral and other functionaries. These thousands had come not only from Coverley itself, but from as far away as London or even cities of the northern shires, most of them by waggon, those who could afford it by railtrack or express-omnibus. They were the early arrivals, and they waited not only for a sight of royal, ecclesiastical and noble magnificence, but also for the Archbishop's benediction, which those other thousands, now lining the way to Headington Palace, must to their spiritual hardship go without.

The sun shone down, illuminating to advantage the rather severe facciata of the Chapter-House, pleasantly warming the multitude, which would, however, have assembled just the same

9

in a snowstorm. On a different sort of grand occasion – a royal wedding, an anniversary of the Holy Victory – there would have been noise and bustle and trafficking, fiddlers, jugglers, acrobats, comedians, balladiers, vendors of hot patties and ginger beer, sharpers and pickpockets too. If there were any such here today, they were not plying their trade, but stood quietly alongside the worthy men who worked in the fields, forests and mines, in the provision of food, drink, clothing or furniture, in domestic service and in that profusion and variety of humbler lay offices required by the Church. When, as expected, Great Dick began to toll, indicating that King Stephen now lay at rest among his forefathers in the cathedral vaults, a groan of grief ran through the crowd and subsided. Again they settled down to wait, until the tall bronze doors of the basilica slowly opened.

At a dignfied pace, the members of the congregation began to emerge and to take up their preordained places along the broad marble steps. Above them, the sculptured figures of Vanbrugh's tympanum, a boldly inventive representation of St George and the Dragon, caught the sunlight here and there, and above everything soared the twin Brunel spires, each of them overtopping by several feet that of Ulm Cathedral in Almaigne. The Archbishop ascended his tribunal popular, and it would be some minutes yet before all were in position to receive his blessing. His snow-white vicuna pallium, and beneath it the chasuble of black velvet adorned with gold, were an emblem of the austerity to be seen almost everywhere on this day. The Royal Palatine Guard in their azure and violet, together with the carmine uniforms and capotes of the Papal Cohort, provided the only patches of vivid colour. None could be found among the people, nothing but the dullest tones of moleskin, corduroy or hessian.

The Benediction Popular as an established Church practice was a comparatively recent innovation, dating back little more than three centuries. It was not confined to the English Isles, but flourished also in the Netherlands, in Brunswick-Brandenburg and in other northern states of Almaigne. To the learned, it symbolized the union between the two degrees of divine favour, the Twice-Blessed, in the persons of those who had received the Benediction Devotional at the conclusion of the Mass, and the

Once-Blessed as represented by those who filled the square; so also the union of the two conditions of society. But to the unschooled of the lower degree and the lower condition, it was one of the most important of the very few ways in which grace could be acquired by an act of will, since it was effective upon those in a state of sin.

The Archbishop proceeded to deliver his blessing. He spoke in high ecclesiastical Latin, a language unintelligible to the great body of his hearers despite the theoretical similarity of some of its forms to phrases they heard every day. But this did not matter to them, any more than it mattered to many of those present that His Eminence's voice reached them as a faint murmur, or to very many more that they heard nothing of it whatever. To be present meant to be within sight of the source of benediction; all that was required besides was to think seriously upon Jesus Christ; on these points doctrine was firm.

The ceremony reached its end. The Archbishop vacated the tribunal, received the King's obeisance, raised him to his feet and escorted him to the royal baruch. In continuing silence – there would be no trumpets today – His Majesty took his seat, but the wheels did not turn until His Eminence was settled in the carriage immediately to the rear. The declining sun drew glaring reflections of itself from the gold leaf of both vehicles, fast-shifting points of varicoloured light from the cut-crystal with which they were embellished. Preceded by two Papal outriders, a troop of the Palatine Guard, their black-pennoned lances dipped, moved at a slow walk before the line of baruches, each drawn by black-plumed horses and hung with black streamers. Hooves, iron tires and harness made the only sound. In the year of Our Lord one thousand nine hundred and seventy-six, Christendom would see nothing more mournful or more stately.

'Bring the lamp over, would you, Fritz?' asked Lupigradus Viaventosa in his squeaky voice. 'This confounded gas gives no real light.'

'Very well, but please finish your prinking,' Mirabilis's voice was as high-pitched as his friend's but turned the hearer's mind to an upper woodwind instrument, say a flute, rather than to a slate-pencil. He took the oil-lamp from its hook in the smoke-stained ceiling and put it down on the toilet-table. 'We must not be discourteous to the Abbot.'

'It would be the very depth of discourtesy for us not to appear at our best.'

'How could the state of your mustach constitute a discourtesy to the Abbot? He has never seen it before.'

'I beg you, Fritz, allow a foolish old man his vanity.'

The two spoke in the language of Almaigne, where they had been born. To do so was a mild but continuing pleasure after so many years of constant Italian diversified with Latin. Each had lived in Rome since boyhood and now held a high position in the musical hierarchy there: Viaventosa, some fifteen years the senior, was director of the Sistine Choir, Mirabilis a leading singer in the secular opero. It was the former's first visit to England; the latter had been many times before. As a renowned exponent of Purcell, he was likely to be in demand whenever the Royal Opera House at Wheatley staged a new production of *Dido and Aeneas* or *Majorian.*

Although it was not a cold evening, both men were glad of the log fire that glowed steadily and cheerfully in the grate between their beds. On the wall above these there hung in each case the statutory crucifix and devotional picture: an Annunciation and a St Jerome with a demented-looking lion. They showed some skill and taste, to be expected in a first rate bed-chamber at the Inn of the Twelve Apostles, King Stephen II Street, Coverley. The room was furnished in conservative Great Empire style: the rugs and heavy silk curtains from India, the jade candlesticks from Upper Burma, the tiles of the hearth from Indo-China, the mahogany prie-dieu from the Soudhan, as, rather irreverently, was testified by the low-relief carvings of lion, crocodile, elephant and hippopotamus.

Viaventosa finished at the looking-glass. 'Have you ordered a public?' He used the English word, which, in the sense he meant, was current throughout civilization.

'Naturally. No doubt it awaits below at this moment.'

'Nonsense: we should have been informed of its arrival ... Well?'

As invited, Mirabilis surveyed the controversial mustach, a sparse, fine growth now darkened with kohl so as to suggest what might sprout from an adolescent's upper lip; then took in the frilled lilac shirt, the purple velvet jacket and black breeches, deftly tailored to hide something of their wearer's plumpness, the high-heeled leather boots. 'Most commendable. You do yourself credit.'

'You also. The wig is a great success after all and those cuffs are most distinctive, though I might have preferred a little more colour at the throat. Yes, we're no disgrace, either of us, considering what we are.' Viaventosa's ample jowls shook slightly.

'My dear Wolfgang, both of us have had quite long enough to reconcile ourselves to what we are.'

'Have we? Would a lifetime be enough for that? I'm sorry, Fritz: this is foolish of me. Seeing that boy today brought so much back to me that I'd thought was safely buried.'

'I understand. I share your feeling.' Mirabilis gripped the other by the arm. 'But we must try to suppress it.'

'Yes, of course. You're wiser than I am, Fritz.'

The whistle of the speaking-tube sounded at that moment and Mirabilis, no less portly than his companion but light of foot, hurried to answer it; Viaventosa took the opportunity to dab his eyes with a white lace pocket-napkin.

'Yes? ... Thank you most kindly: we will come down at once,' said Mirabilis in the excellent English his studies and visits had brought him. 'Die Public ist hier, mein Lieber.'

A public (in full, a public-express) was actually the least public of the three modes of powered public transport available, the other two being the express-omnibus and the railtrack train. All these used the method of propulsion developed by the great inventor Rudolf Diesel. The fuel was petroleum from the wells of northern Mexico, Louisiana and, in the last few years, the New Spain province of Venezuela; ignition was achieved merely by compressing petroleum vapour to a certain density, without the introduction of a spark. That suffix was vital, for the only practicable known means of producing a spark was an electrical one, and matters electrical were held in generel disesteem. They were commonly regarded among the people as strange, fearful, even profane; the gentry smiled at the terms of this view while not missing its essential truth : electricity was appallingly dangerous, both as it existed and as it might be developed. No wonder that its exploration had never received official encouragement, nor that persistent rumours told of such exploration by inventors in New England.

The vehicle that waited at the portico of the inn was a typical public, squarely and stoutly built, bright with brass at its edgings, handles and lamps. Viaventosa and Mirabilis, with the aid of the driver's arm, climbed on the step and were soon settled against the soft leather upholstery. The clockwork motor whirred, the engine began its drumming and they were off. Even at forty miles an hour progress was smooth, thanks not only to the air-filled tires of Malayan rubber, but also to the level stone with which all the main streets of the capital were faced. There was some traffic on this one : other publics, an express-omnibus bound for London, several expresses. (Mirabilis had never got over his first feeling of amused irritation at the English illogic whereby a public-express was called a public and a privately-owned express an express.) And of course, the people's horse-drawn waggons and traps were everywhere.

Viaventosa had strapped down his window and was keenly attending to the buildings they passed. How different from Rome and its ordered antiquity ! That theatre – its gasoliers extinguished on this day, though bills that promised a presentation of Thomas Kyd's *Hamlet* were to be seen – was an embarrassing survival of the Franco-Arabesque style that had been all the rage a century earlier, but at least it stood for something different from the lath-and-canvas structure beside it, a pattie-shop and all too evidently popular swill-shop in one. A little further along, a Court tailoring establishment in the latest ornate style, complete with single-window glazing, was separated by no more than a narrow passage from one of the exquisitely varicoloured brick-built churches for which middle England was famous. Two elderly clerics emerged from its portal into a passing group of young men whose dingily-hued attire proclaimed their social condition. To be sure, they moved apart to let their betters through, but with neither the alacrity nor the air of respect that would have been common form elsewhere. To Viaventosa, the tiny incident stood for much of what was to be seen and heard of England: careless, bumptious, over-liberal, negligent of order.

At some point between the outskirts of Coverley and of Headington, the public reduced speed and turned off to the left. The quality of the roadway soon deteriorated; several times the passengers braced themselves or were sent groping for the straps; but it was only a couple of minutes before progress steadied again and the two were set down outside the main gate of the Chapel of St Cecilia – not in fact a chapel at all (though needless to say it incorporated one), but the choral school that served the cathedral and provided some teaching facilities for students from other parts of England and from the Empire.

Mirabilis handed the driver eightpence, which was acknowledged with a low bow and more than perfunctory thanks. Inhaling deeply, he caught the scents of the countryside – there was no other building to be seen – but also the hint of petroleum fumes, together with something else acrid and unnatural, something else man-made: a distressful product, it must be, of the manufactories that had been springing up in the area between here and Coverley itself over the past twenty or thirty years, most of them engaged in the production of express vehicles, including, most likely, that same public which had brought him here. It seemed to him that he could recapture in full those odours, normal then to the neighbourhood of any habitation, that had reached his nostrils on his first visit to St Cecilia's in 1949, those of tallow-fat, bone-stock, horses and humanity. He was forty-six years old and an age was passing.

With Viaventosa breathing heavily at his side, he set going the clapper of the gate-bell. There soon appeared a young man in the black habit of the Benedictines, presumably a lay brother.

'Salvete, magistri,' he said in his flat English accent.

'Salve, frater. We are guests to supper with the Lord Abbot. Masters Viaventosa and Mirabilis.'

'Welcome, sirs – please to follow me.'

As he stepped over the sill of the wicket, Mirabilis thought he saw a vehicle approaching, but paid it no attention. The Abbot's invitation had specifically said that there were to be no other guests tonight.

The shadows were gathering in the central courtyard, and the pale yellow of candlelight showed behind some of the little square windows. The three crossed a circle of turf, thick and beautifully taken care of, with at its centre John Bacon's piastraccia statue of the saint, one of the most famous English products of the late eighteenth-century classical revival. Apart from their footfalls, and those of a servant crossing from the buttery with two pots of ale, there was almost total silence, with compline over and all practices and lessons cancelled for the day.

Abbot Peter Thynne sat in his parlour above the arch that led from the courtyard to the stables, the brewery, the bakery, the wood-house and ultimately the small farm that supplied the Chapel. A tall, upright, handsome man of fifty, with high cheekbones and with cropped grey hair under his skullcap, he wore as always the strictest Benedictine black, a relatively unusual choice of costume at a time when clerics in his elevated position were given to luxuriating in coloured silks and velvets. If asked, he would say that it was God Who had led him to music, which he saw in its entirety, even in its avowedly secular forms, as praise of the divine. But his style of looks and dress indicated no asceticism, were belied by the splendid Flanders tapestry that covered most of one wall, such pieces as the French writing-table of sycamore with Sèvres inlay, and the presence and quality of the glass of sherry on its marble top.

He rose slowly to his feet when the lay brother showed in Mirabilis and Viaventosa.

'My dear Fritz,' he said with measured cordiality, extending his hand from the shoulder. 'Welcome back to Coverley.' (He pronounced it 'Cowley' after the old fashion.)

Mirabilis bowed and took the hand. 'I am pleased that we meet again, my lord. May I present Master Lupigradus Viaventosa?'

'This is a great honour for all of us, master.'

'Your lordship is too gracious,' said Viaventosa, producing one of his smallish stock of English phrases.

'Now – let me bring forward my Prefect of Music, Master Sebastian Morley, whom I think you'll remember, Fritz, and my Chapelmaster, Father David Dilke, who joined us last year.'

There were further salutations and compliments. Apart from his powerful square hands, Morley, with his peasant's face and broadcloth attire in sober brown, could not be said much to resemble a musician, but in fact he was one of the most eminent in the land, a brilliant performer on the pianoforte who had given up that career in order to devote himself to the teaching of musical theory and composition. His merits in these fields were such as to have overcome the natural antagonism to the preceptorial appointment of one of the laity. He was respected and liked by Mirabilis, who was not at first greatly taken with Dilke, a comparative youngster, slight, fair-haired and given to nervous twitchings of the eyelids, though he seemed amiable enough.

'Some sherry for our guests, Lawrence,' said the Abbot, but before the grey-clad servant could move the lay brother had returned.

'A thousand excuses, my lord, but there are two gentlemen who wish to speak to you.'

'Oh, merciful heaven.' The Abbot closed his eyes and lifted both hands in front of him. 'Tell them I'm engaged.'

'They are the New Englander Ambassador and the Archpresbyter of Arnoldstown, my lord.'

'Are they so, indeed? In that case I suppose I had better not be engaged. Fetch them.'

'This is surely rather discourteous at such a time,' said the Abbot after the brother had gone, 'if my expectations are not too high. But I hear very little good of Schismatic manners.'

What he had heard proved a poor guide to the behaviour of the two New Englanders when they were admitted. The Ambassador's unaffected, manly address and direct blue eyes made an immediate good impression, while the Archpresbyter showed a quiet dignity that could not have come easily to one of his faith in his present circumstances.

'I'll take up as little of your time as is consistent with politeness, my lord,' said the Ambassador when introductions were complete. 'First, my excuses. I sent no advance notice of my wish to talk with you because I was afraid it would be rejected. I reckoned it would be difficult for you to order an ambassador off your doorstep, even one from New England.'

The Abbot gave a slight brief smile. 'Some sherry, Your Excellency.'

'Thank you, my lord. Now my request. It wasn't only my official duties that took me this afternoon to St George's, nor even my personal desire to pay my last respects to your late lamented sovereign. I went for the music too. May I say, Father Dilke, that the singing was of a quality I expect never to hear surpassed?'

Dilke blinked a great deal and glanced quickly at the Abbot. 'That's very kind of you, sir.'

'No more than just, Father. I was particularly struck, as I'm sure others were,' – the Ambassador, who seemed to know who everyone was, turned his blue eyes on the two men from Almaigne – 'by the performance of the solo soprano in the Agnus Dei and elsewhere. That young man has a voice from Heaven. And he's a musician besides. Splendidly trained, to be sure, but there were things in his performance that nobody but himself could have put there – isn't that so, Father?'

'Oh yes, Your Excellency, yes.'

'Forgive me, sir,' said Morley in his harsh voice, 'but are you yourself a musician?'

'I was about to be one, sir, until I discovered my lack of capacity. All that I have now is the most cordial interest. Which brings me back to my point at last, my lord Abbot. I beg the favour of a few minutes' conversation with the genius of St Cecilia's. Then I'll have something to tell my grandchildren, something worth telling, too – I say that with surety. I insisted that the Archpresbyter should come too, as a favour to him. Also to lend me moral support for my hardihood.'

'Your request is unusual, Your Excellency,' said the Abbot after consideration, 'but I can find no sufficient reason to deny it. We still have a little time before the supper-bell.' He beckoned his servant. 'Lawrence, fetch Clerk Anvil here at once. Let him know he's to meet some, uh, eminent visitors.'

'I'm most profoundly grateful, my lord,' said Cornelius van den Haag, 'but I had in mind something rather more private than this concourse, which may prove intimidating.'

The Abbot gave another small smile. 'Your sensitivity does you credit, sir, but Anvil isn't soon intimidated, as Father Dilke will tell you, and if he were he must learn to overcome such weakness. But I'll see to it that you have your private word with him.'

As the Abbot had foreseen, Hubert Anvil was not intimidated by his summons, but he was startled and, on arrival, overawed: not so much of either, however, as to restrain him from taking in what he saw and heard.

There were four strangers in the parlour. Two were New Englanders, speaking English naturally enough, but far back in the throat; the grey-haired, broad-shouldered, elderly one was some sort of bishop, but the taller, younger one with the tanned face was more important, perhaps as important as the Abbot himself. Both wore black, with white linen; in this their clothes resembled his, but in style were strict and quite foreign. Although they tried hard, neither could altogether hide a sense of constraint. The ecclesiastic, indeed, did not want to be here at all.

The other pair were plump, dandified and unhealthy-looking. One had moist eyes and an absurd mustach that might almost have been painted or pencilled on; his companion, despite his pallor, seemed shrewd and full of life. Their names showed that they came from Rome, their accents that they had not been born there. That was normal and natural; the reason for the high pitch of their voices, if neither normal nor natural, hardly needed to be guessed at; what faintly disconcerted Clerk Anvil was the look each of these two gave him when he was brought forward to them – a considering, measuring look. He remembered being in the library at home when a painter had been starting work on a portrait of his father: the man had scrutinized his sitter in something of the same careful but unobtrusive fashion.

All four of the visitors proceeded to make laudatory remarks about Clerk Anvil's performance in the Requiem that day. He was used to compliments on his singing, in the sense not that he was unmoved by them but that he had learned how to receive them, and so was able to make part of his mind free to observe that the most considered comments were offered by the shrewd, pale man and the warmest by the important New Englander. It was with the latter that he found himself standing slightly apart when the Abbot took the rest of the company off to admire his tapestry.

'May I know your first name, young master?'

'Here in this Chapel, I'm only a clerk, my lord. My Christian name is Hubert.'

'Now it's my turn to correct you, Hubert. I am nobody's lord. Being the New Englander Ambassador means I'm sometimes My Excellency, and then sometimes I'm Citizen Cornelius van den Haag, but with you I reckon I can just be sir.'

'Very well, sir. Van den Haag sounds like a Netherlander name.'

'And so it is, or was. My ancestors were transported from that country over four hundred years ago, along with . . . But enough of my concerns; yours are far more interesting. What age have you, Hubert?'

'What age? Oh – ten years, sir.'

To the man as he listened to it earlier, the most distinctive quality of the boy's singing voice had been instantly noticeable but resistant to definition, hidden somewhere among pairs of antonyms: full-grown yet fresh, under total control yet spontaneous, sweet yet powerful. A close view of the owner of the voice soon suggested a word for the quality: agelessness. Hubert Anvil's face, with its full lips, prominent straight nose and eyes deep-set under heavy brows, had no maturing to do; he would grow in height, but presumably he would retain his short neck and the ample rib-cage that must help to give his voice that power. Van den Haag felt suddenly protective; come to think of it, he had felt some such thing in the basilica, a sense of the vulnerability of art. He said,

'I want to tell you, while we talk together, that I wasn't paying you empty compliments just now. I meant every word.'

'I knew it at the time, sir.'

'Good. You intend to continue as a singer, I hope, when you're a man?'

'My lord the Abbot and Father Dilke would like me to.

Master Morley thinks otherwise.'

'And you yourself?'

'I have no opinion, sir. And I need have none for some time yet. But . . . I do want to see something of the world. Rome, of course. Then Vienna, Naples, Salzburg, Barcelona. And further away – India and Indo-China. The Bishop of Hannoy told my father that it's like the Garden of Eden there.'

'Well, nobody is better enabled to travel around than a famous singer . . . I noticed you didn't put anywhere in the New World on your list.'

'Oh, I should have, sir. Mexico. Québec, New Orléans . . . and Arnoldstown, of course.'

The New Englander chuckled, but his eyes were keen. 'Thank you, my boy. You may not know it, but you're right – that's one place you have to visit. And there are plenty of others in my country: New Amsterdam, Haverford, Wyclif City . . . Enough: I mustn't go on.'

'Please do, sir. What's it like in your country? We hear so many strange things of it which can't be true. Not all of them.'

'It's beautiful, Hubert, which nobody believes who hasn't seen it. And various, because it's so extensive. Seven hundred miles from north to south, four hundred miles across in places, three times France. In the north-east in winter, everything freezes solid for three months; in the south, there are palm trees and lions and swamps and alligators . . .'

Hubert's inner eye saw much more than that. There passed before it a series of images drawn from story-pamphlets and the drawings in them, from photograms and facsimiles, from talk among his mates: a lake of blue water that stretched to the horizon, a tall mountain isolated on a broad plain, a river crowded with boats of all sizes, a whaling-fleet putting to sea, a city of wooden houses, a forest of enormous trees, a party of men in furs hunting a grizzly bear, a blue-uniformed cavalry squadron at the charge, a cluster of strange tents among which moved dark-haired women with babies on their backs, a farmhouse all alone in a green hollow. All this was so intense that Hubert missed some of what was being said to him, until a striking word recalled him to it.

'Our inventors are the finest in the world: not long ago, two of them . . .' Van den Haag stopped, then earnestly continued, 'We have no king, only a First Citizen. That man over there is the head of our Church, but by his dress and by how he lives you couldn't tell him from a village pastor. And of course we have laws, strict laws, but each of us is free to decide what to do with his life. But I go on again.'

'No, you interest me greatly, sir.'

'Another time. This place, this Chapel. Is it your school or your home or both? Or what is it to you? Forgive me, but there's nothing like it in my country. We have no need of it.'

'It's my school, sir, and it's as much my home as any school could be. My father and mother live in London, and I often go to them, but the Abbot is like a second father to me, and some of my friends are like brothers. And there's my work, and all the life here, and the farm.' Through the rear window, some moving object could be dimly seen in the distance, beyond the corn-mill, the fish-ponds, the dove-cote: a small, whitish, four-legged shape that hurried, steadied itself, hurried again and disappeared among some bushes. 'I think I'm the luckiest person I know.'

After a pause, van den Haag said, 'My embassy is in London, of course, but I have a house in Coverley. My family and I would much welcome a visit from you, Hubert. Perhaps you might care to meet my daughter, who's just your age. If you'd sing for us . . . Would you like to do that? Would you be allowed to?'

'Yes, sir – yes to both questions. You're very kind.'

'I'll fix it with the Abbot. To whom I must say a few more words before I take my leave.'

Later that evening, in a small dormitory he shared with three other clerks, Hubert Anvil was pressed for details of his visit to the Abbot's parlour.

'This New Englander you saw,' said Decuman, the strong boy with the thin, down-turned mouth whom the other three half-willingly accepted as their leader – 'I expect he carried a pistol and smoked a cigar and spat on the floor and said "Goddam"?'

'I beg you, no blasphemy, Decuman.' This was Mark, who

looked a little like a fair-haired mole.

'By St Veronica's napkin, I'll blaspheme to my heart's content in this room. And I wasn't blaspheming myself anyway – I was talking about what somebody else might have said.'

'Oh, very well. Your soul is your own affair.'

'Let Hubert tell his tale,' said the fourth boy, Thomas, the dark, fine-featured, quietly-spoken one.

Hubert nodded gratefully. 'To answer you, Decuman – no, there was nothing of that sort. Do you think anybody would spit on the Abbot's floor?'

'A New Englander might. They have bounce enough for anything.'

'Well, this one didn't. He was a gentleman.'

'A gentleman! Shit!'

'He was very correct in his talk and manners and he loves music and he invited me to his house to meet his daughter.'

'Now we see, don't we? Little wonder he made himself popular. Hubert dreams of a young miss in a deerskin frock who'll feed him cookies and teach him the lasso and rub noses with him.'

'And a very pleasant dream it is,' said Thomas.

'And if the girl needs eyeglasses badly enough it may come true.'

'Is that a good joke, Decuman?'

'No. Hubert, did your new friend come to the Chapel just to seek you out?'

'I don't know.'

'Of course he did,' said Thomas. 'You forget that we're used to Hubert's voice. A stranger would – would *hear* it differently.'

'Perhaps. I grant Hubert can sometimes sing in the right key, but it still seems to me out of the common, this visit. But then, a New Englander . . .'

As they talked, the four boys had been undressing and putting on their nightshirts. The two candles (one the housekeeper's issue, the other illegally introduced by Decuman), the low ceiling and the proximity of other bodies kept each of them warm enough. Hubert hung up his jacket and breeches in his part of the closet and stretched his stockings over the rail at the foot of his bed. In the distance, a hand-bell sounded and a high monotonous calling came slowly nearer.

'Down on your knees, unhappy children. Pray to God to remit some small part of your dreadful punishment. Ask His divine mercy for the grievous sins you have wrought this day. Limbs of Satan, deprecate the just wrath of God. While there is yet time, beg His indulgence with a contrite heart.'

The Prefect of Devotions (who thought he was being funny) passed along the corridor outside the room, and silence fell, broken only by small mutters and murmurs. Hubert knelt on a strip of matting worn threadbare by generations of such use.

'... that I made no mistakes and that everybody sang well and that the band played well, for all this I heartily and humbly thank Thee. And I thank Thee too that Thou didst bring the gentleman from New England today, and I pray Thee that his daughter will like me. And I petition Thee not to let me become proud of anything I do or puffed-up when men praise me, because I know that everything I do is Thy work. And I ask Thy favour and protection for all men in this house, and for all the children too, especially Thomas ... and Decuman and Mark, and for my father and mother and Anthony, and, oh, I pray for the peace of the soul of Thy servant King Stephen III, and I ask Thy favour and protection for myself and for my soul, through Jesus Christ Our Lord. Amen.'

There was a sigh that seemed to come from everywhere at once, a deeper silence than before, and then again the Prefect's bell.

'Into your beds, miserable sinners. Dowse your lights, and if after one minute I see the smallest gleam the offender will receive a foretaste of the pains of Hell. Into your beds ... Dowse your lights ...'

Hubert lay under the rough blankets and waited in the dark. What happened next, whether anything happened next, was up to Decuman. Perhaps he was tired after the day's events, which had necessitated a good deal of standing and waiting about. Hubert hoped not: he himself was still too elated to think of sleep. Minutes went by before Decuman spoke.

'Hubert.'

It was enough; he got out of bed, rummaged sightlessly in the closet, hung the kerchief on its inconspicuous nail so that it covered the squint in the door, and prodded the rolled bolster-cover into position along the sill.

'Done.'

He was back in bed before Decuman had relit one of the candles with a phosphorus and the other two boys had sat up.

'Now let's see what we have here.' Decuman brought a small canvas bag out from somewhere under his blankets, and successively from the bag four slices of bread and four pieces of cheese. With gestures of conscious lordliness he tossed one of each to his three companions. There was a minute of eating noises. Then, still eating, he said,

'Well, Thomas?'

In the same theatrical spirit as Decuman, Thomas looked warily over at the door, then produced from his bedding a small, battered, coverless book, which he held in the air like a trophy.

'How did you come by it?'

'Ned, the brewer's boy. Of course he can't read, so he must act as a go-between, but he refuses to say where his goods come from.'

'Hit him,' suggested Decuman.

'You hit him. He's fourteen.'

'So. How much did you pay?'

'Sixpence.'

'By St George's sacred balls! We expect something hot for that.'

'We have it – this is as hot as shit.'

'Read us some,' said Hubert.

'Think what you do,' said Mark.

Decuman slowly clenched his fist and glared at Mark 'You may remain as you are and listen, or you may lie and pretend to sleep and listen, but listen you will. Read, Tom.'

'I think it would be best if I told you the first part in short. It's not easy and I had to go slow.'

'Very well,' said Decuman. 'First let us know what it's called.'

'*The Man in the High Castle*, by Philip K. Dick.'

'A strange name. It is TR, I suppose?'

'If you count CW as TR.'

'CW, is it? Yes, indeed I do. Say, then.'

'The story starts in this year, 1976, but a great many things are different.'

'Are they so? We all know what CW is. Get on. What things?'

'I'll tell you if you stop interrupting. Invention has been set free a long time before. Sickness is almost conquered: nobody dies of consumption or the plague. The deserts have been made fertile. The inventors are actually called scientists, and they use electricity.'

'Such profaneness,' said Mark, listening with close attention.

'They send messages all over the Earth with it. They use it to light whole cities and even to keep folk warm. There are electric flying-machines that move at two hundred miles an hour.'

'Flying-machines always appear – this is no more than ordinary TR,' growled Decuman. 'You said it was CW.'

TR, or Time Romance, was a type of fiction that appealed to a type of mind. It had readers among schoolboys, collegiates, mechanics, inventors, scribes, merchantmen, members of Convocation and even, it was whispered, those in holy orders. Though it was formally illegal, the authorities were wise enough to know that to suppress it altogether a disproportionate effort would be necessary, and contented themselves with occasional raids and confiscations. Its name was the subject of unending debate among its followers, many of whom would point to the number of stories and novels offered and accepted as TR in which time as such played no significant part. The most commonly suggested alternative, Invention Fiction, made a beguiling acronym, but was in turn vulnerable to the charge that invention was no necessary ingredient of TR. (Science was a word and idea considered only in private: who would publish a bawdy pamphlet under the heading of *Disgusting Stories*?) CW, or Counterfeit World, a class of tale set more or less at the present date, but portraying the results of some momentous change in historical fact, was classified as a form of TR by plenty of others besides Decuman, if on no firmer grounds than that writers of the one sometimes ventured into the other.

Thomas answered Decuman's objection. 'Wait: what has happened is first of all that the Holy Victory never took place.'

'What impiety,' said Mark, his little eyes wide.

'Prince Arthur didn't father Stephen II or anybody else on the Blessed Catherine of Aragon. When Arthur died, Henry the Abominable married her and continued the dynasty. No Holy Expedition, because there was no true heir to set at its head. No War of the English Succession and so, of course, no Holy Victory. England became altogether Schismatic under the next king, Henry IX, and so, instead of being a place of exile and punishment for Schismatics and common criminals,' – Thomas's brown eyes were fixed on Decuman – 'New England was at first a colony under the English Crown, then, in 1848, declared itself an independent republic, and now, in 1976, it's the greatest Power in the world, under the name of the Union of –'

'Wish-wash!' said Decuman loudly, pulled himself up and repeated quietly, 'wish-wash. That mean little den of thieves and savages the greatest Power in the world?'

Hubert spoke up. 'It's not so little, Decuman, even as things are. Seven hundred miles long, my friend was telling me, bigger than –'

'And as things aren't it's bigger still,' said Thomas with some firmness. 'It conquered Louisiana and Québec and took away the top part of Mexico and it covers the whole of North America except New Muscovy and Florida. Now: the Old World is different too. As well as England, all sorts of other places become Schismatic: Brunswick-Brandenburg, Helvetia, Denmark and the Netherlands. You remember the other day we learned about the Three Northern Popes, starting with Germanian I in 1535, and how when he was elected he said he wasn't worthy, but would serve for the sake of the unity of Christendom? Well, in this type's world, he was never reconciled to Rome – he never even went there: he stayed in Almaigne for the rest of his life as plain Martin Luther. And so, of course, Hadrian VII was never anything but Sir Thomas More.'

'The Martin Luther in the story – why did he never go to Rome?' asked Hubert after a pause.

'It says here he was afraid to. He thought they might burn him as a heretic.'

Decuman stroked his nose. 'The real Martin Luther had more

courage and more wit. He went to Rome and said, "If you burn me you'll have to burn thousands of other folk too, not only in my country. But if you make me Pope and promise the English it's their turn next and so on, all my followers will come round – and if I have to I'll declare a Holy War on Henry and restore Prince Stephen." It must have been like that. Something like that.'

'The Holy Father is appointed by God,' said Mark, crossing himself. 'Not by arrangements between –'

'The Holy Father is a man,' said Decuman, 'and so are the members of the College of Cardinals. They plot and scheme like other men.'

'Schismatic!'

'Fuck a fox. Go on, Tom.'

'I haven't read much further. How somebody called Zwingli preached Schismaticism to the Helvetians. Rather heavisome, I thought. But there are some good grins here and there. One for you, Hubert – Mozart died in 1799, just after finishing *Die Monderforschung*, but your friend Beethoven lived until 1835 and wrote twenty symphonies.'

'I don't call that a grin.'

'Well, the author enjoys it.' Thomas turned a page. 'Oh yes. There's a famous book which proves that mankind is descended from a thing like an ape, not from Adam and Eve. Can you give me the title?'

The others shook their heads.

'*The Origin of Species*!'

Even Mark joined in the laughter, which was quickly shushed by Decuman.

'Who is the man in the high castle?' asked Hubert.

'He hasn't come in yet,' said Thomas, 'but he must be wicked and very powerful. A sorcerer, perhaps.'

In the Abbot's refectory, dinner was over. The servants had taken away the sixteenth-century pewter plate, piled the fires and filled the baskets with apple logs, left fresh candles and departed: only Lawrence remained on call.

Mirabilis unbuttoned his jacket and glanced ruefully down at his paunch. On its inside were rather large amounts of sorrel soup, salmon trout, Gloucestershire lamb baked with rosemary and served with new potatoes and young carrots, geranium cream and, inevitably, Stilton cheese, together with a couple of pints of audit ale. When entertaining foreign visitors, the Abbot made rather a point of providing only the best English fare. In a spirit of polite response, Mirabilis passed over the offered claret and malmsey in favour of the walnut cordial that, like the ale, was made on the premises. He sipped and looked into the delicate Waterford glass.

'The herb is still a secret?'

'I'm afraid so.' The Abbot spoke with what sounded like real and deep regret, adding in alleviation, 'It grows only in the country hereabouts.'

'Very distinctive . . . What of his intelligence, my lord?'

'Ah, we think highly of it, Fritz, and I trust I can say we do what we can to foster it. We've put him in company with three slightly older lads, one of them a confounded rogue, but all capable of thought. And his studies prosper, notably his Latin : a safe guide.'

'He seemed to me a little . . . stolid. Not dull, but not active.'

'That's his looks,' said Father Dilke. 'Poor Hubert – when you see him it's hard to believe that a quick mind lives in that head, but it does. If I put a point to him at practice, he grasps it before half my words are out.'

'Oh, musically, of course, that's obvious.'

Morley had said nothing in the last few minutes. Now he spoke up with some asperity. 'But musical intelligence is intelligence, master. We should need only the music of Valeriani, for example, to know that he was a most unusually intelligent man. And, in what at the moment is naturally a smaller way, the same is true of Anvil. Perhaps nobody has told our distinguished guest that Anvil, apart from possessing a remarkable voice and remarkable powers of execution and interpretation, is also a composer quite out of the common. Later, perhaps, the Abbot will permit me to play you one or two of Anvil's studies for piano-forte. They will answer all your questions about his intelligence.'

'This at ten years old?'

'Ten or so. He's a prodigy, sir. Could anyone less have come to understand his way from Bach to Wagner in eighteen months?'

'Was hat er gesagt?' muttered Viaventosa.

'Anvil ist ein begabter Komponist.'

'Nein, wirklich?'

'And at the keyboard it's the same, Master Morley?'

'In honesty no, sir. Serviceable and deft, deft enough to guide his compositions, little more. There's no conflict there.'

'But there's conflict here, yes?'

Whether by accident or not, the form of words seemed to fit the fact. Morley looked grim, almost glowering. Dilke faced him, his long fingers pinching repeatedly at the point where his nose met his brows. The Abbot's handsome face was watchful. (Viaventosa was fairly busy with a bunch of hothouse grapes.)

'Have you considered this as I asked you to, Sebastian?'

'Yes, my lord.'

'Say, then, but in short if you will. It must be decided tonight. I should much prefer it so.'

Morley nodded. His red complexion looked redder than ever in the light from fire and candles. 'Anvil would surely prove a composer of repute, an ornament to Coverley and to England and with a place in the history of his art. But –'

'And a credit to you, master,' said Dilke in a friendly tone.

'No, Father. He was there all the time; I was merely the one who found him. Now: if it were to happen that Anvil should continue as composer, it might be that he would go beyond mere repute. He might take – he might one day have taken his place with Weber, Schumann, even Valeriani. I can't give you chances: I'm not an operator. All I can tell you is that it would have been fully possible. Is that short enough for you, my lord?'

'Yes, Sebastian, and thank you. But you speak as if the outcome were already resolved.'

'So it is, my lord.' The harshness of Morley's voice was more than usually evident. He gave the two visitors an odd look, one in which hostility was mingled with something like compassion.

'Are you quite yourself, old friend?'

'A touch of melancholia, my lord – it's my nature. Forgive me, I beg you.'

'Why, of course. What have you to say, Father?'

'Very little out of my own mouth, my lord. Hubert is the finest boy singer I've ever heard as regards both musicianly and physical endowment. But my experience is rather limited. Master Morley's word will stand of itself; mine needs support.' Dilke spoke as one stating a fact. 'And God has seen to it that there are those on hand who can give that support. Master Mirabilis, would you care to repeat to the company what you said to me earlier?'

'Gladly, Father. Indeed, I'll extend it. I state roundly that I've listened to the work of every singer of mark in Christendom, in most cases several or many times: I couldn't live in Rome for twenty-five years without doing so. Your Clerk Anvil surpasses any other of his condition. He has six or seven superiors who have what only the years and experience can bring. And Wolfgang here has something to add to what I say.'

'I heard Fritz when he was ten years old,' squeaked Viaventosa, expressing his own sentiments in the terms his friend had coached him in, 'and this boy is better. Not much, but he is better. I remember well and I am sure.'

'Thank you, masters,' said Dilke after a short silence.

The Abbot looked grave. 'It seems,' he said, 'it seems to me that we have a possibility on one side and something not so far from a fact on the other.'

'We'll find that possibility is closed,' said Morley, quietly now. 'But if it had ever come to fruition, we'd have had something immense. And even if not ... A composer belongs to the world and to posterity; a singer by comparison can reach only a few and his voice dies with him, leaving no record behind except in the words of those who heard him. My regrets, masters, but it's true. It's true.' His voice tailed off.

Viaventosa had followed part of this. He nodded, frowning, his eyes shut.

'But are we faced with a choice?' asked Dilke. 'Surely Anvil can be composer and singer by turns?'

Morley said, 'An active career as singer has always in effect ruled out serious composition.'

'But an active career with violin or piano-forte hasn't always.'

'Conceded. What of it?'

'Anvil may be the first exception,' said Dilke, with a quick glance at the Abbot. 'Another possibility, eh?'

'We need none of your jesuitries tonight, Father.'

'That'll do.' The Abbot's troubled look – perhaps it had never been more than a look – was gone. He poured himself claret with a small flourish. 'You've put your case, Sebastian, and I commend you most strongly for your moderation. Yes, I do. But you could scarcely have argued otherwise. The decision is clear. Anvil goes to the surgeon as soon as the formalities are complete.'

Morley shrugged his broad shoulders. After a moment he said, 'Certain of those formalities may not be simple matters of form. The boy's father is of high condition.'

'A London merchantman, with an older son near marrying age,' said Dilke. 'Uh, what of it, master?'

'This of it: he will know, or will soon discover, that boys chosen for this treatment are normally of low parentage. He may see the proposal as a slur upon him, and his consent is of course required by law.'

'True,' said the Abbot: 'Clerk Anvil's case is in that way somewhat exceptional, but then so are his talents. He will be celebrated and rich before very long. That should carry weight with the father. And if not, as a pious man, which I myself know him to be, he'll have in mind his duty to God. Or can easily be put in mind of it.'

'There'll be no difficulty, my lord,' said Dilke, carefully choosing a sweetmeat from the silver bowl before him.

Later the Abbot said privately to Mirabilis, 'If I may ask you, Fritz – do you think we were right?'

'In what respect?'

'The decision about Anvil's future isn't an ordinary one, you see. There can be no going back afterwards.'

'No indeed, my lord, but I still don't quite understand.'

'It's simply that not even the wisest of us is infallible. Suppose that in a few years Anvil's powers decline. There was such a case – at any rate, if it should so turn out, what do we say to ourselves then?'

'What you have just said, that none of us is infallible. Let me put your mind at peace, my lord. There are these, these declines you mention, but they're very rare, too rare to be allowed for, and your duty to music and to God is too great. No, whatever should happen, anybody who knows the full truth must see that you were right in your decision.'

'Thank you, dear Fritz, that's what I wanted to hear.'

Later yet, Lawrence escorted his master's two guests across the quadrangle to the gate and assisted them into the small four-wheeled carriage that was waiting there. Mirabilis gave the man a sixpence – he enjoyed overtipping on his travels – and watched him and his lantern disappear. All St Cecilia's, all that could be seen, was dark. The driver whipped up his horse and they moved off between the tall hedgerows. The going was quiet, quiet enough for Mirabilis to be able to hear without difficulty the little rapid snorts and sniffs coming from his companion. They held a familiar message, and experience suggested that it should be heeded without undue delay.

'A pleasant and distinguished evening,' said Mirabilis with an air of contentment.

Further sniffs and snorts.

'That young priest, Dilke: I must confess I didn't care for him at first, but he has more depth than I suspected.'

'H'm. H'm.'

'Does something trouble you, Wolfgang?' Parts of marriage must be rather like this, thought Mirabilis.

'No. Nothing.'

'Tell old Fritz about it.'

Viaventosa was a fat bewigged shape in the watery moonlight. 'There's a boy asleep somewhere in that place,' he squeaked after a moment. 'An ordinary English boy, with all his boyish dreams. No doubt he pictures himself journeying to Mexico to win the hand of the Emperor's daughter, or rescuing a Christian princess from the Turks . . .'

'No doubt he does, Wolfgang.'

'And steps are about to be taken which will confound those

dreams for ever.'

'Really, very few English boys can hope to win the –'

'Please, Fritz. His youth is to vanish, with his manhood, and his humanity. He'll be what we are, a gelding, an ox, a wether, a capon.'

'And a singer at the summit of his profession, a –'

'Not as great as Velluti. No one could match Velluti.'

'Shame on you, Wolfgang: your grandfather could not have heard Velluti.'

'My great-grandfather did, as a young boy. I told you before.'

'Be done with your great-grandfather, and with Velluti. We talk of Anvil, and I say he'll be admired, deferred to, welcome wherever he wishes to go, above all possessed of something more valuable than any crown: to have as the centre of his life the delight that comes from the exercise of skill.'

'There are other things more valuable than crowns, and other delights.'

'How can you know?'

'I can't know, but I have eyes and ears. And feeling.'

'I share it, my dear: you know that.'

'H'm. H'm.'

Your feeling is too much for yourself at this moment, thought Mirabilis, but what he said, in a gentle tone, was, 'What did you think of the boy's piano-forte studies? Some of those modulations were too violent for me, in spite of what Morley said. Oh, the days are gone when music was supposed to sound pleasant . . .'

At St Cecilia's, the next day was one of leisure. According to Decuman, this was actually a device for extracting more work from the inmates than usual: morning studies began with a solid two hours of Latin during which (so he said afterwards) the preceptors behaved as if all knowledge of that tongue were about to be removed from their minds the moment the bell sounded, and they must convey everything they could before it struck. Church history was similarly accelerated, with popes, idolators, martyrs, heretical bishops jostling one another across the scene like characters in an extravaganza. Forenoon choir-schooling sternly eschewed anything that could be called music and set the clerks to struggle with uncouth intervals or eccentric time-signatures. But, with dinner, the march of instruction halted; Hubert, for instance, was to have the afternoon to himself until his private hour with Master Morley at five o'clock.

Activity on the dormitory floor was intense but almost silent: a reckless guffaw or yell was apt to draw the attention of a monitor and lead, perhaps, to a withdrawal of leisure-privilege. So it was in a kind of bursting mutter that Thomas invited Hubert to join him, Decuman and Mark in an expedition to a pool where there were supposed to be trout, and in a similar mode that Hubert conveyed his thanks and regrets – he had to write letters to his family, he said. But, as the other three did, he changed from the chapel dress to the garb permitted for the leisure hours of leisure days: coloured cotton shirt, a furious indulgence for those limited on all occasions to white, and, in theory, to spotless white at that; loose trousers reaching to the ankle, an escape no less precious to habitual wearers of breeches and stockings; and rubber-soled canvas shoes instead of the constant polished leather.

Decuman gave Hubert a perhaps over-cordial buffet on the shoulder and led his fishing-party from the room. All the way down the tiled corridor to the stairhead, the receding swish and squeak of rubber could be heard, diversified by the recurrent bang of a door, smothered giggle and louder shushing. Soon there was silence but for a creak or two of woodwork as the building warmed up in the sun. It was a hot day for the time of year: from the dormitory window, Hubert had a view of grass and treetops, shining almost yellow in the strong light, and caught a stray sparkle from the distant spires of Oxford. For some time he stared without blinking, without looking except vaguely. The waxed windowshelf was warm and moist under his hand. His writing materials were in his desk in the day-room on the ground floor, but when at last he moved it was through the momentary coolness of the tiny stone-paved hall of that part of the building and out into the sunshine.

He crossed the courtyard and went through the arch under the Abbot's lodging. In the farrier's shop, the ring of beaten metal could be heard; otherwise, the various offices seemed asleep or empty. Hubert paused at the carp-pond and peered through the shifting glare at the mud-coloured mass that showed itself only now and then, for a moment, to be a crowd of individual fish. When the time came, each and all of them would vanish down the gullets of hungry folk at dinner or supper in the Chapel refectories. That was not shocking, or rather it ceased to be so on consideration. Human beings had absolute God-given rights over dumb creatures; it was part of the principle on which the world worked. Less extremely but no less strictly, it applied to divisions within mankind: Christians and Mahometans, clergy and laity, gentry and people, men and women, fathers and children.

At the dove-cote, Hubert paused again. Coos, flutterings and a good deal of activity on foot carried between them an air of urgency, of resources strained near their limits, though whether in the direction of disaster or triumph it was, as always, quite unclear. Then, slowly, head lowered, he entered the farmyard. The duck-pond here was far less grand than the carp-pond, being nothing but a large hole full of dirty water; on the other hand, it had ducks on it and near it, dozens of them, far too many for more than a fraction to benefit from the scraps of bread he had saved from refectory. While he was doling these out, Smart the collie bounded up to him. The growls he made meant only that here came somebody of rank and mark, and soon changed into grunting noises that meant that somebody of rank and mark was being affable to somebody less well placed. After a few moments of this, Hubert heard an uncertain step on the stretch of dried mud between him and the main pasture. He looked up and saw approaching a calf he had become slightly acquainted with over the past few weeks. It (he had not discovered the animal's sex) was mostly white, with a large black patch on one flank and two smaller ones thrown as if at random on to its face, giving it a clownish look. With many a protestation of friendship, Hubert went up to it step by step. He had not reached it when it backed, wheeled away and trotted on to the grass, but it had let him come at least a yard nearer than last time. If he had been a country lad he would have known what to offer – a carrot, a handful of hay – as a token of good will; since he was not, good will itself and patience would have to serve, but serve they surely must in the end.

Calling to Smart to follow, he walked at the same slow pace as before along the edge of the pasture and reached the foot of a long bright slope overgrown with furze and heather. Smart did follow as far as here, but no further, which was quite right, because he belonged to the farm. Hubert moved on. Every dozen paces he turned his head and found the dog in the same position as before, looking at him alertly and yet blankly, until all once he was nowhere to be seen.

At the top of the slope a wood began. It must have been there for a long time, to judge by the trunks of the trees, which were thick and bulging and quite often split, and by the fact that some of the taller trees had spread their boughs so densely as to keep out the sun in patches. This was still Chapel land, the source of fuel for the ovens, and rabbits, pigeons and partridges for the refectory tables. Hubert had no wish for company that afternoon; he settled himself in a thicket with his back against an ivy-covered stump and stared at the irregular tiers of foliage, some of them brilliant with reflected light, most of them in shadow, all of them hardly moving in the still air.

After a few minutes, what Hubert had been keeping at the back of his mind – so far back that none of it had any pitch or duration: it was more like a buried memory – rose all at once to his attention and began to gather shape. But the shape would not come right, not everywhere. There were two melodies that immediately and necessarily involved the same harmonic structure, but they would not fit within it together, and each resisted alteration to make it conform with its fellow. Both in turn proved impossible to drive out. Hubert frowned and sweated and began to feel the passing of time. What he had so nearly grasped was on the point of slipping away from him when the third melody appeared and, in the act of doing so, revealed itself as the air on which the other two were variations. The sooner, perhaps, for having been held in check by his discreditable slow-wittedness, there came to mind the outline of two further variations and a central episode in the tonic minor. Should he write out the whole piece and win Master Morley's praise for his apparent diligence, or produce only half and save himself thought for the next half-week?

He was considering this point, not very actively, when he heard voices approaching along the path that ran within a few yards of his nest in the thicket. An instinct implanted by experience at St Cecilia's and elsewhere made him stay where he was and keep quiet: in this deep shade, he would be likely to be seen from the path only if he were being looked for. The voices came closer, turned into a chuckle and a giggle, went past him a little way and stopped. Then, through birdsong and the hum of insects, he heard a faint rhythmical murmur as of someone pleasantly half-asleep. It ceased, and two people, bending low, came into his view twelve or fifteen feet away at the far end of a sort of accidental tunnel of greenery, and stayed there.

Hubert recognized one of them as Ned, the brewer's boy who supplied Thomas with TR. Ned's companion was a girl, but it was difficult to be certain of anything beyond that because, as they knelt face to face, his arm and shoulder and head were so much in the way. They were kissing, though the word seemed wrong, inadequate to their energy and singlemindedness, to the greed or desperation with which they clung to each other, as if trying to display a fear of being parted for the rest of their lives. Were they playing a game?

When Ned's hand pushed at the girl's bosom through her clothes, Hubert pretended to himself not to notice; when the hand went beneath the clothes, he drew in his breath with a wince; when they were gone and she was bare to the waist, he forgot about breathing. Then they both sank to where his eye could not follow them, and he panted a few times to recover air. What Decuman had described more than once to an incredulous, rather appalled Hubert was about to happen, or was already happening. Why? How could it? This was Ned, somebody he knew, somebody who had never shown the least sign of wanting to behave like this or being capable of it. Hubert was excited, aware of but not attentive to a stirring in his body, absorbed and full of guilt and dread.

Very soon, Ned rose to his feet, still fully clothed, and moved behind a bush with thick, broad leaves on it. Then the girl sat up; without being able to see, Hubert knew she had all her clothes off now. He had a clear sight of her face for the first time, and stared at it hard, eager for some clue. Whether she was beautiful or ugly or anything between quite passed him by. She was looking over at Ned with an expression Hubert strove to read. He thought he made out what he found hard to believe could be there: dejection, defeat, pleading, and a fixity that suggested to him that her mind was on other things. But that last was surely impossible.

Ned came back with nothing on and Hubert did not look at him. In a moment, the pair had again disappeared below the level of his view, and again there was silence but for the noises of the woods. For the first time Hubert felt embarrassed, but this did not last long because his head was too full of questions without answers. He would understand when he was older, Decuman had said. Would he? Did they?

From the ground those few feet away Hubert heard a voice cry out, but so strangely that he was never able, either then or afterwards, to decide whose voice it had been. And what did it express? Relief? Astonishment? Triumph? Despair? Not despair. Pain? No, not pain. Pleasure, then. It must be pleasure: Decuman had laid great stress on that. All this would be something to tell him and the others when the candles were relit that night, something to discuss, something he had that they had not. And yet that would be wrong. Indeed (it occurred to him with sudden force), watching and listening these last ten minutes, being here at all, had been wrong, wrong enough to be a sin. He had seen earlier no alternative to remaining hidden, nor did one occur to him now, but that did not make it any less of a sin: teaching was very firm on such points. What was this a sin of? Impurity was a safe guess. So, although he did not feel impure (in fact rather the contrary, if his desire to forget what he had seen and heard was to be considered), he muttered some words of contrition and then, more and more drowsily, an unknown number of Hail Marys.

Hubert waited for some minutes, still drowsily, until Ned and the girl had put on their clothes and moved out of earshot. Then, distant but clear, he heard the St Cecilia's clock strike four and jumped up, startling a large grey bird which startled him with the abrupt whir of its wings. Master Morley would have to be satisfied with, at best, Theme and Variations 1 and 2. Theme ... For a moment Hubert's mind was quite empty. In deep dismay, he checked his stride and abruptly, without any thought, laid his hand on his chest just below the base of the throat. The moment soon passed and the piece was there again, exactly as it had been. But nothing like that had happened to him before.

He reached the edge of the wood and was at once calmed by what lay below him: the uncultivated slope, the pasture and its herd, the farm buildings, the Chapel in the form of an H with its upper half closed. What had happened in the wood was over, and had never been anything but senseless and on its own.

CHAPTER TWO

Master Tobias Anvil's house stood on the north side of Tyburn Road near its junction with Edgware Road. A generation ago, this had been in effect the north-western corner of London, with Bayswater Station, the railtrack departure-point for the capital, to be seen across open fields. But nowadays, with the population of the city well above the million mark, manufactories were springing up round the advantageous station site, and the dwellings of the people came with them. It was forecast that, within another generation, London would extend as far as the former villages – now the thriving small towns – of Kilburn and Shepherd's Bush. Already, those among the gentry who felt or professed a disdain for city life had begun to settle down by the river in Fulham and on the northern heights of Hampstead.

For the moment, Master Anvil was very well content to stay where he was. The position was convenient. His express took him to the consular district round St Giles's Palace in no more than five minutes, to his counting-house by Bishopsgate in well under fifteen. (It was alleged by his enemies that the much closer proximity of Tyburn Tree was an attraction, but this must have been malice or humour, since no felon had been executed there since 1961, and the last Act of Faith dated as far back as 1940.) The house itself had many points in its favour. Separated off from the highway by wrought-iron gates and a pair of lawns on which fountains played, it was an impressive three-storey building of Kentish ragstone with window-arches and chimneys of hand-moulded Reading brick. To the rear lay two and a half acres of garden in the Danish style, with large formal lily-ponds, an orangery and a small aviary. It had been built by the present occupant's grandfather about the year 1900 at a cost of nearly three thousand pounds, and today the whole property was valued at something not far short of three times that amount.

The breakfast-room was sited at the south-eastern corner of the house to catch the early sun, which, one fine morning in late May, gleamed and glinted with rare brilliance on the white-

and-gilt furnishings. The scent of wallflowers and azaleas, fresh-cut from the garden an hour before, mingled pleasantly with the odour of hot bread. Four persons sat at the long mahogany table: Master Anvil himself, his wife Margaret, their elder son Anthony, and Father Matthew Lyall, the family chaplain. Usually at this hour – eight o'clock – Tobias was about his business, but today he was expecting visitors, so could indulge himself with a third panino and honey, a fourth bowl of tea and an extended reading of the newspapers.

He was forty-eight years old, thin and thin-faced, with abundant black hair reaching to his shoulders after the usage of his social condition. His grave demeanour, in particular the habitual intentness of his gaze, went with his taste for a plain, almost severe style of dress to give him something of a clerical aspect. His conduct was in keeping: few merchantmen were stricter in their observances, on better terms with the clergy in general, or – as was testified by the gold candlesticks and gold-threaded altar-cloth at St Mary Bourne, his parish church – more liberal with donatives. Lowering his black brows at the front page of the *London Observer*, the organ of the Papal Cure, he said in his clear, rather sing-song tones,

'The Turk announces his departure from Greece in 1980. This follows his sending his High Delegate to the obsequies of his late majesty.'

'An encouraging development, master,' said Father Lyall, a chubby, youngish man whose upper lip was always dark no matter how closely he shaved.

'Is it so, Father? Never forget that our adversary isn't bound by his word as Christians are. He means us to disarm ourselves to the point at which he may safely recross the Danube. Already his policy of "pacific concomitance" has had frightening effects. You must have seen that the Papal and Patriarchial forces along the north bank are to be reduced further. And I hear talk of a Bill to be laid before Convocation intended to diminish our own navy. The argument's familiar enough: why should we English exert ourselves in that quarter when Naples and Venice and Hungary do so little? How else are we to show the spirit of detensione? Liberal cant! I should very much like to know the number of secret Mahometan agents among our governors. Oh, this battle has continued for more than six hundred years, whether the state of affairs at any one time was called war or peace, and Christendom will never be safe until the Turk is thrown back by force into Asia and the Imperial Patriarchate restored at Constantinople.'

'I'm sure many Christians share that dream,' said the priest.

'But not you yourself.'

'Oh yes, sir. Indeed, I devoutly wish it were attainable.'

'It will never be attained while there are such as you within the Church, fortifying the cause of the heathen.'

'Master Anvil, I do no such thing. I ask only that we reserve our efforts and the blood of our young men for achieving what can be achieved. And I remind you that there was One who commanded us to forgive our enemies.'

'It was He who advised the people that when a strong man in arms holdeth his palace, his goods are safe; but when one stronger than he shall come upon him, then . . .'

'That's an argument for continuing to be strong, for maintaining defences, not for –'

'My argument precisely, Father. I deplored our weakness and our reduced defences.'

'And went on to advocate the violent expulsion of the Turk. Now attend, sir. The true strength of our Church lies not in armies or fleets but in the souls of her children.'

'By St Peter, I'm glad you're not Secretary of the War Chamber.'

'It's my duty to instruct you as I have, master.'

'Very well, Father, very well. Have I your permission to continue reading?'

'Of course.'

The post of private chaplain to the Anvil family had had half a dozen incumbents since Tobias had been in a position to institute it. Father Lyall had already lasted in it longer than all of them put together. He had seen at once that his employer regarded himself, or wanted to be regarded, as a latter-day zealot so extreme as to satisfy the most ardent ultramontanist in the Church hierarchy and the most Romanist of politicians

– so very extreme, in particular, that he needed constant doctrinal sedation to hold his missionary enthusiasm within bounds. Instead of tamely submitting to Tobias's extravagances, then, Lyall called them in question, disparaged them, rebuked them. The colloquy about the Turk had ended after the usual and preferred pattern, with the layman accepting but not embracing the advice of his spiritual counsellor and conspicuously reserving the right to return to the charge at any more or less appropriate time.

In itself and in its applications, the arrangement suited Lyall. After fourteen years in orders he felt no particular disapproval if a man took elaborate means to secure his position with Rome. He himself had entered the priesthood partly through motives of self-advancement. As it had turned out, his career had not prospered: he lacked both the skill and the energy to make the right friends or become known for the right opinions. When the Anvil appointment fell vacant, he had recognized it without trouble as an insurance of comfort and security. The duties were not onerous: ministering to the souls of an unremarkable household, acting as social secretary, running the kind of errand for which a servant was deemed unsuitable, keeping Dame Anvil company, and being on hand to abate her husband's fervours. The positive rewards included good food, good wine, and the occupancy of a room above the express-house where, thanks to the presence of a separate staircase, young women could be entertained in seclusion. All that troubled Father Lyall, and that not often or so far to any effect, was a resentment against those faceless and largely nameless persons whom he considered to hold the real power in and over his Church. They had not admitted him to their number; more than that, they were not true servants of God.

Rather perfunctorily, Tobias had been glancing through the *English Gazette*, the organ of Convocation: it came to his breakfast-table only because he felt it incumbent on men in his position to have access, at least, to both national newspapers. But again his notice was caught, perhaps more closely than before.

'Attend to this,' he said. ' "The physicians and inventors who conferred on the outbreak of plague in East Runton in Norfolk last month have delivered their findings to the Secretary of the Salubrity Chamber. They state that the disease, from which 88 persons died in a single night, is of no known origin, but that consultation reveals a similarity with the sickness which, in February last, launched 110 souls into eternity at St Tropez in France. In neither case, however, had the disease spread to the surrounding country, and its recurrence was not to be feared." So. Well, Anthony, what do you think of that? Is it possible?'

Since he had not so far been spoken to since the beginning of the meal, Anthony Anvil had not so far spoken. At twenty-one years old, he was a well-grown youth with a healthy skin, wide dark eyes and a full mouth which, whatever his father might and often did say, tended to fall open in repose. He wore collegiate black with white bands, since he would shortly be on his way to pursue his studies at St Clement's Hospital in the Strand. On being addressed, he shut his mouth tight, then opened it cautiously to say,

'If it's reported in the *Gazette*, papa, then it's possible.'

'I'm not a nitwit, sir! I ask you if you think it's possible that a sickness can strike at two such widely-separated places as these, leave no hint of its nature, and yet be altogether discounted as a future threat.'

Anthony could not for the moment see what was the required answer to this question, or series of questions, so it was with continued caution that he replied, 'The two places are widely separated in distance, but not in kind. Both are small fishing-villages.'

'But a plague of unknown origin?'

'All plagues are of unknown origin when they first appear.'

'A plague from fish? Is that what you suggest?'

'It wasn't believed for a long time that other plagues were brought by rats.'

'But rats are warm-blooded creatures like ourselves. A plague that kills in a few hours?'

'Some in the past have died in less than a day. Forgive me, papa, but you asked if it was possible and, from what I know, it is.'

'What do you say, Father?'

'I? I have no knowledge and therefore no opinion, master.'

'It would be useful,' said Anthony after a pause, 'to know whether in truth the disease has not spread to – what was it? – the surrounding country.'

Tobias lowered his brows again. 'You doubt the voice of Convocation?'

'No, sir,' lied his son: 'only that of the physicians and inventors who weighed the matter. From what you read to us, the *Gazette* does no more than record their words.'

'Well said, Anthony – and we know how much trust to put in them. Physicians may be all very well, but what of inventors? Half of them are no better than scientists who daren't give themselves their true name. This affair has every sign of an experiment in science. Recklessness. Disregard for human life. Above all, an inclination to usurp the power of the Creator. Whether or not these outbreaks were indeed isolated, we must fear a recurrence. We're all in danger. And will remain so until our heads of State look to their duty of protecting Christians.'

'Yes, sir.'

The priest stroked his bluish upper lip to cover traces of a smile: he had wondered a little how his master would reach his preferred theme from such an unfamiliar starting-point.

'The case is no better with our spiritual lords,' continued Tobias. 'Some of them are positively worm-eaten with tolerance. The Holy Office must bestir itself and set out to eradicate the ulcers that afflict us. When was the last scientist examined? I think at the very least a letter to the Editor of the *Gazette* . . .'

Before long, Master Anvil had finished with science and scientists for the moment and, after grace and a word with Father Lyall, left the room. Anthony embraced his mother and also departed. The two servants who had attended all this time in total silence came forward and began to clear the table.

Margaret Anvil had likewise said nothing throughout. This was normal and, in a general sense, so regarded by her. What seemed to be exceptional about her relations with her husband was their intimacy in private. He treated her as she imagined he would a valued friend, telling her of his activities, asking about her own, sharing little jokes. In the marriage-bed itself he showed her every consideration: never once had he had his way with her against her will. He was a good man and she was proud to be his wife.

Except in the fullness of her figure, Margaret did not look her forty-two years. She had a fine natural complexion, auburn hair touched no more than lightly with grey, and excellent teeth. A man might have taken her for a countrywoman unless he observed the severe set of her mouth and the diffident glance that went oddly with it. When she rose from her chair her height was noticeable, as was also the richness of her quilted turquoise breakfast-gown against the plain black, white and grey worn by everyone else present.

As usual, Father Lyall was at the door, and as usual he said respectfully that he would attend her in due course in her sitting-room. But, not as usual, she looked up at him as she passed, and found him looking at her in a way that she could have defined only by saying that it was not respectful.

Ten minutes later, by arrangement, the priest came to his master's library on the first floor. It looked like the abode of someone distinguished for both worldliness and piety, being expensively panelled and carpeted, furnished with massive teak and leather, hung with Indian brocades and Siameses silks, and yet profuse in large canvases of scriptural scenes, devotional statuary, brass-edged volumes of theology and hagiography. The two interests were most fully combined in the great solid-silver Crucifixion on the east wall and, below it, the plush-upholstered ebony prie-dieu, well placed (it had occurred to Lyall in a refractory mood) for any occupant whose spiritual needs might at any time suddenly become too urgent to allow recourse to the more than adequate chapel at the other end of the house.

Tobias was behind his vast oak desk. 'Sit down, please, Father.'

'Thank you, master,' said Lyall, deciding on an upright chair as the least unconducive to his making some show of sacerdotal austerity. 'May I know a little more about what you require of me this morning?'

'I'll tell you what little more I know myself. I await a visit from the Abbot of St Cecilia's Chapel, whom you've met, and his Chapelmaster, a certain Father Dilke, whom I think you haven't? No – well, they don't reveal their purpose, but it must be something that touches Hubert.'

'Some misdemeanour?'

'The natural inference, but I'm inclined to doubt it. A misdemeanour grave enough to bestir the Abbot would have fetched me there, not him here. Accident or other misfortune he rules out.'

He wants something from you, then, thought Lyall, but said only, 'And you need me here to . . .'

'To perform your usual function, my dear Father Lyall.' The momentarily heightened intentness of the glance that came from under those heavy brows suggested that some more than superficial understanding of that function might be common to both men.

'Just so, sir.'

'And the Abbot specifically requests your presence . . . Come.'

A servant appeared, announced the two visitors, and soon brought them in. There were greetings and the necessary introductions. Bowls of chocolate were offered and declined. First inspecting it carefully, the Abbot settled back in one of the deep chairs, and Dilke sat on the edge of another.

'I hope your journey was tolerable, my lord?'

'Oh, better than that, master. Far, far better. These new parlour-baruches are really very pleasantly appointed, and the rapid completes the journey well within the hour.'

'Impressive.'

'I think so. Let me at once open to you the matter of our interview, if I may.' The Abbot paused long enough to quench thoroughly any doubts he might have had about whether he could assume that it was indeed legitimate for him to go on. 'Your son Hubert: he's well and happy and in good favour. And more than that. Yes, more than that. It's a question of his abilities as a singer. Now you've heard me say many times in the past that these are exceptional, outstanding, prodigious, and the like – terms of the highest praise, that is, and honestly intended, but lacking in value because they lack any fair measure or comparison. That has recently been supplied. Hubert is, simply is, the best boy singer in living memory and one of the best singers of any age to be found anywhere.'

After a silence, Tobias said, rather mechanically, 'The Lord be thanked for His gracious gift.'

'Amen,' said the Abbot. 'But that's not all I came to tell you. No. Master Anvil, I hope you see it as our sacred duty to preserve this divine gift that has been entrusted to our stewardship. Such is my own view, you understand.'

'And mine too, my lord. Of course.'

'Good. I'm pleased. Now: there's only one way whereby to bring it about that the gift we've mentioned shall be preserved. This is what it is. Surgery. An act of alteration. Simple, painless, and without danger. Then, afterwards, a glorious career in the service of music, of God and of God's Holy Church. Any other course,' said the Abbot, looking quite hard at Tobias, 'would be a positive disservice thereto. The career I spoke of is assured, as certainly as any such matter can be. I tell you altogether openly, master, I'd give much to have a son with such an opportunity before him.'

'You say Hubert's future . . .' Tobias's voice was less distinct than usual and he cleared his throat before going on. 'You say his future is assured.'

'I repeat, as far as it can be. If you'd like details of my information . . .'

'No. No. My lord – suppose for a moment that this surgery is not carried out, what then? Hubert's voice will break, yes. But couldn't he continue then as a – a male singer, a tenor or . . .?'

The Abbot started to turn to Father Dilke, who said rapidly,

'There are two answers to that, Master Anvil, sir. One is that a mature treble or soprano of this kind is something rather out of the common these days. There's only a handful of them in all England and perhaps a hundred and fifty in the whole world. We at St Cecilia's have had none for . . . some time. Most places must make shift with boys of Hubert's age or a couple of years older. But who could count the number of those you call male singers? And many of them are of great excellence, whereas Hubert will come to stand alone. An abundance of music exists that only he will be able to sing as it deserves, as (I think I can say) God would have it sung.' Dilke glanced at the Abbot, who nodded approvingly. 'Your indulgence, master, but this is my conviction.'

'I understand you, Father. Is that your two answers or only the first?'

'The second, sir, is that, if a voice like Hubert's is allowed to break, it never afterwards recovers its distinction. In my father's time there was a boy called Ernest Lough. Does the name . . .?'

'I know nothing of these matters, but continue.'

'Lough was a clerk at one of the London churches, where he became famous for his performance in *Hear my Prayer*, in effect an anthem by Bartley of no great import in itself – all the same, folk would come from Coverley and further on purpose to hear him. My father used to say he had purity rather than power . . . Well, later he showed himself a most accomplished musician and sang as a baritone, but he never attained the mark that he –'

'Enough, Father: I take the point.'

There was silence again. Furtively, Lyall looked from one to the other of the two visitors. The Abbot pursed his lips, leaned forward, and said with a smile,

'You give your consent, then, master?'

'What is this consent?'

'Your signature to a simple document authorizing the surgery I spoke of. I have it with me here.'

'One moment, my lord, if you please. There are some circumstances I must take into account. First: has my son been told anything of what you tell me?'

'Not yet. It was felt, I felt, that you might care to let him know yourself.'

'I see. Now: this act of alteration may be safe enough in itself, but can we be satisfied of its consequences? The chief consequence is not in doubt; I ask if there are any others we should notice. I think for instance of the physical health of such a person.'

'Oh, unimpaired. There is, I believe, a slight tendency to stoutness in later life, but reasonable moderation should forestall that. And the chief consequence you mention shouldn't trouble one such as you, with another son to continue the family name and line.'

'Quite so, quite so.' Tobias was a little abrupt; then his manner grew thoughtful or reluctant, and when he went on it was in a similar style. 'My lord Abbot: when I was a young man, there was a common saying that there were only three ways in which a man of the people could buy himself out of his condition: by letting his son go for a prizefighter, an acrobat or a singing eunuch and possessing himself of the spoils. It may not be true now, it may not have been true then, but it's still believed. Some of us have to live in the world, and it's a cruel place, and I should hate to have it said that I'd behaved like an ambitious cobbler or a greedy coal-miner or a . . .'

'We all have to live in the world, master,' said the Abbot rather sternly, 'and we make with it what accommodation we can. What if you should be reprehended for having sold your child? You and I know that the truth would be different, and not you and I alone. Are pretty slanders so hard to bear?'

'No such consideration would sway me from my duty to God,' said Tobias.

'Or to His Holy Church,' said Father Lyall, but not aloud.

The Abbot caught Dilke's eye. 'Nobly and piously spoken.'

'Thank you, my lord.' Tobias gave a deep sigh. 'May I see your document? Most concise, isn't it? Three clauses only, and a . . . There seems to be space here for a second signature.'

'That of the habitual confessor of the family in question, the parish priest or, as in the present case, private chaplain. A wise and necessary precaution against fraud or folly. That's not needed between you and me, master, but there is the legal requirement. Your Father Lyall will do the office, which is why I asked for his attendance on us here, do you see.'

Tobias gave a satisfied nod and picked up an ink-stylus from the tray on his desk. 'Well, then . . .'

'Wait,' said Father Lyall.

'What is it, Father?' asked Tobias, frowning. 'It's all quite clear.'

'I won't sign, sir, and I advise you not to either.'

'Why?' The Abbot sat up from the depths of his chair. 'Why do you give such advice?'

Lyall felt he could not say he was not sure which of two things was harder to put up with, the Abbot's conversational style, with its bland coherence and assumption of severely limited cogitative powers in the hearer, or his recurrent look of pleased surprise as each fresh piece of evidence of his wisdom or moral worth turned up, but between them they were likely to implant in certain minds a hardy seed of revolt. There were other things Lyall felt he could not say: that he intended to enjoy using to the full this unexpected gift of a fragment of power, a small weapon against the Church's self-perpetuating hierarchy, and, by way of a footnote, that the look Dame Anvil had sent him at the end of breakfast was an encouragement to any and every sort of assertive behaviour. And he did not say that there might be some sort of natural case against mutilating a child for the greater glory of music or God or His Church or anything else whatever, because no such thought occurred to him. So what he did say was,

'We have in our hands the mortal life of a child of God, my lord. Are we to dispose of so much of it after such little consideration?'

'What further consideration would you have us give, Father?' The Abbot sounded honestly puzzled.

'I don't know, sir. It's not five minutes since I first heard of this proposal – how can I weigh it fairly? I ask for a postponement during which I can consult my conscience.'

'I'm advised that time is pressing.'

'But Hubert isn't yet eleven years old, and surely all of us have heard boy trebles of thirteen or fourteen whose voices were still unimpaired. Must we be so precipitate?'

'Father, be so good as to give me credit for knowing something of this matter, which has arisen before in my experience. Those of thirteen or fourteen have gone beyond the age at which alteration will have the desired effect. By then, it's too late. We haven't years to spare, as you seem to imply.'

'But we must have days to spare, at least.'

'Can I be of help, my lord?' asked Dilke. 'As one in holy

orders and – I hope – of good repute, well conversant with the matter in hand . . .'

The Abbot smiled faintly. 'You are all you say, Father, and more besides, but this provision is quite specifically laid down in the relevant Act of Convocation. The crucial word is "habitual" attached to "confessor". You've never once, I believe, had occasion to confess Master Anvil, and Hubert seldom. We must abide by the letter.'

'Yes, my lord.'

There was silence once more. Twice in quick succession the window-fames shook slightly at the passage of express-omnibuses or other large vehicles: the traffic in Tyburn Road was heavy that day. Tobias looked grim, also apprehensive, no doubt at the prospect of again being asked to sign the document and having to cross either his own spiritual guide or the Abbot. Lyall was already regretting his hardihood, and would have withdrawn his objections on the spot if offered any reasonably dignified means of escape. But the Abbot gave him a cold glance and said,

'Would a week be long enough for you to finish consulting your conscience, Father?'

'Yes, my lord, I'm sure it would.'

'Let it be a week, then.'

Nothing was said of the possibility that at the end of that time Lyall's position would be unchanged, and it might well have seemed to be ruled out by the making of an arrangement that Hubert should visit his home at the week-end to be told what was in store for him. As soon as they were alone, Tobias said to Lyall, in wonder rather than anger,

'In Christ's name, Father, what do you mean to do?'

'No more than I said, Master Anvil.'

'Your conscience and so on. How will you deal with it?'

'Prayer and meditation are sure to guide me.'

'A week of that?'

'There are other things to be done, master.'

'What things?'

Rather than have nothing to say, Lyall said, 'Naturally I must consult Dame Anvil.'

'My wife? Consult my wife?'

'Yes, sir.'

'But' – Tobias spoke as one stating a seldom-contested fact – 'a woman's opinion on a matter of this kind is of no import whatever.'

'Hubert is her son, master.'

'He's my son too: that's what signifies ... But again, Father, what do you mean to do? Abbot Thynne is a very eminent man. You can't simply defy him.'

'We shall see.'

'All too clearly, perhaps. But I don't think you mean to continue to defy him. I think this is a sort of game. All you mean is to savour the thrill of defiance without any actual risk. Let me know when you've had enough of your game. You place me in a most uncomfortable posture.'

Good observation but bad policy, thought the priest, and said, with as much fervour as he could summon, short of sounding ridiculous, 'This is no game, Master Anvil.'

Tobias raised his eyebrows. 'Bravely spoken, Father Lyall. Well, I must be about my business. When you're not praying or meditating or consulting my wife, I ask you to bear in mind who it is that employs you.'

A more than usually smart express, its walnut panels stained a dark crimson and its front and rear trimmed with placcas that bore the initials CD (Corpus Diplomaticum), was twisting its way along King Stephen II Street in Coverley through the horse-drawn traffic. Its only passenger was Hubert Anvil. He wore chapel dress with the permitted addition – since he was on extramural precept for the afternoon – of a coloured scarf, and was sitting well forward with the window down in order to see and be seen. The foot-passengers, the other vehicles, the great shops and grand public buildings were all a delight to somebody who lived most of his life within the same stone walls, but Hubert also wanted to be the subject of questioning glances, signs that it was being said or thought of him, 'Who's that young boy in the handsome express? How can he be of so much mark? What high mission of Church or State is he upon?'

Nothing of the sort showed itself. There was little to be seen of the gentry, and that only for moments at a time: the tall old man in the vermilion jacket and pink breeches entering a tea-house, the two ladies with bright bonnets and sashes halted at a jeweller's window – none could have reason to spare him a glance. As for the people, they strolled along by the thousand in their greyish or brownish tunics and trews, their glances moving over him with the same indifference they showed towards everything and everybody, even one another. They betrayed no envy of the attire or adornments of their betters, nor any resentment of the expensive inns and ristorantes they passed and would never enter or of the displays of fine goods they would never own or consume. Well, after all, they were the people, resigned to their God-appointed lot, too coarse of soul and sense to want what their betters enjoyed as a right: offer any one of them a bottle of first-harvest Chichester, say, instead of his usual mug of swipes, and he would not thank you. That, at any rate, was Hubert's father's view. Hubert himself was less sure that that was an end of the matter; and if it was not, he reflected now, there was something unworthy in his presenting himself as though for admiration, something close to a sin of pride. He sat back against the cushions of the express.

After a little, the vehicle turned off, sounding its bell and causing a drably-clad group to scatter out of its path; Hubert forgot his pieties and chuckled at the sight. This was Hadrian VII Street, where some of the most magnificent houses in the city were to be found, and it was into the paved courtyard of one of them that he was shortly driven. There were stone pillars with a blue-painted pediment, an ornamental astrolabe on a bronze pedestal, a great many flowers and some clumps of strange tall grass. The driver helped Hubert down. He was strange too, tall and muscular in trim red-and-blue livery, but narrow-eyed and dark-complexioned; his straight black hair had a blue sheen on it. He said in a strange accent,

'Please to mount the steps, young master, and to use the

55

knocker on the door.'

'Thank you.'

'It's nothing, young master.'

The man who opened the door, though older and not so strong-looking, might have been the driver's brother, but Hubert had little time to consider him, because Cornelius van den Haag, hand outstretched, was striding across the lofty hall.

'Welcome, Hubert! So they let you out, eh? Wonderful! Let me bring forward my wife, who says she must see for herself the person I talk of so incessantly – and my daughter Hilda.'

The New Englander had managed to indicate that formal bows were not called for, so Hubert just shook hands with Dame van den Haag, a pretty, dark-haired, smiling lady in a sober but rich-looking gown, and with Hilda, who was almost exactly as beautiful as he had hoped and almost persuaded himself not to expect. She had blue eyes like her father's, a curved mouth and a very straight nose, and her hand was warm without being moist. Rather to his disappointment, she wore a green short frock cut high at the throat and made from something that could not be deerskin. But of course he was excited and happy, struck by the foreign way the New Englander family had come out into the hall to greet him instead of waiting while he was fetched in to them by a servant. It must be a result of being brought up in log cabins, and was very kind and undignified of them.

'Does this contain what I hope it contains?' asked van den Haag, taking the leather satchel that Hubert carried. 'Good. But that will come later. We have a few minutes before the other guests arrive, so we can all become acquainted. Well, Hubert, this is our home. Do you like it?'

Hubert was not used to being asked if he liked things like homes, and had had no time to notice more about the room in which they now sat than that it was cool and dark after the sunlight and that it had Italian windows opening on to a garden. He looked hastily round in search of some object to praise, but saw only a painting of a bald man with eyeglasses and thick mustache who was evidently Joseph Rudyard Kipling, First Citizen 1914–18. He murmured a few words that depended more on their sound than on their sense before curiosity, all the stronger for being pent up, had its way.

'Those men, sir, the one who drove me here and the one who let me in – what are they?'

Van den Haag said at once, 'They're Indians, Hubert. Descended from the folk who lived in the Americas before the white man came.'

'I thought they rode horses and hunted buffaloes and lived in tents.'

'They did at one time, or some of them did, but no longer. Now they work in the mills, in the fields, in the mines, in the fishing-fleet, and some as servants, like Samuel and Domingo whom you saw.'

'Domingo – isn't that an Italian name?'

'Spanish, or Mexican more truly. Yes, they come to us from all over the continent and further, from Louisiana, Cuba, Florida, even from South America and New Muscovy.'

'Why do they come from so far?'

'For the good life we offer them, Hubert, so much better than they've known. And we pay their journey costs. It makes the other countries angry – they say we steal their best folk. Only last month, the Viceroy of Brazil issued a decree forbidding any further –'

'My dear Cornelius,' broke in Dame van den Haag, 'you imagine that this is the House of Commissioners. Hubert is here to be entertained, not instructed.'

Her husband smiled. 'He knows my weakness from our first meeting. I'm in England only since a year. Soon I expect to be able to speak of more things than my country and my countrymen. Yes, Hubert?'

'Your indulgence for another question, sir, but I notice you say you're in England since a year. That must be a New Englander expression, yes?'

So it was, by van den Haag's account: one of a number of ways in which the speech of his nation had been affected by that of its French-speaking neighbour, Louisiana, whose Indians had turned out long ago to be peculiarly well fitted to serve as nursemaids to white children. Hubert was interested enough to hear this, but he had asked his question chiefly in order to help the talk follow the course it had been given. He knew that his host had started explaining about Indians in such detail not only because the subject was one of his favourites, but also in order to give him (Hubert) a chance to become accustomed to his unfamiliar situation. That was kind, and necessary too: it had been quite a shock to hear Dame van den Haag actually interrupting her husband in public, even though she had spoken amiably and he had taken no offence. No doubt that log-cabin upbringing had been at work again. What it might have done to somebody like Hilda was impossible to estimate. At the moment, her knees raised as she sat on a low stool, her glance neither seeking nor avoiding his, she seemed very much like most girls of her age, only more beautiful. But then she had not said anything yet.

Hubert tried to rectify this when the mention of languages led to a discussion of studies. Describing his own on request, he threw in several cunning phrases about different children liking different subjects, some not liking any at all, etc. To no avail: the man and his wife agreed with him, thought his studies remarkable for their scope and volume, declared that nothing of the sort would ever be attempted in their country; the daughter might have echoed all these sentiments inwardly, but all she did was sit as before and look several times at the toes of her slippers. So Hubert fell back on looking at her as often as he dared. Quite soon, he had decided that the best thing about her was the way her crisp dark hair grew out of and across her forehead, and the next best thing the tiny blue veins in her eyelids.

At about that time, he heard the front-door knocker, and the Indian who had opened to him brought in a series of other guests. Some were quite old and very serious, like bishops in lay dress; some were foreign, with French or Netherlander names and accents; some were children, and van den Haag brought each of them forward to Hubert, but did not indicate that he and they should move apart from their elders. That suited him; he stayed at Hilda's side, and then, just after a pale, curly-haired little boy of about eight had been steered up to him and mercifully steered away again, she turned and looked straight at him for the first time.

He immediately said what he had had ready for the past ten minutes. 'Do you like living in England, Hilda?'

'Yes, I do. We were in Naples before, and it's so hot and dirty there.'

Her voice was wonderfully hoarse, but he could not tell her that, so he said, what was true enough, 'You speak just like an English person.'

'Why not? I go to school in Coverley, and most of my friends are English.'

'But you've been here only a year.'

'That's enough time. My ears are quick.'

Quick or not, they were thin and slightly pointed, and seemed to Hubert more intricate than most other folk's ears. 'Did you learn the language when you were in Naples?'

'Yes, of course – some of it.'

'Say something to me as they say it there.' He was not making conversation: he wanted to hear how her voice sounded with foreign words. 'Say, "I have a pretty blue frock just like this green one." '

'Oh, no.'

'Please, it can't be difficult.'

'I don't want to.'

He thought from her demeanour that his coaxing pleased her and that she meant to yield to it in the end. 'You've forgotten how to say it.'

'Yes, I believe I have. Why oughtn't I?'

'If you've forgotten how they speak in Naples, you must surely have forgotten how they speak in New England. How the people there speak, not your father and mother.'

'Trash, I remember well. We were home after we left Naples and before we came here.'

'Then say something as they say it. Anything – whatever you choose.'

'I don't want to.'

'If you won't say something, I shan't believe you remember

59

how to.' The smile with which Hubert accompanied this had faded by half-way through.

'Have you truly only ten years, young master?'

'Eleven in July. But I'm –'

'You don't look ten or eleven,' said Hilda van den Haag with her blue eyes wide open. 'You look like a little man.'

'Do I so?' Hubert felt himself flush : in one sense he did not understand her, because in his world it was childish looks that were to be scorned; in another he understood well enough and to spare. Without any volition, he added, 'I'm sorry.'

'Sorry, trash. How can you be sorry for what isn't your blame? Now I go to help my mother.'

The help turned out to have to do with the big afternoon table that had been prepared, and in particular with attending to the wants of one or two of the younger children. As she did this, Hilda looked kind in a serious way, and sweet; perhaps she really was, thought Hubert, and tried to find justification for her harsh words to him just now. However she might appear, she must be shy; he had pressed her in a way most boys would not have resented, but a girl well might. He would find her again later and do what he could to make her like him; meanwhile, there was the table.

Here two maidservants stood, not dark of skin but recognizable as Indians by their eyes and hair. By a procedure unfamiliar to Hubert, guests were served with their preferences and carried their own filled plates and glasses to seats scattered round the room. The fare, once again, was strange : Hubert perforce went by appearance and found, on inquiry, that he had chosen pecan pie, molasses cookies and Mexican bridal cake, together with a cold drink called Calvina mint tea. All were delicious. He ate and drank in a chair near the Italian windows, next to a thin dark boy of twelve whose name was Louis, or Luis, and who, having soon established that Hubert had never visited Asia, told him in some detail about places in that continent. Hubert listened to quite a lot of this, though Louis seemed to have had the bad luck not to have come across much of interest on his travels, and, out of politeness towards his host, who glanced every so often in his direction, made a show of listening to it all. He was content: a careful survey had shown him earlier that there was no one present with the watchful yet withdrawn look he had come to recognize as the sign of a possible new friend or leader, and there was only one girl who appealed to him, and she was still looking after overgrown babies.

While the remains of the meal were being cleared, van den Haag came over. The boys got to their feet.

'I see you two have found plenty to talk about. Good – it doesn't always happen that way at these shows. Well now, if you'll give us leave, Louis, I must take Hubert off. We have some preparations to make.'

'Forgive me, sir,' said Hubert a moment later, 'but are you sure this is the right occasion? Your guests are here to enjoy the company and the –'

'My guests will feel mightily balked if you don't give them what I promised them, be assured of that.'

'The young children won't enjoy it, will they?'

'Any child, young or not so young, who does not will be removed into the garden: I've given instructions. So . . .'

Van den Haag's gesture indicated the piano-forte by which, having mounted a low dais at the far end of the room, they now stood. It was handsomely cased in rosewood; more important to Hubert, it was one of the new six-octave instruments by Satie of Paris. Master Morley would have approved, and perhaps shown some surprise.

'This a very fine piece, sir.'

'I'm glad you think well of it, Hubert.' Van den Haag handed over the satchel Hubert had brought. 'What's your selection to be? You can hardly give us everything you have there.'

'I thought you might advise me, sir.'

'No, it must be what you prefer, my boy.'

'Thank you, sir. Then . . . the little Mozart song, "L'alouette en haut", the Schumann, "Nun muss ich fort", and the Valeriani, "I miei sospiri". A mixture of the . . .'

'Of the familiar and the less familiar, just so. May I see the Mozart? Ah, of course, K.308b, the third of the set. I think I may be able to handle that. Yes, Hubert – you shouldn't stare so, it isn't very gladdening – I mean to accompany. I won't disgrace you, I undertake.'

Hubert's recital was a great success. He knew himself he had never sung better, and it was obvious to him why: he had never in the past had anybody to sing for as that afternoon he had Hilda. Yet Hilda was nowhere to be seen – perhaps she was hidden behind someone else, perhaps she was listening from outside the room. At the end of the Valeriani he bowed briefly three times, waited for the considerable applause to die away, thanked van den Haag for his accompaniments, which had indeed been deft for a dilettante, and stepped down from the dais to signal the end of his performance. There were many calls for an extra, but he knew from experience that the attention of an audience of this kind would not remain intact after fifteen minutes at the most. He received personal congratulations from a Polish dignitary, from a priest with a Scandinavian accent, from a member of the Royal Opera House Company, even from Louis; not from Hilda. Then suddenly he saw her in the sun at the threshold of the garden doorway, and without thinking started towards her. Van den Haag was quickly at his side.

'Hubert will need to relax himself after his efforts, my dear. Will you kindly conduct him round the garden? And well-minded, nay?'

Two pairs of blue eyes looked into one another for a moment. Then the girl said,

'Oh, best. Ya ya, paps.'

The garden was quite unlike the one behind the house in Tyburn Road. Except for two paved walks and a circular area partly surrounded by a clipped hedge of some yellowish shrub, it seemed almost wild, although there was colour enough. Hubert noticed a ground creeper with large purple-and-white flowers like inverted bells. He said, pointing,

'Is that a plant from New England?'

'Yes, I think so.' Hilda spoke with encouraging friendliness. 'Many of the plants here come from home.'

'Did your father put it there? It must grow quickly.'

'It was there when we came. My father says New Englanders are living here since over a hundred years. The first was a man called Jefferson Davis.'

'Oh, yes,' said Hubert sagely, and added with as much conviction as he could muster, 'This is a very pretty garden.'

'Thank you. Did the folk enjoy your singing just then?'

'I think so. Everybody was polite.'

In silence, the boy and girl crossed the circular space, which had nothing at its centre, and left it on the further side through a gap in the hedge. They were not the only two in the garden, but nobody else was near. Abruptly, and in a flat tone, Hilda said,

'I didn't hear it.'

'Forgive me?'

'I didn't hear your singing. Well, I heard it in the distance, but I didn't listen to it. One of the little children was unhappy, so I carried him out here and talked to him and told him stories and gave him flowers.'

They had reached what amounted to a small wood, mainly of young trees. One of them had suffered some minor malformation during growth such that, a yard or so from the ground, its trunk leaned over at almost forty-five degrees for another yard before resuming the vertical. Hilda went over to it, joined her hands round the inclined part and hung back at the length of her arms, looking up through the branches.

'That was kind of you,' said Hubert. 'To look after the little child.'

'It was nothing.' She began rhythmically pulling her body up so as to touch the trunk with her chest, then lowering herself again. 'Are you disappointed that I didn't listen to your singing?'

'Yes.'

'Why?'

'Why? Surely you can see why. Singing is what I do best. If you had listened to me, you might have begun to admire me, and after that you might have begun to like me.'

Without stopping her exercise, Hilda brought her head down and looked at him. He felt in himself a kind of tension he had not known before; it was touched with bewilderment and a vague but powerful longing. As abruptly as a moment earlier, but in a different voice, she said,

'Copann a me, thart a precious honest cooly, hoke. Kisahkihitin.'

'What? What do you say?'

'That's how the people talk in New England. See, I haven't forgotten.'

'But when I asked you before . . . What does it mean?'

'That you're honest.'

'Thank you, but I understood that – it was all I did understand. But you said more than that. What was that last word? Was it a word?'

'It was Indian. Now don't ask more.' She released the tree-trunk and stood facing him a yard away or less. 'You don't look like a little man. That was trash. You simply look more than ten years.'

Hubert felt a tingling at the back of his neck. Although neither of them made any move, he was always to say to himself afterwards that they would have kissed then if no one had come along. But someone did: Louis in his frilled shirt and chequered stockings, smiling, swinging his arms.

'So you hide in the woods,' he said amiably. 'Come back to the festa, Hilda. There's to be a game of Old Mother Broomstick.'

'Oh, that I mustn't miss.'

She started for the house with Louis at her side and Hubert following.

Father Matthew Lyall struck a phosphorus and lit the gas-lamp in his room above the express-house. At first sight it was very much a priest's room: small, low-ceilinged, barely furnished, containing indeed only a bed, a chair, a writing-table, a press and a chest-of-drawers in unvarnished wood, a prie-dieu and some hundreds of books. The walls, done over with a dark wash, were bare except for the legally-required crucifix and pious picture – in this case a Virgin and Child identical with millions to be seen throughout Christendom in the habitations of the people. The bed was somewhat larger than one person might have been expected to have a use for, but Father Lyall was a restless sleeper and needed the extra space, or so he would say. The chair was unusually comfortable, but that was no more than the due of a man given to meditation. It was far less obvious that the books, except for a few dozen in unlettered bindings, never left their places on the shelves, and not obvious at all that the press hid several suits of decidedly secular clothing, a couple of bottles of old geneva, and a store of preventative sheaths.

Lyall screwed up his legs and yawned: it was late, past ten o'clock, and supper had not been an easy occasion. That morning, Dame Anvil had responded with a violent display of passion to the news, delivered jointly by her husband and Lyall, that the alteration of her younger son was proposed. At table, Master Anvil had addressed her only on indifferent matters, and so she had had to keep her emotions to herself, or rather had not spoken of them: she had made them plain enough in other ways. Lyall took her behaviour for little more than a piece of feminine self-assertion, and it would certainly be useful to him if he were to decide to carry further his obstruction of Abbot Thynne's wishes; at the same time, it had done nothing to improve his relations with Anvil, who had made it equally plain that he saw Lyall as the instrument, if not the instigator, of the lady's capriccios.

But (the priest told himself) he must not be uncharitable towards somebody who suffered: if Dame Anvil really felt one-tenth of what she professed to feel, she was to be pitied. He would pray for her mind to be eased, not an altogether straight-forward task. Praying for her had recently become apt to turn without apparent transition into thinking about her, thinking thoughts too that ill suited the occasion.

He had taken off his gown and was just unfastening his collar when he heard quiet footsteps on the steep right-angled stairway that ran up from the corner of the express-house. There was a tap at his door.

'Who is it?'

'Dame Anvil. May I come in?'

Discretion pointed two opposite ways: for her to be in his room at night was bad enough in itself, but what might she not do if refused entry in her present state? Inclination settled the matter.

'Of course,' he said.

Carrying a bare candle, she stood on the threshold as if there was nothing left of whatever impulse had brought her so far. The priest hurried over, shut the door behind her and took and blew out the candle.

'Dame, this is most unwise. What if you were discovered here?'

She smiled, showing her fine teeth. 'You're my spiritual guide, Father.'

'Much heed your husband would pay to that.'

'My husband has gone to the gaming-rooms down Tyburn Lane. He won't be back before midnight.'

'The express is below.'

'He walked. And nobody in the house knows where I am.'

'What do you want with me? Can't it wait till the morning?'

'Come now, Father, you know what I want with you, and if it could wait I should have let it.'

'Very well. My excuses, dame, but you startled me a little. Please sit down. And try to be calm.'

'I am calm. I haven't come here to say all over again what I said this morning. I've come to ask you about something I didn't know then. When my husband told me that he and all the men at St Cecilia's, that everyone concerned had agreed on this thing, you were silent. And you were silent when I called it a barbarity and an abomination and fit only for Turks and whatever else I called it. But I've since learned that you had already refused to sign the document authorizing it.'

'Your husband and I had differed on the matter earlier. It would have been improper for me to continue the argument in your presence.'

'I understand that, Father. It wasn't what I meant to ask you about. There was something to the effect that you had some days to decide finally whether or not to give your consent. You will of course persist in withholding it?'

66

'I've not yet had time to consider the issues fully.'

'But what is there to consider?'

'The . . . interests of the child, your own feelings . . .'

'You know what they are, the interests and the feelings and everything else. What could induce you to change your mind and sign? What made you refuse at the outset?'

The answer to the first of her questions was easy to formulate but hard to deliver. The true answer to the second was in the same case, but false answers could at least be attempted. With the best show of firmness he could put on, Lyall said, 'The first concern of us all, as ever, is our duty to God. We speak of that as of a simple and obvious thing, and sometimes indeed it is so. But at other times we have to walk with caution and seek for guidance. That guidance may come –'

'Oh, is that all?'

He did not need to look at her to feel the weight of her disappointment.

'You must allow me to know more of these matters than you, my child.'

'Yes, I suppose I must. One last question, Father. If at the end of this period you were to remain steadfast in your refusal, what then?'

'Then,' he said, with real firmness this time, 'I should soon be removed from the office which gives import to my refusal, and a more pliant person would be substituted.'

'My husband would be compelled to dismiss you and to appoint . . .?'

'No compulsion would be necessary. Master Anvil is an exceedingly devout Christian, and is known to be one. A word from the right quarter acquainting him with the divine will in this business, and that would be an end of it.'

She nodded without speaking. After a moment she said in a lifeless tone,

'There must be some right of appeal, to the Archbishop or Convocation.'

'Right of appeal, well and good, but no surety that an appeal will not be dismissed without even being heard. No substantial grounds for appeal that I can discern in this case. And unsuccessful appellants are not well regarded in our polity.'

'In other words, you'll do nothing.'

'If I thought I could be of the least –'

'Enough.'

There were tears on Dame Anvil's face as she left the chair and made slowly for the door. Father Lyall barred her way, taking her gently by the upper arms. She lowered her forehead on to his chest.

'My child,' he said several times. To begin with he said it like a priest, but only to begin with. When she lifted her face in one of her brief timid glances, he kissed her. Her lips shook, then steadied, then responded, then withdrew.

'But you're . . .'

'A sinner,' he said, smoothing her tears away with his fingertips. 'That's nothing so terrible, I promise you. There are plenty of us in this world.'

Some time later, a voice rose in what sounded like, but was not, a theatrical prelude to a sneeze, followed by what sounded like, but was not, a long cry of grief. 'Blessed Lord Jesus,' said Margaret Anvil without much clarity. 'What happened to me then?'

Holding her in his arms on the bed, Lyall made an instant deduction, one that called for no great cleverness or insight, merely for some experience of married women of the higher social condition. 'It was love,' he said.

'Love? But love is what we . . .'

He put his mouth on hers. They lay there a few more minutes in the dim light from the lowered gas-lamp. The tower clock struck eleven.

'Father, something troubles me.'

'I see no bar to your calling me Matthew now.'

'Yes, Matthew. Something troubles me.'

'Don't begin to repent just yet. Have your sin out. It will have lasted such a short time.'

'It isn't the sin,' she said urgently, pulling away from him. 'God will take care of that. What you think of me is important too.'

'Of course it is. I think you're beautiful.'

'Oh, Matthew, do you? But you distract me. What I must

say to you is this.'

For the moment, however, Margaret did not say what she must say, presumably because, in one quick movement, Lyall had thrown the bed-covers aside, altogether exposing her naked form. Her right hand flew to cover her crotch; her left forearm went across her breasts. Without touching her, without stirring, Lyall looked her in the eyes. Her head jerked away, then slowly came back till she could glance down at her own body. Another jerk, another return, this time to Lyall's face and away again. After a minute of this, she was looking straight back at him, eye to eye, and her arms were at her sides.

'I must make sure you are beautiful, all of you,' said Lyall. 'I may have spoken too lightly, out of nothing more than instinct ... Well, if so, it was sound enough. You are entirely beautiful. But your most beautiful part ... is here.'

He reached out and stroked her temple and cheek. She caught his hand, kissed it, and said in a shaky voice,

'Nobody has ever looked at me like that before.'

'You haven't allowed it?'

'No, just – nobody has ever looked at me.'

'I'm glad I was the first.'

'So am I.'

After putting back the covers and waiting for a moment, he said, 'Well?'

'Forgive me?'

'There was something you must say to me, I thought.'

'Oh. Oh yes. But it seems of less import now.'

'Since you were distracted from whatever it is by my telling you you were beautiful, you may forget it for ever and not ruffle me.'

'No. No, I must say. Here it is. Matthew, it may seem to you that all of my talk of Hubert and the document was a pretext, and I called on you only to come to your bed.'

'That is not so.'

'No, it's not so, but do you believe it's not so?'

'I believe it.'

'Swear that you do. Swear by Almighty God.'

'I so swear,' said the priest, making the Sign of the Cross as he lay naked on his back. Nor was this a false oath: it was a quarter of an hour or more since he had discarded the view he had just denied. 'Now, is that better?'

'Half better. Only half better, because I must talk to you again of Hubert and the document; I must try again to persuade you to help me. And this may make you believe something different, but still bad. Matthew, I didn't come to your bed to make it harder for you not to be persuaded.'

Both manners and policy dictated his answer to that. 'No, Margaret, I'm sure you didn't.'

'Are you? Your voice isn't the same. This time you're thinking. You spoke without thought before. Now, you consider whether you've heard the truth or not. Isn't that so, Matthew?'

'Yes.' Lyall had indeed been thinking, to the effect that only a bold and devious woman would have ventured to raise openly the point about persuasion, let alone press it, and that Margaret Anvil was not bold and very likely was not devious either.

'Say, then.'

'I swear by Almighty God that I truly believe that you came to my bed out of no ulterior motive.'

She sighed but said nothing.

'Where's your persuasion?' he asked after a time.

'Here it is, now that you ask – to begin it at once would have been too vulgar. As Hubert's mother I have a duty to protect him, a duty laid on me by God and nature. But, in this world, what can a woman do? I must have a man by me who will –'

'You have a man. I'll help you, so far as I'm able. That may not be far, but there's something in the wording of that document which gives room for debate, and two years ago a friend of mine was in the Archbishop's directorate. I must discover if he's still there.'

'You said nothing of this before. All was hopeless.'

'That was before.'

'And now you see things differently.'

'Yes.'

This was broadly true. What he did not see differently was Hubert's interests: fame, money, position, divine favour and –

hardly less important – ecclesiastical favour were surely a rather better than fair exchange for the sexual and parental functions: the one would in this case never be missed, and the other, to judge by the families one came across, brought no great joy to anybody. It was now clear, however, that the feelings of the boy's mother, reasonable or not, extravagantly expressed or not, were as near genuine as most feelings were. This and the fact that he was in bed with her had done something to Father Lyall's hitherto lukewarm, half-whimsical desire to flout the Abbot and what stood behind the Abbot.

'When I . . .' Margaret stopped and tried again. 'You said it was love then. You remember.'

'Yes, of course.'

'I don't understand, Father.'

He waited for her to correct the appellation, but she did not. When he put his arm round her shoulders, she looked nervously into his eyes and away again at once, but turned towards him.

'You must be patient, my child,' he said.

CHAPTER THREE

'Will it hurt?' asked Hubert.

Tobias Anvil shook his head emphatically. 'You will feel nothing. You'll be deeply asleep when it takes place, and afterwards – soft bandages, soothing ointments ... For just a few days. Then you may leave your bed and never think of it again. The surgeons will be the most skilful in the land. I talked to one yesterday: an old friend of mine. In these times it's not regarded as a serious action: they have so much experience. There's no risk, even of pain.'

'Where does their experience come from, papa? You told me this was rarely done.'

'With children it is. It's sometimes necessary with ... others, for their own good.'

'Their own good?'

'And that of the State. You needn't concern yourself with them. Have you any more questions, my boy?'

'When will it happen?'

'Within a fortnight or so. By then you'll be quite used to the idea.'

'Yes, papa, I expect I shall.'

'Good ... Well, Hubert, you may leave me now, and consider what I've said to you. When you've done so, you may find there are other things you want to ask. Come to me and I'll answer them.'

Tobias patted his son's head affectionately and saw him to the library door. Outside, Hubert was at once approached by a servant, no doubt set there for the purpose, and asked to attend his mother in the bower at the end of the garden. He thanked the man and, with lowered head, went slowly down the curving staircase, across the hall, through the parlour and into the open. He was trying to think, and finding it hard. His father had been at great pains to make himself understood; Hubert believed everything he had been told, but he had not been told anything about the most important part of what was to happen, about how the world would seem to him when he was a man in years. There seemed to be no words for that part, only for what it was like: to be living in a country of which nothing was known except its position.

Hubert passed the orangery and the aviary, went down the walk between the lily-ponds and reached the bower, a recess in a grassy bank under a hooped wrought-iron framework entwined with climbing plants. Here his mother sat in a canvas chair with Father Lyall standing beside her. Not for the first time since arriving home that morning, Hubert was struck by how pretty she looked, how much like his earliest memories of her. Although he had left her barely half an hour before, he put his arms round her neck and kissed her.

'Your father told you everything, dearest?'

'Yes, mama: everything he could. I followed it.'

'What did he say?'

He sat down at her feet on a three-legged wooden stool. 'That I had been chosen by God and it was a most notable honour and I must be grateful and it was for the glory of God and of His Holy Church. And I should be admired and respected all over the world. But I couldn't have a wife or children. But it wouldn't hurt, being altered. But I . . .'

There were no words again. His mother drew in her breath sharply, as if startled. Father Lyall said in a grating voice,

'I'll leave you together.'

'No, Father, please stay, I beg you.'

Hubert was glad that the priest, whom he thought amusing and intelligent, had not left: at the moment, he would have welcomed the company of almost anyone he knew. But he wondered why the two had arranged beforehand their piece of talk about leaving and staying.

'Papa said' – he found he could go on now – 'that it was a pity I couldn't have a wife, but that there were very many men without a wife, like priests and monks and friars, and I should be better off than they, because I should never want a wife and they often do, papa said. Do you ever want a wife, Father?'

'Yes, Hubert, sometimes.'

'Does it make you unhappy, that you mustn't have one?'

73

'Again sometimes, but then I remember my promises to God, and I pray to Him to comfort me, and then I ... But there are priests and others who are often unhappy, I believe.'

'I knew papa was right. Another thing he said was that he was very happy with you, mama, but that he knew men who were very unhappy with their wives, and they must simply go on being unhappy unless they could have an annulment, and that's only possible for very pious servants of the Church. I expect I knew something like that, but I never thought of it before. Oh, and he spoke of the sins of ...'

'Go on, Hubert,' said Father Lyall gravely. 'You may say whatever you please to your mother and to me. God won't be angry with you.'

'Fornication and adultery. I shall never commit those, and I shall never want to, and wanting to is another sin, isn't it, Father?'

'Yes, my child.'

'What else had papa to say, dearest?'

'He talked of love, mama. He said there were many kinds of love: love of friends, love of brothers and sisters, love of parents, love of children – I shall be able to love children, the children of others. And there's the love of virtue and the love of God, the highest kind. And of course the love of men and women, which is not the highest kind, papa said. He was right, wasn't he?'

'He was quite right, Hubert.'

'Forgive me, Father, but I must know what mama thinks.'

'Papa was right,' said Margaret, and looked down at her hands, which were clasped in her lap.

Hubert gazed at her. 'Tell me the truth, mama.'

'It is the truth.'

'In the name of God, mama.'

'In the name of God and of the Blessed Virgin and of all the saints, it is the truth. The love of men and women is not the highest kind of love and that's the truth.'

'Then why do you say it as if it's a lie?'

'Your mother means that there are –'

'My mother will tell me what my mother means.'

'Hubert, dearest, I can't tell you anything more.'

'But there is more to tell, isn't there? I must know what it is.'

'You could not understand it.'

'Tell me and I'll see whether I do.'

'Very well. The love we speak of is not the highest but it is the strongest and the most wonderful, and it transforms the soul, and nothing else is like it.'

'You talk to the wrong tune again, mama. This time you try to make something very interesting sound silly and heavisome. But I understand just the same: that's easy enough. You mean that what I shall miss by being altered is so important that it would be quite wrong to alter me.'

Hubert's mother burst into tears faster than he would have believed possible. He was not too agitated at this to notice Father Lyall laying his hand gently on her shoulder, nor to find something in the way she responded that, just for the moment, made him think she was used to being touched in that sort of way. But this was soon driven from his head by puzzlement and concern.

'Why do you cry, mama? Please stop.'

'I tried so hard not to tell you, but I couldn't help it. I wanted you to believe it was right that you should be altered, but then you asked me for the truth and I told it you, God forgive me. I tried to hide it . . .'

'Why must God forgive you for telling the truth?'

'There are some truths it can be better not to know. You would have been happier if I hadn't spoken.'

'I think not.' Hubert held out his hand and his mother grasped it. 'You mean I might never have known what I shall miss by being altered. But there would be so many other ways for me to hear of it, and other folk to tell me. And after all, mama, I shall never *know*, shall I?' Getting no answer, he went on, 'It is decided, is it? I must be altered?'

'Yes, Hubert,' said the priest at once. 'Your mother is against it, as you hear, but nothing can –'

'Are you against it, Father?'

'It's better that I don't answer that. But if I were against it ten times over, it would make no difference. Neither of us, nobody at all, has any power to resist what has been decided.'

'I understand.'

'Say nothing of this to your father.'

'I understand that too,' said Hubert, and went on directly, 'I think I should like to be alone now.'

'Pray to God, dearest, and to your saint.'

'Yes, mama, I want to, but I don't know what to pray for.'

'For God's favour.'

'I already have that, as papa said. It might be better to pray for His protection.'

Hubert turned and walked slowly back the way he had come. As soon as he was out of hearing, Lyall said,

'Don't blame yourself, Margaret. You could have done nothing else.'

'If only Tobias hadn't talked of love to the boy. Why did he? There was no need.'

'Your husband is a very fair-minded man in his way.'

'Yes, he is. You did better than I, my love, not to raise Hubert's hopes that we might still prevent this from happening.'

'His hopes? I wonder what they are.'

Margaret waited until Hubert had disappeared into the parlour; then, reaching furtively behind her, she took Lyall's hand. 'It was strange, his saying that he already had God's favour. Was that irony, do you think?'

'No. Only a man could be ironical in such a case, and Hubert is wise enough for his years, but he isn't a man yet. Now I must go and pray too.'

'For Hubert.'

'For Hubert first.'

Hubert's prayers were fairly brief, though they took him a little while to deliver. Even at the best of times, with his mind set on some simple objective like begging pardon for having blasphemed or petitioning to be made to grow tall, the words would slip away from him and become sounds, displaced most often by sounds of a different order, his own music or another's. There was not music in his head this afternoon, and as he felt at the moment there might never be again, but he could still offer real prayer only piece by piece. He asked God's guardianship against harm, then found himself deprecating the artifices of the Devil, who surely had no discoverable part in the matter in hand; he had no sooner pleaded for a stout heart than he began to solicit a serene conscience, not his most pressing requirement. He did rather better with St Hubert, who had been chosen for him out of a so far vain paternal hope that he would interest himself in hunting, but whom he had come to see quite clearly as a grey-bearded, good-hearted old man leading a horse with gentle eyes and a curly tail.

What did God's protection mean? It was not to be regarded (he had been taught) as any assurance against physical harm, though not to invoke it on the battlefield or in a region struck by plague would be the direst folly. The more important meaning, as always, had to do with the fortunes of the soul. God answered prayers of this sort in the same way as He rewarded pious meditations and virtuous deeds: by elevating the status of the soul concerned and preparing a place for it among the ranks of the blessed. Neglect of prayers, sinful thought or action, worked to the soul's eventual disadvantage. But, in the meantime, while it was on the way to its destination, its owner had no idea of what would happen to it, whether it was secure or in danger, what direction the various agencies bearing upon it had caused it to take. Anyone who knew where his soul was going must be a sort of god himself.

Hubert got up from his knees and wandered idly round the small room, gazing at and handling objects of past or present interest: his once-beloved dandle-monkey in real skin, a totum of carved bone that had belonged to his grandmother as a little girl in India, a pair of child's foils and masks, a tennis-racket, a model railtrack-tug and four cargo vans hand-painted in the black and crimson of the Coverley and North-England Line, a set of Turks and Christians in ebony and ivory (the gifts of his rich second cousin, now Bailiff of Estates to the Bishop of Liverpool), an old-fashioned book-cupboard with sliding shelves. His eye passed over *St Lemuel's Travels* and *The Wind in the Cloisters*, slowed down at a collection of Father Bond stories, and rested finally on *Lord of the Chalices*. But instead of reaching for the volume he moved to the corner window, which looked out to the south and west and gave a view of the side entrance to the house.

From here, too, he could see the tops of the inn, the Cistercian hospice and the other buildings on the west side of Edgware Road. The road had been there many times as long as the buildings, since the days when the Romans had linked Dover with St Albans and Chester. This part of it ran along the firm ground between the valleys of the Tyburn – finally covered over from the Thames up to St Mary Bourne Parish in 1925 – and the Westburn. Once, it had skirted the great Middlesex forest, of which little now remained except the hundred square miles or so between Harrow and the outskirts of Staines. There the wild boar was – at some trouble – preserved for the King to hunt.

What Hubert had been waiting for happened: the foreshortened figure of his brother Anthony came in at the side gate and passed out of view below. Hubert waited a little longer, until he heard a neighbouring door shut, then moved towards the sound.

The walls of Anthony's room were covered with pictures, mostly expensive facsimiles of works of the modern graphic school. Their subjects, or professed subjects, were orthodox in the extreme: scenes from Holy Writ or the lives of the saints, with here and there one of the more familiar mythological incidents. The treatment of these matters, on the other hand, often seemed inappropriate, even perverse, showing Salome in the back seat of an express-omnibus with the head of John the Baptist on her lap in a market-bag, filling two-thirds of the space with a caterpillar on one of the roses in St Elizabeth's apron. The case was different with the large, colourful and popular Adam and Eve by the illustrious Netherlander, de Kooning. Here the artist had plainly not tried to furnish anything that might be called a portrayal of our First Parents; what he had tried to do, with great success, could be seen in the relegation of Adam to a dim shape half-obscured by grasses and, more positively, in the treatment of Eve's flesh at the bosom and other parts. The band of hair above her crotch, or rather above the serviceable poppy that just hid her crotch, was said to have been decisive in inducing the Archbishop of Amsterdam to attach the original under a writ of non permittimus. It was of course not known exactly why or how the writ had fallen, but the fact of that fall was enough to cause Master Tobias Anvil to content himself with glowering at the facsimile whenever he saw it instead of ordering its immediate destruction. Now, as always, Hubert looked at Eve with sly enjoyment and wonder, but that afternoon he quickly looked away again.

Anthony had taken off his jacket and bands and was washing at the china basin. He gave an unsmiling glance that was not at all unwelcoming. Without knowing him very well, Hubert like and trusted his brother enough to feel as little constraint as possible at what was in prospect; he hoped only that Anthony would not do as he sometimes did and say things he had just thought of and did not mean.

'May I talk to you a little?'

'You may continue to. About your alteration, yes?'

Hubert was surprised. 'Papa told you?'

First glancing at his brother and away again, Anthony said, 'I think he wanted reassurance that the action is as safe and as painless as he'd been led to believe. He must regard my learning more highly than it would seem. Well, I could tell him in conscience what he wanted to hear. As I can you. You'll feel nothing and be in no danger.'

'But what happens? Oh, I know what the action consists of, and how my voice won't change, and I shan't be able to have children, or do what's done to make children . . .'

'Did papa describe to you in full what's done?'

'No, but he went on until he could be sure from what I said that I knew enough. Not everything, but enough.'

Now buttoning a silk shirt, Anthony nodded slowly. 'That's his way. You ask what happens. You mean inside your body?'

'Yes, I think so.'

'It may be easier to describe what, because of your alteration, will not happen. Elements in your blood we call conductors would in time cause your voice to become deeper, hair to grow,

79

on your face and body, and your private parts to render you capable of mating. These elements come from what will be removed from you.'

'And the same elements would keep me thin and healthy unless I ate too much.'

'Why do you say that?'

'The other day at the Chapel I saw two men who'd been altered. They were fat and they didn't seem well. They . . .'

'Yes?'

Hubert had remembered how the two had looked at him, and understood now that they had been considering him as someone intended to share their condition, understood too what the Abbot must have wanted from them that evening. But there was no reason to explain this to Anthony. 'Just that they seemed sickly. Unsound, not . . .'

'That's no consequence of their alteration. Their fatness may have indeed come from overeating. It must be a temptation to them.'

'Why?'

'My dear Hubert, do please forgive me and sit down. Now, may I tell you anything more?'

'Yes, Anthony, if you will. I want to know about mating.'

'You said you knew enough.'

'Enough for papa, not for me.'

'Very well. Say how I can –'

'What happens? I said that about the alteration, didn't I? This is not so different. I've been told what goes where, and that something comes, and that the something will make a baby. But what I don't understand is why – I mean, why folk do it, why they want to do it. I see that they must if the human race shall continue, which is God's will. But then, as every-body knows, they'll mate even when they must wish as hard as they can that there'll be no baby.'

'True.' Anthony looked up from the drawerful of cravattas he was turning over. 'It's an instinct from our nature, and wonderfully strong. It doesn't touch our reason, so we can't talk of why as we do in other matters. Consider that we eat because if we fail to we die, but it isn't that that makes us eat, it's hunger, a feeling in us.'

'Is this like hunger, a feeling in us that makes us uncomfortable? Like thirst?'

'Well . . .'

'Does it grow until we can think of nothing else?'

'No.'

'I shall never understand.'

'I'm sorry, my dear, but I might as easily explain the colour red to a blind man.'

'So it appears. We might do better with what else I have to ask, if you're not tired of questions.'

'Of course not. Say, then.'

'You've done it, haven't you, Anthony? You've mated? Let's be straight – you've fucked a girl? I'll say nothing to papa, by Our Lady's crown.'

'See you keep your oath. Yes, I have.'

'So. Try to explain to me how it is.'

Anthony had been carefully tying a pale green cravatta at the looking-glass on his toilet-table; now he stopped doing this and turned to face his brother. 'Isn't it best that I don't?' he asked gently. 'It's a part of life that you can never meet with.'

'Then I must discover as much as I can from one who has met with it.'

'In Heaven's name, why? It could only –'

'I want to know where I'm placed. As far as I can. I beg you, dear Anthony.'

'If you must . . . Simply, it's the most intense pleasure the human body can feel.'

'Pleasure?'

'Of course pleasure. Why so surprised?'

'I'm not surprised. At least, I've heard it said before. But I can't –'

'No mystery there at all.' Anthony spoke sharply, but Hubert recognized that the sharpness was not directed at him. 'They do their best to keep it hidden.'

'Who are they?'

'Everyone in our polity. The priests, the accursed friars and monks – though they see to it they're in no ignorance themselves. The preceptors, even the surgeons. All those set in authority over us. The whole of Church and State in every land throughout the world.'

Hubert said nothing, not wanting to prolong this unhelpful digression.

'They conduct a tyranny and call it the Kingdom of God on Earth. Oh, let it go – there's one place they can never reach. That pleasure is safe.'

'Does it happen all the time, the pleasure? During the . . .'

'There is some all the time, but the big pleasure's at the end. When, as you said, something comes.'

'How long does it last?'

'A few seconds.'

'Oh.'

'It seems much longer. It seems to last for an indefinite time.'

'I see.'

Anthony was brushing his hair. 'Let me try again. What's your favourite food?'

'Chocolate ice-cream,' said Hubert without hesitation.

'Can you imagine an ice-cream so wonderful that it made you call aloud?'

'I think so. And it's like that . . . down there.'

'Yes. Now imagine . . . You've played with yourself down there, haven't you?'

'Oh yes.'

'And you like girls. You want to kiss them.'

'Yes.'

'Well, think of kissing a girl while it feels like playing with yourself but it's like the wonderful ice-cream.'

'I must have done something like that before, many times. But it's so vague. I can't really think of a girl when I do that, and I can't think of that when I see a girl, even a very pretty one. I can't bring them together.'

'You must try harder. If you want what you tell me you want.' Now Anthony's manner changed, as if he was moving from what he thought he should say to what he really wanted to say. 'But there are other things that are wonderful. A

82

woman's body, a woman's skin, is the most delightful thing to touch that was ever made. Look at Eve in that painting there.'

'Yes,' said Hubert, not doing as invited.

'That should give you a notion. And yet all this is only a kind of beginning. Something strange, something unique takes place.'

'The soul is transformed?'

'Who said so?'

'I forget. I must have found it in a book.'

'It's meaningless to me. How can what we know nothing of be transformed? No, I speak of the entirely physical. Or the super-physical: a state of bodily cognizance compared with which all other states are – how can I put it? – unsubstantial and heavisome and bloodless. The man and the woman are so close that nothing else exists for them and they become almost one creature. They're closer to each other than they can ever be to God.' Anthony paused, his dark eyes apparently vacant, his mouth a little open. 'Perhaps you think I blaspheme.'

'No, I don't think that.'

'What if I do blaspheme? They blaspheme the name of man and women. And while we live, man and woman compose the world.'

After another pause, Hubert said, 'Thank you, Anthony.'

'For what service?'

'For doing as much as you could to answer my questions.'

'Mind this,' said Anthony in his sharp tone. 'Resign yourself to whatever must happen. Whatever you think or feel or discover, you're to suffer alteration. They . . . they'll see to that. You can do nothing.' Then his manner changed once more. 'My poor Hubert. Think of your blessings. Papa said you're to be famous. And consider that to lose what you've never had is only half a loss. And, if it signifies, I'll be with you whenever you want me.'

'It signifies, my dear.'

Hubert went over and kissed his brother on the cheek and the two held each other for a moment. Soon afterwards they parted: Anthony had an appointment (with a girl, clearly) and Hubert went back to his room. He felt that at one point in their conversation he had been only a phrase or so away from the understanding he sought, but he could no longer remember which, and now he doubted whether that feeling had been valid. He could have wished that Anthony had spent a little longer on trying to find helpful details and comparisons, but, again, it was impossible to imagine what could have been helpful. Red was the colour of blood and fire and not of trees or the sky, of the dress of soldiers and cardinals and not of monks or servants; think of the sun, not the sea, an organ, not a choir, hard work, not indolence. Yes, but what was it like to look at something red? To know nothing whatever of women or girls and to know of them what a ten-year-old boy might know were different: as different as blindness and total colour-blindness. He went over in his mind the best part of what Anthony had said, with additions of his own. Kissing a girl – kissing Hilda van den Haag – he had forgotten how it had felt to be about to kiss her, and had to imagine it – kissing Hilda with no clothes on while it felt like playing with himself but like the wonderful ice-cream and she behaved like a very friendly cat – that would have to do for now, and perhaps parts of it were right.

Anthony had said very little that could be judged true or false: indeed, only one such remark stayed in Hubert's mind. This was the statement that there was nothing that he, Hubert, could do to avoid alteration, and it was false. But the thought of doing it filled him with fear, and under that stress he could not make up his mind whether to do it or not. So he knelt beside his bed and prayed for courage.

Hubert went back to St Cecilia's Chapel by the early-morning rapid on Monday. He took with him a letter-packet from his father to the Abbot, on whom, at the ten o'clock interim, he called as instructed to deliver it. After a brief wait he was admitted to the cabinet by Lawrence, the servant. At once the Abbot dismissed his secretary, to whom he had been dictating, sent Lawrence off to fetch Father Dilke, and in a kind voice asked Hubert to sit down. Then he opened and read the letter. At one point the habitual gravity of his expression grew deeper.

At last he looked up.

'Well, Clerk Anvil . . . Hubert, your father lets me know that you fully understand what is to befall you.'

'Yes, my lord.'

'Do you also understand that it's a sign of God's special favour for you to be able to serve Him in this way and that you must be grateful?'

'My father used almost those exact words, my lord.'

'And you understand them.'

'Yes, my lord.'

'And you believe them. You recognize God's favour and you are grateful.'

'I think so, my lord.'

'It's not enough to think so, Hubert,' said the Abbot, still kindly. 'He who only thinks he's grateful feels gratitude with only half a heart.'

'I'm sorry, my lord. I mean . . .'

'Yes?'

'I know it's glorious to have God's favour and I'm as grateful for it as I can be, but I can't prevent myself from wishing it had taken another form.'

'You'd choose among God's gifts?'

'Oh no, my lord, not that. I try all I can not to wish what I wish, but it's too hard for me.'

The Abbot looked sad. He had not yet answered when there was a knock at the door and Father Dilke came in. After bowing to the Abbot with a very serious face, he gave Hubert an affectionate smile and laid his hand on his shoulder instead of just motioning to him to sit down again.

'God bless you, Hubert.'

'May He bless you besides, Father.'

'I came as soon as I could, my lord.'

'Naturally. Consider this for a moment if you will.'

Father Dilke took and quickly read the proffered letter from Tobias Anvil. His face changed in the reading, more markedly than the Abbot's had done. 'This is unfortunate,' he said.

'Or worse.'

'Oh, I think not, sir. Master Anvil's course is clear and easy.'

'We'll confer upon it later. Our excuses, Hubert — we speak of a matter that doesn't touch you in the least degree. Now, Father: it appears that Hubert, while (what shall I say?) sensible of what it signifies to be elected for God's service by the means we all know, finds it difficult to respond contentedly to everything this will entail. Is my account fair, Hubert?'

'Yes, my lord. But may I ask a question?'

'Of course.'

'Isn't it quite certain that I'm to be altered?'

'Quite certain,' said the Abbot steadily.

'Then . . . how can it matter what my feeling is? If I said I'd sooner be beheaded, what difference would it make?'

The Abbot's steadiness hardened into sternness. 'Creature of God, what is at stake here is not your feeling but your immortal soul. Its salvation might depend on whether you go to be altered in gladness, in free and joyful acceptance of God's will, or with contumacy of spirit and mundane vexation. Give your counsel, Father.'

Dilke blinked his eyes for some moments before he spoke. Then he said, 'My dear Hubert. You know that my lord Abbot and I love you and wish you nothing but good. Were there anything in what has been designed that might not tend to your welfare in this world and the next, you would find none more implacable in opposition to it than my lord and me. The action in itself is harmless. A part of your body will be gone, and the animal that is in all of us must shrink from that, but reason tells us it is not to be feared. Your celibacy will be absolute. Is that such a sacrifice? At least it's not a rare one. Every year thousands of young folk in England alone vow themselves to celibacy of their own free will. And in their case . . . What is it?'

'Forgive me, Father,' said Hubert, 'but I find there a substantial difference. A monk does indeed become a monk of his own free will. He chooses to. My celibacy is to be necessitated.'

'But you are a child.' The Abbot was patient. 'A child has no competence to choose, except whether or not to commit a sin. Such is the only choice he may make. You know that, Hubert.'

'Yes, my lord, I know it.'

'May I ask you to be so good as to continue, Father?'

'Yes, my lord. I meant to grant that there is a difference between this case and that of a monk, but to state that it's a rather different difference from the one he cites. A monk, Hubert, is subject to fleshly temptation; you can never be. And that temptation can be a dire burden; you'll never have to bear it. Weigh that.'

Hubert did as he was told. He thought of saying that there was, or would be, a third difference between himself and the generic monk: the latter could choose to break his vow of celibacy at least as freely as he had taken it. But that that monk never did break that vow was always taken for granted, except by those like Decuman, according to whom no monk did much else. It seemed wise, then, to nod sagely at Father Dilke.

'Very good. Now, all I've done so far has been to deny what might be thought contrarious. I must go on to affirm your advantages. First, those of this world. In your altered state, but only in that state, you'll become one of the foremost singers of this century, one the like of whom hasn't been known to anyone now living. Can you conceive of a more precious gift?'

Hubert could without difficulty, but had no reason to think he could ever attain it, so this time he shook his head.

'And you'll use your gift directly to the greater glory of God. That is to be given a second gift, no less rare if not rarer than the first, and infinitely more precious. Do you believe that God rewards those who glorify Him?'

'Yes, Father,' said Hubert, and meant it.

'And do you then accept to perform His will joyfully and gratefully?'

'Yes, Father.' Hubert meant that too, but would not have cared to affirm that he would still be meaning it the day after.

The Abbot gave Dilke a nod of considerable approval. 'Let us pray,' he said.

The two clerics and the boy knelt down on the scrubbed oak boards: there were no elegances here in the cabinet. All made the Sign of the Cross.

'In nomine Patris et Filii et Spiritus Sancti.'

'Repeat after me, Hubert,' said Dilke. 'Most loving and merciful God, hear Thou the voice of Thy child.'

'Most loving and merciful God, hear Thou the voice of Thy child.'

'Implant Thou in my mind and heart the full meaning of Thy grace . . .'

After one or two more clauses Hubert's attention had wandered, but not into the void. It was firmly fixed on the thought that he must now after all submit to what was required of him by authority. To have refused to pray would have been terribly difficult, but to have failed to refuse meant that any scheme of defiance would amount to breaking a promise to God, and that was not only dangerous but dishonourable. Well, this way was easier: it meant an end to the search for something he would not recognize if it were put into his hand. And surely God would cherish one who kept faith with Him.

'. . . sitque tecum benedictio Domini,' said the Abbot.

'Amen,' said Hubert.

'So when is this to be?' asked Decuman.

'A week from this morning.'

'So soon?'

'It must be soon,' said Hubert in a blank tone. 'Father Dilke made that plain. The changes in our bodies begin before we see signs of them, and by then it's too late.'

There was silence in the little dormitory, as there had been more than once after Hubert had made his announcement. It was a still night: the two candle-flames scarcely wavered. Decuman took his time over stuffing back into his canvas bag the considerable remains of the boys' illicit second supper; the salame and biscottos had been palatable enough, but appetite seemed to have failed. At last Thomas looked over at Hubert.

'Are you content?'

'I change from hour to hour. Sometimes I see myself being acclaimed at Chartres or St Peter's or at our own opera house. And then I think of fifteen or twenty years' time, when all of you will have children and I'll have none. But mostly I can face the prospect.'

'Face it!' Mark sat up straight in his bed. 'You're called to

God's service and you're to be a celebrated man besides and you talk of being able to face it. You should be –'

'It's very well for the likes of you,' said Thomas rather fiercely. 'You cackle of God at every turn. If you were the –'

'Quiet, the two of you,' snarled Decuman, shaking his fist. 'Do you want the Prefect in here? This must be conferred on in an orderly fashion, one speaker at a time. So . . . say, Mark.'

'What more shall I say? Except that even if Hubert were not to be a celebrated man he should still be grateful that God has chosen him.'

Decuman curled up his mouth. 'Wish-wash. The Abbot and Father Dilke have chosen him.'

'The Abbot and Father Dilke are the mortal instruments through whom God has made His will known,' said Mark. 'Do you expect Him to send an angel with a trumpet?'

'If He did, we should at least find out for certain what His will was. As it is, we have to take the word of two men who each stand to gain considerably from bringing forward somebody who'll become a great singer.'

'Gain! How gain?'

'Not in riches, you noodle – in credit, in mark, in fame. They're men like any others.'

'Decuman, I must warn you for the sake of your soul to cease this impious *cackle*. My lord Abbot and the good and learned Father are not like any others. They're priests, and one of their powers as such is that they can discover God's will.'

'You mean they've known Him longer than we have.'

'Schismatic!'

'Oh, bugger a badger.'

Thomas broke in. 'Leave God's will and consider Hubert's. I want to ask him – Hubert, can't you stay as you are and continue as singer like one of us?'

'I can, but I should be no more likely to become a great singer than any other clerk in this place.'

'And you mean to become great?'

'Well . . . good. As good as possible.'

'Then surely you should be glad to be altered. Already you sing wonderfully well, and to do anything wonderfully well must be wonderfully pleasant. And now you can become a great singer or as good a singer as possible or the sort of singer you must very much want to be. Would you throw that away for the sake of . . . being able to fuck, which you might not even like? Can anyone be sure of liking it? From what I hear of it, I'm not sure.'

Mark nodded his little head rapidly. 'Tom's right, Hubert. At least, his reason goes the same way as mine. Answer me. Are you a Christian?'

'Yes.'

'From where does your gift of singing come?'

'From God.'

'And what will He think of you if you doubt the value of his gift?'

'You talk like the Abbot.'

'Thank you, Decuman. Well, Hubert? Say.'

There was silence. Somebody in the next dormitory laughed and was immediately hushed. The cry of what might have been an animal came from far off, too far for it to be identified. Decuman leaned forward in his bed, his upper lip raised from his teeth.

'Now attend to me, Hubert,' he said. 'And you other two attend. Near my father's house in Barnet there's a monastery, at a place called Hadley a little outside the town. Last year, a monk was caught in an act of unchastity – adultery or fornication, I don't know. The Prior showed him great lenience. Instead of bringing him before the Consistory, he awarded him a summary punishment of twenty lashes and warned him that, if he offended again, nothing could save him. Four months later, the noodle did offend again and was again caught. The Consistory examined him for flagrant and incorrigible unchastity, found him guilty, and handed him over to the Secular Arm. It was quick after that; he went to the pulley.'

'Oh, Mother of God,' said Thomas.

'May She comfort his soul,' said Decuman, staring grimly at the other three as he made the Sign of the Cross. 'Attend further, you. This man knew all along the penalty he faced. Perhaps the first time he was rash or indiscreet. Not the second time. He preferred the risk of being pulled to pieces to not fucking. That tells us something, yes? We still don't truly know what it's like, but we do know how much he wanted to do it.'

'Those who are altered never want to do it,' said Hubert.

'The worse for them. From knowing how much that wretched monk wanted to do it, we know how important it is. More important than anything else.'

'Men do such things in war,' said Mark. 'I mean they face such hazards.'

'Very well, very well. This is as important as war, then, and we already know how important war is. War against the Infidel, Mark. So, Hubert, not only will you never do it, you'll never so much as want to do it. Never so much as want to do a thing of such tremendous importance. You'll live only half a life, my dear.'

'Singing is important,' said Hubert.

'When did a man hazard his life sooner than not sing?'

'You offer poor comfort,' said Thomas.

'I mean to offer none. And I've another story to tell. What do you know of Austell Spencer?'

Thomas acted as spokesman. 'A . . . an altered singer, once of this Chapel. Dead some years ago by an accident here.'

'Dead in 1964,' said Decuman, with a nod of something like satisfaction, 'at the age of twenty-one, having fallen from the belfry-tower. A rare misfortune indeed, with no reason for his presence in the tower and nobody else there at the time. Yes, I asked among the servants as soon as I heard of him, when I first entered as a clerk, but I forgot the tale until now. Austell Spencer committed the unforgivable sin . . .'

The other three gasped and Mark crossed himself.

'. . . because he so much regretted that he'd been altered.'

'You guess,' said Thomas.

'I know. He left a letter to the Abbot, but not in a packet – he must have wanted everyone to hear. Someone saw the letter and told someone who told the buttery-boy, who told me for a ha'penny. Austell Spencer said that his alteration had been in vain. His voice had fallen off and he could no longer find high notes with any surety. He was about to lose his post, or that was what he thought, that was what he wrote to the Abbot. He was fit for no other function and had given away his manhood for nothing. What should he do but kill himself, Hubert?'

'This was only one man,' said Thomas before Hubert could speak. 'He might have been mad or –'

'The only one we know of,' said Decuman. After a pause, he went on, 'Now for more discomfort. Granted that your voice does hold, Hubert, what would you be at twenty-one, thirty-one, forty-one? Not merely a man who has never fucked. Not merely a man with no wife and no children: there are plenty of such and it's no shame to them. You would not be a man at all, but a human ox. Those you met would be respectful to your face, but behind your back what would they say? What would they think of you? Wait – there's one thing you might not have heard. Now an altered man doesn't change as he grows up, he gets no hair on his face, his complexion stays the same, like a boy's, and of course his voice stays like a boy's, yes? Or like a woman's. What you might not have heard, Hubert, any of you – I only heard it from somebody my brother brought to the house who keeps doubtful company in Rome – well, it seems there are certain oddities who, instead of just chasing after boys or other men, chase eunuchs because they're men who look and speak like boys or women. How that's desirable I can't tell, but to these types it is. So, Hubert, even friendship would be difficult for you. Any man you deal with might be an oddity of this sort, or be said to be. Behind your back.'

'Be quiet, Decuman,' said Thomas, who had been trying to break in for some time. 'Hubert is helpless: he must be altered. Therefore all you do is –'

'I defy that notion.' Decuman's expression now resembled a gargoyle's. 'There are a dozen things he can do, and my purpose is to encourage him to do some one of them. Hubert: you can appeal to the Cardinal-Archbishop, you can look for sanctuary, you could even tell the Abbot you've changed your mind and just see what happens, or you can run away to North-England or West-England, you can hide in the woods above the farm and we'll bring you food. You can fight, whatever happens at last. You must fight.'

'This is the Devil's counsel, Hubert,' said Mark.

'No,' said Decuman. 'No. It's the counsel of almost everyone and everything we really understand, whether we feel we understand it or not.'

'Remember your feeling as you sang in the Agnus Dei, Hubert,' said Thomas.

There was a longer silence than before. Finally Hubert said, 'Is there any TR for us?'

'Nothing new,' said Thomas. 'I must go to Ned again.'

'I'll go,' said Hubert.

CHAPTER FOUR

Brother Collam Flackerty, friar of the Augustinian Order, sat behind his cabinet desk in the Archiepiscopal Palace of Westminster, an extensive Egidian building situated half a mile up river from the Cathedral of St Peter and the House of Convocation. He was a small, narrow-framed person with carefully-combed fair hair at the fashionable shoulder length and cheeks rouged perhaps a little more than was fashionable. Today he wore an olive-green cassock, selvedged with the traditional black, that had cost him four and a half guineas at one of the new bottegas in Chelsea village. He also wore an expensive scent that was too delicate to contend with the emanations of the lilies of the valley, pink moss roses and reseda hanging in baskets from the blue-starred ceiling or lining the window that looked out over the Thames. Before him was an open manuscript book to which he occasionally referred or added a note. With his hands clasped against his chest and his head on one side, he said in a voice that held no trace of a West-English accent, though he had been born in Dublin,

'So let me sum. Here's the order – not easy to come by, as I expected. The Abbot goes at first to the Domestic Office of Convocation and fetches his document, his paper. When he has it signed, he takes it back to the Office and takes in return another paper. This gives the surgeon leave to act; it's a non senza. Now, the point where the order can be checked is when the first paper goes back. The Office may call it void and refuse to grant the second paper, giving no reason. The Abbot may then appeal to the Lord Intendant, who may, or may not, place a tribunal, citing whom he pleases. There's no appeal against whatever the tribunal finds.'

Father Lyall nodded and rubbed his upper lip. 'This question of the refusal of the second paper. Would the grounds I attest be sufficient? – that I and only I am qualified to sign the first one and that any other signatory must be an impostor.'

'If that other signatory is your Master Anvil's chaplain in

succession to you, how is he an impostor?'

'He can't be the established confessor of the Anvil family – the word in the paper is "habitual". Can duties discharged only for a matter of days be called habitual? It must be that the provision was designed to prevent just such a contingency.'

'It might be, and it might or might not be so arguable.' Flackerty looked down at his notebook. 'Why has Anvil not sent you away before this?'

'That I've considered. He dislikes the course of replacing me by a man who'll follow his wishes. That would make him his enemy, and to have an enemy in the Church, of however little mark, would trouble him. He'd prefer me to change my mind and sign, and he hopes and believes that at last I will.'

'But you won't.'

'No.'

The Augustinian was watching his former fellow-seminarist closely. 'Why not?'

'I have my reasons.'

'Oh, merda. What reasons? If I'm to move at all I must hear them. And don't say your conscience or anything that touches the child, who for all I see will do no less well without his stones than with them.'

'It's the Abbot. Crossing him tickles me. Him and that bum-kissing choirmaster of his.'

'No doubt you are tickled, but the spite in your nature isn't strong enough to beat the sloth. I know of only one force that is. I deduce that Dame Anvil is both good to look at and strong-willed.'

Lyall grinned without replying.

'And given to whims and conceits, or she'd simply be glad at the chance for her son, no? Come on and tell me the whole tale, Matthew: we've plenty of years in common.'

'The lady's past experience of men has been small and disappointing.'

'I catch.'

'But as things now are she's set on not having the boy denied that part of his future.'

'You must indeed have pleased her.'

'It's more than that, Collam. She loves me.'

'Well, so she should.'

'No: I mean something more serious. She talks of her soul being transformed,' said Lyall in a neutral tone.

'I hope you rebuke the blasphemy as often as you hear it. And the dire use of words. What scrawler does she read?'

'She means what she says.'

'Tanto peggio. And what of it?'

'It's this love that the boy must not miss, not the carnal pleasure alone.'

'She must give you a pot of the latter if you're used to letting her sing such airs.'

'Well, you know what women are like.'

'I hear tell,' said Flackerty, polishing against his cassock the fine emerald on his left ring finger. 'Again, what of it? How does her transformed soul bear upon you?'

'You asked me my reason for resisting this design. That's the chief one.'

'Is your soul transformed too, or only your brains?'

'Collam, I tell you just this, that because of her love I must do all I can to help her.'

'Must? How must? You fancy you must.'

'I can't see any difference. Now say what I can do.'

'You can do nothing, my dear. You can go to the Office and lodge a suit, which is to do nothing. Even if you reach the man you need, you'll be either too soon or too late.'

'Then I beg you to act for me. No doubt in your post here you have connections with folk in the Office.'

'Some. Of no great rank or mark.'

'Great enough to cause the Abbot's first paper to be called void?'

'Perhaps. The Abbot on his side is of a certain rank and mark and has his own connections. And lately they down there aren't best pleased with us up here. There was a sharp knock over a vacant canonry when the Lord Intendant's choice was barred by His Eminence. There are always such things.'

'I believe you. But will you do what you can?'

First smoothing his hair with both hands, Flackerty got up

and crossed to the window, where he sniffed at several moss roses before strolling towards the far end of the room. As he talked, he continued to move at intervals, his kangaroo-leather sandals making no sound on the thick rugs, so that Lyall could not have predicted just where the next words were to come from except by constantly turning round in his chair. The friar knew well enough that this behaviour might be called theatrical, but he thought none the less of it for that, and had found it of excellent service at interviews in compensating for his physical smallness. Even on occasions like this, it was well worth while to put the other party at a disadvantage from time to time. He spoke now without hurry or much emphasis.

'Go back no more than four hundred years or so. Over all the time since, Christendom has been a tyranny of a rare sort. By way of the soul it rules the minds of most and the acts of all. As effect, no wars throughout Europe but the one, a war with long breaks of peace, a war against a power that can never be crushed and can be held in only by standing in arms from year to year: the best possible form to draw off any will to rebel or quarrel. And, in the last fifty years, Christendom has finally drubbed a power much more awful than the Turk could ever be, one that now lives on as it can in New England among boors and savages: science. God be praised.'

'Amen,' said Lyall automatically.

'Amen to amen. It was a close thing. A little longer, and science would have abolished God and brought our world to ruin.'

'You don't mean abolish, you mean take attention from, leave on one side.'

'I mean abolish, I mean deny, I mean disprove. Come, Matthew.'

'I must rebuke your blasphemy, Collam, and call upon you to abnegate it at once.'

'Again must. You may say what you please.'

'You never showed much reverence, and I suppose your work here has –'

'Let me show you some now. I feel nothing but wonder and gratitude when I look on so many centuries of patience, hope, content, trust, constancy, restraint and certitude, so much art, letters, music, learning, all founded upon one great lie. Ah! – no words, Matthew. At first a lie nobody had the smallest need for, since become the sole necessity. Its lasting makes me wish I had someone to thank. More reverence for you. But to go back whence you switched me. With the victory over science, the tyranny begins to afford to seem a little soft. Seem, not be. Don't mistake, my dear. Today there's talk in Convocation and even in the Church that thirty years ago would have earned the scaffold. The commonest felons are no more than gaoled. A man can be known to take to his bed whom he pleases and still escape if he's wary and in good regard. But the tyranny stays. I'm obliged, because tyranny alone can let men be safe and serene. None the less, to set against it is the act of a noodle. If you do so, it'll stretch out as far as the moon or the planets to snap you.'

As he ended, Flackerty settled back behind his desk. Lyall, who had managed to sit still throughout, looked at him hard.

'You overstate.'

'I don't, Matthew, I don't. All you know is the Church, and that not far. Be assured there's more than rebukes to be faced. I ask you most gravely to sign that paper as soon as you can.'

'Or you mean you're afraid to act in my behalf.'

'No. I've held my post for nine years, and before the third of them was over I'd learned how to act at a distance in such a way that I could never be named. It's you that should be afraid.'

'I am,' said Lyall, 'but not enough to check my purpose. Will you act for me, Collam? Or not?'

'Yes, I'll act, though I promise nothing.'

'I understand. I catch. Thank you.'

'One hard condition; you must do nothing more. Make no other move. Approach no one else. Say not a word.'

'I won't.'

'Swear it.'

'To you? In the name of what you call a lie?'

'For yourself.'

Lyall made the Sign of the Cross. 'I so swear, by Almighty God.'

When his friend had gone, Brother Flackerty at once took a key from the ring at his waist and unlocked one of the bottom drawers of his desk. Opening it caused the ignition of gas-jets in its asbestos-lined interior. With a neat movement, he ripped from the manuscript book his notes on the Lyall matter and dropped them among the flames. As soon as there was nothing more to burn, he shut the drawer, thereby releasing a stream of compressed air. This blew the ashes through a fine wire mesh, so that when the tray underneath came to be removed for emptying, nothing would be left of them but a grey powder.

In the afternoon of the next day of leisure at the Chapel, Hubert went through the courtyard arch and strolled over to the brewery. From it came a steady but intermittent creaking noise. One door stood open: Hubert peered round it and saw Ned in his usual brown work-shirt and trews, a dirty kerchief knotted at his throat, his hand on what was evidently a pump-handle. After a few minutes it had become clear that the brewer himself, unless in hiding or unconscious behind one of the coppers, was either on another floor of the building or altogether absent. Hubert stepped inside; Ned nodded morosely at him and went on pumping. He gave off a powerful odour, or mixture of several that was not actually unpleasant. His height, muscular arms and slight mustach made him seem older than fourteen.

'Where's your master?' asked Hubert.

Ned grunted and screwed up his face in such a way as to suggest that they were in no danger of being interrupted, but that he was perfectly indifferent to this state of affairs.

'What are you doing?'

'Water got to go atop or a come down again.'

'I see. Have you any of those books?'

'Ah no.'

When Hubert brought out and displayed two threepenny bits, the other, without the least change of demeanour, stopped his pumping at once and led the way to a metal ladder bolted to the wall. Up they went, through a cut-out in a wooden floor that supported a pair of large tuns, and finally to a space under the roof where there was a tank and a pile of sacks. From beneath a corner of this pile Ned produced something that had to be called a book, though it was very near returning to its constituent parts. Hubert looked at the crumpled title-page: *The Orc Awakes*, by J. B. Harris.

'Sixpence,' said Ned.

With no delay or objection, Hubert handed over his two coins. It seemed that Ned was surprised enough at this to show some momentary approval: his mouth twitched and he nodded several times as he released the book.

'Ned, would you tell me something?'

'What would you know?'

Hubert said quickly, 'What happens when you fuck? What do you do?'

'You don't hear nothing to that of me, you don't.' The boy's tone was startled, but not hostile. 'Nor speak and rue wasn't never my proceeding, no. That Prefect would hear.'

'Don't tell me who or where or when – just what, no more. Nothing for the Prefect to hear.'

'Find another, little sir. Ask another, eh?'

'I ask you. But I lose my time: you can tell me nothing. You haven't done it. Well, I win my sixpence back off Thomas – he wagered you had.'

'By Christ, that I have,' said Ned angrily. 'Here it is, now. I grapples her and I near kiss her bloody mouth off the face of her and I gropes the cunt of her till her's all stewed and ready, see? Then I haves the clouts of her and I lays the fusby on her back and I shove my pen all the way up her fanny artful and I bang and bang, see?' For a moment longer, he appeared to Hubert angrier than ever, the corners of his mouth drawn tightly back as he puffed out the words. 'I goes on at her cruel till my knob start to whack her tripes and her cry me mercy, see? Then I feel a start to ... Christ, I could ...'

Hubert, who had been watching his face, caught sight of the distension at the crotch of his trews just before Ned snatched at it and squeezed it, wincing loudly as if in pain; his body was bent at the waist. Within a couple of seconds Hubert had reached the top of the ladder and begun going down as fast as he could. He heard Ned run across the floor above him.

'Ah, would you? Let the fucking Prefect hear, would you? I'll stop your mouth, I will. Tear your fucking head off I will, little sir. I gets my hands to you, you wish you never been born, I swear to Christ.'

With his pursuer close behind and still shouting, Hubert reached the ground and ran for the doorway. He was through it, but he would be caught in seconds. Then Ned's footfalls stopped abruptly, and at the same time Hubert saw the bulky figure of the brewer approaching from the arch that led to the courtyard, a curved piece of metal pipe balanced over his shoulder. Hubert hurried in the other direction. He only stopped gasping and trembling when he had reached the farmyard and Smart had rushed across to greet him. Today the collie had perhaps had an unusually good dinner; at any rate, he put himself out to entertain Hubert with a display of fierce growls and pretended snaps at his sleeves. When he left it was at top speed, to show that there were other tasks calling for his attention.

Hubert stood and looked in the direction of the ducks on and round the pond. At a now reduced rate, phrases moved through his head: Ned was mad, Ned was not mad but had only wanted to fuck when there was no girl, Ned was rude and low, Ned might be rude and low but he had been telling the truth, Ned was only a boy, Ned was indeed a boy but in the one important way he was a man too. There were other phrases besides.

A hoof sounded on dried mud. The white-and-black calf came up and halted just a few paces off; Hubert moved towards it with the utmost caution. Soon he was near enough to stretch out his hand at an inch a second and lay his fingertips on the hide of the animal's nose. It shifted its footing, but did not turn or edge away. By degrees, he moved further until he was standing at its shoulders with his hand on the back of its neck. There was an interval while he sent a hurried prayer to St Francis to see to it that no duck should quack too loudly or make a flurry in the pond. Then, after a gentle blowing through its nostrils and a few shakes of its head, the calf pressed its cheek against his chest; he lowered his own cheek on to its neck.

A minute or so later, a questioning moo was heard from the pasture. As if by prearrangement, Hubert straightened himself and the calf trotted off; contentedly, he watched it out of sight. Only now did he remember *The Orc Awakes*: he must have dropped it somewhere in the brewery. Well, there was no going back for it. Should he walk on up to the woods? No: if he did, he would have to think about what he had seen there the previous week, to compare that with what he had seen just now and as much as he had understood of what he had been told, and from all this to try to imagine himself in Ned's case, and he shied away from such a task. He would go instead to the study-room and write out the little improvisazione he had thought of coming up in the rapid.

While the clock was striking five, he carried the completed manuscript across a corner of the quadrangle to the small concert-chamber where composition was usually taught. The ceiling and four wall-panels had been painted with scenes from the life of St Cecilia, including what was now known to be her unhistorical martyrdom in the year 230. The artist was supposed to have been a mid-eighteenth-century Prefect of Music at the Chapel, and although it was also supposed, or at least hoped, that he had been a better musician than artist, most folk enjoyed what he had painted. Hubert did; as he mounted the low platform and sat down at one of the two piano-fortes there, he gave the figure of the saint's husband, known to generations of clerks as 'the tipsy Roman', an affectionate glance. Raising the lid of the instrument, he began to play the Prometheus Variations, Beethoven's last complete keyboard work. It would never do to be caught tinkling some trash of one's own.

Presently, Master Morley hurried in, his footfalls heavy on the wide elm boards. Hubert stopped playing and stood up.

'My excuses, Clerk Anvil: the organer kept me at the oratory. Now what have you for me today?'

'Here, master.'

At his work-desk to one side of the platform, Morley turned over the sheets of music-paper at a fair speed to start with, then more slowly. Twice he went to the nearer piano-forte and, without sitting down, played short passages. Halfway through a second study of the manuscript he spoke, in the voice that was as heavy as his tread.

'How long was this in the writing, Anvil?'

'In the writing down, master, no more than –'

'My question was ill drawn. How long in the composing?'

'It's hard for me to tell, master. Six minutes or seven.'

'It'll be that long in the playing.'

'Forgive me, master, of course it was much longer in the composing.'

Morley stared past Hubert at one of the wall-paintings. 'Anvil,' he said at last: 'I know you meant six or seven minutes in the composing. What did you mean by composing?'

'I . . . My mind was those minutes in going through it. Or . . .' Hubert hesitated, but the Prefect still stared. 'Or it was those minutes going through my mind.'

'You tell me it came to you from somewhere else.' The voice was at its harshest now.

'No – no, master, it was inside my mind already when I . . . looked.'

'Very well. These F naturals here.' Morley pointed with a stubby finger. 'And again near the end.'

'Oh yes.' Hubert sang a short phrase.

'Why did you have your hands in front of you then?'

'Did I so? I expect because it's the clarinet – I was . . .'

'What clarinet, Anvil? This is a keyboard piece.'

'Yes, master, but I heard that voice as a clarinet.'

'And the other voices too, you heard them as flutes and violas and horns and so forth?'

'No, sir. Two oboes, two clarinets and two bassoons.'

'So this here is a keyboard transcription of a wind-sextet movement you haven't put on paper.'

'Yes, master.'

'Are all your keyboard pieces transcriptions of non-existent originals?'

'Oh no, master: the theme and variations was for pianoforte.'

'Indeed. Now at last to these F naturals. The key is G major, and elsewhere, here for example, we find the F sharp we expect. Well?'

'They're different places, master.'

'When I protest that the leading-note of G major is F sharp, what's your answer?'

'That where I've written F natural nothing but F natural is possible.'

Morley was silent for nearly a minute. Then he said, 'They let me know you go soon to be altered.'

'Yes, master.'

'I'm sorry to hear it. Oh, it means an eminent career for you and I wish you well. But it also means an end to your activities as composer.'

'Surely not, sir.'

'As surely as can be. Name me six pieces of any kind that a singer of the least eminence has written. You see? Consideration will show that a singer's life is too much lived with others, too remunerating in other ways than financial, simply too full to allow of composition. So I'm a little dismal, because you're by far the best pupil I've ever had. But in any case I must lose you soon as pupil: soon I'll be able to teach you nothing more.'

'You are too gracious, master.'

Again Morley stared at the painting. 'Why is it, Anvil, do you think, that St Cecilia is the patron saint of the blind as well as of music?'

Anything Hubert might have had to say to this was never heard, because just then Lawrence came into the concert-chamber and up to the two on the platform.

'Your indulgence, master,' he said, and then, 'Clerk Anvil, my lord Abbot wishes you to come to him at once.'

'What have I done?' asked Hubert in fear, thinking of his encounter with Ned.

'Nothing ill that I know of, clerk,' said the servant, smiling slightly. 'You're to go to Rome.'

As the other two moved off, Morley sighed and nodded his head, his eyes shut.

The Eternal City Rapid pulled out of Bayswater Station, its

only stop between Coverley and Rome, at 6.25 a.m., and moved slowly, through networks of points and round tight bends, across London, across the river and into the north-west corner of the county of Kent, which was still virtually co-extensive with the ancient kingdom. There the track straightened itself, changing direction only in the longest and shallowest of curves, its continuously-welded rails on their cushioned sleepers moving through natural obstacles, not round them: the work of the great Harrison. The half-mile-long train – three triplex tugs, 30 passenger baruches, 38 cargo vans – accelerated steadily, but it did not attain its top speed of 195 m.p.h. until the towers of Canterbury were to be seen out of the windows on the left side. Soon came the famous moment when it emerged from the Dover cliffs and entered on to the Channel Bridge, Sopwith's master-piece, 23 miles 644 yards of road and railtrack carried between 169 piers. Little more than half an hour's travel on the French side took the Rapid as far as Clermont, the slipping-point for Paris where it freed itself of its rearmost quarter. As mid-morning approached, tunnels became longer and more frequent, but all were left behind in a matter of seconds except the 15-odd miles of the Bognanco itself. The track ran downhill through Milan, crossed the Po on stilts 200 feet high, climbed again into Parma and moved finally towards the coastal plain. The journey ended in the Stazione S. Pietro at 1.32 – nearly a quarter of an hour late.

It had all impressed Hubert enough to distract him from more than one troubling or puzzling question, of which not the least was the reason for his summons to Rome. The cabin his father had hired was like several parts of a beautiful house combined into one. After the luggage had been settled, the two of them moved to a kind of parlour by the window. Here there were leather chairs with gold-braided velvet cushions, tall potted plants, lithographs of views of Rome, a row of picture-books, a locker containing a chess-set and packs of playing-cards and much else; but Hubert attended only to things on the outside. As the train went faster, nearby objects like hedges or dwellings of the people became an indifferently-coloured lengthwise blur, but he very soon learned to overlook them in favour of more distant and important things: churches, great houses, busy streets and squares, and at different times no fewer than four aircraft, mighty envelopes of gas on the long run to Africa or the Antipodes.

Breakfast was taken at a polished oval table on which the linen, china, silver and glass might have been made the previous day; the bread the Anvils ate with their hurtleberry conserve must have been baked that day, perhaps on the train itself: nothing seemed impossible. The meal was brought in (by two very polite attendants, one stern, the other timid) long after the train had reached its full speed, and Hubert noticed that, probably in consequence, the timid attendant had to take some special care when he poured the tea. The remnants being cleared away, something like a luxurious bedchamber offered itself in the form of couches shaded by silk screens, but Hubert stayed by the windows to see what he had never seen before.

The passage over the Alps was like flying in a dream: the always startling burst into bright sunshine, the huge steady leap between tiers of mountains and its abrupt cessation in the darkness of the next tunnel. When the streams and rivers began again, they had changed their colour from brown or grey to blue, green or turquoise. The countryside was the same as that in the background of some very old paintings Hubert remembered seeing on a visit to the Royal Gallery in Coverley: the sloping fields, the thin dark trees, even the small clouds on their own in the sky. Then, after slowing so gradually that the process could only be seen, not felt, the train came into Rome, where every building that was not a church looked like a palace, and stopped without the slightest jar.

On the pavement beside the track, the Anvils were soon joined by one of the family servants carrying their slender overnight baggage; the man had of course travelled in the narrow cabin allotted his kind at the rear of the baruch. Hubert thought he had never seen so many folk at once: droves of pilgrims, clerics in ones and twos, officials with their staffs, men of affairs like his father, all making their way through crowds of vendors who pressed on them flowers, fruit, patties, flasks of wine, gewgaws, facsimiles of paintings and cheap-looking religious objects. After a short pause at the post of inspection, there was more of the same in the square outside, together with a great concourse of wheeled traffic; every vehicle seemed to make twice as much noise as its English counterpart, just as every Roman shouted instead of talking. The air was hot and damp. Hubert felt relieved when, after only a couple of minutes, a public was secured. Hunger, fatigue, confusion and anxiety weighed upon him. The first two yielded in due time to the excellent dinner provided by the Schola Saxonum, where rooms had been reserved for them, but in other respects he was still uncomfortable when, at ten minutes to four that afternoon, he and his father approached the Vatican Palace on the north side of St Peter's Square.

Nine great windows, each with a decorated half-dome above it, dominated the facciata of the building, the one in the centre distinguished by a balcony and an abundance of high-relief sculpture; it must be from here that the Holy Father gave his addresses to the multitude. Below the windows ran a gallery, and below that, at ground level, an arcade, both of plain stone. The main gate, thirty feet high and flanked by massive granite pillars, was at the end nearer the basilica. Next to it was an incongruously modern and undignified structure, a sort of wooden hut with a flat roof. Here Anvil senior presented himself to a cheerful young monk, produced an identifying document and was evidently found to be expected. The monk nodded to the carmine-uniformed guard who, with shouldered fusil, stood directly at the gate, and the guard opened the wicket. Hubert was stepping over the sill when he noticed a third man who seemed to be stationed at the entrance with an eye to visitors; he was in plain clothes (dark-blue jacket and straw-coloured breeches), but he wore them as if they had been chosen for him.

Inside, there was only one way to go: down the wide path that curved to and fro between masses of trees and shrubs growing so close together that, within a dozen paces, the palace itself could be seen only in stray glimpses and there was no sound except birdsong, some of it unfamiliar. The surface of the path consisted of flat-topped stones about the size of a crown piece, none regular in shape but each perfectly fitted with its neighbours, no two apparently alike in colour, any that the sun caught glinting as if wet. On either side, now and then overgrown in parts by stray foliage, and often a good deal weathered, there stood at five-yard intervals classical statues in marble or bronze, portrait busts on stone pedestals, sections of column with spiral bands of carving, fragments of colossi that included a huge sandalled foot irregularly shorn off above the ankle. Once, the path divided to accommodate an inactive fountain in a basin of some matt black substance; further on, it led straight through the considerable remains of what Hubert took to be a very ancient pagan temple, its walls, floor and low ceiling covered with designs he could not interpret. He scarcely heard his father's expressions of admiration or amazement, except to notice that they sounded genuine; he himself was more and more interested in reaching the end of their journey along the path, which oppressed him in some way.

When at last they did, they had come in sight of a stone staircase at the end of another arcade and leading up to another gallery. From the foot of the staircase, a functionary with a curved sword and a splendid purple sash beckoned the new arrivals by holding out his hand and gently curling the fingers up in the palm. They followed him down the gallery past a series of shut doors, one of which, smaller than the others, had bars across it. Halfway along they turned off at a narrower staircase with a gilded ceiling and low-relief grottescos on the walls. On the second floor they went through a circular chamber in which everything from floor to ceiling seemed to Hubert, in the couple of seconds available to him, to be made of ivory, a square chamber in which everything likewise seemed to be covered with mosaic, and an L-shaped chamber full of more classical statuary, some of which he thought he recognized from books. Next was what must be an ante-chamber. The further door of this was flanked by another guard in carmine uniform and another man wearing plain clothes that seemed not to belong to him. The official with the sword opened this door, or rather half of it, spoke to someone on the far side, again made his courteous beckoning gesture to the Anvils, and withdrew, shutting the door after them.

It was a lofty room with an immense window, no doubt one of the row to be seen from the square; through it, Hubert had a momentary sight of spires and roofs with statues on them, and, further off, domes and towers. Frescos and oil paintings covered the walls. A line of padded benches in carved wood and gilt ran down the wall opposite the window; all were empty. So was the elevated golden throne at the far end. A figure robed in scarlet smiled and spoke, raising his voice as four o'clock sounded from innumerable bells.

'Salvete, magister et magistrule.'

'Salvete, Vestra Eminentia,' said Tobias Anvil, bowing low.

'Dominus vobiscum.'

'Et cum vobis.'

'I am Cardinal Berlinguer. I welcome you to Rome. I will take you to His Holiness. Please to come with me.'

Beside the door they were to leave by, there hung a picture familiar to Hubert from countless facsimiles, Tintoretto's 'Lepanto', one of the most renowned works of art in the world. Hubert did not dare to linger; he just had time for a single glance at his favourite detail, the boarding of a Turkish galley by a lone warrior who was always taken (in England and her Empire) to be Sir Richard Grenville. Then they moved out, up a steep stair, across an enclosed bridge where suits of armour stood in ranks, and finally through another door. Cardinal Berlinguer departed.

Hubert found himself in what might have been the parlour of a small English manor house, with solid oak furniture, chintz covers and what looked like trees and shrubs outside – on a roof? A broad, plumpish man of fifty or more, with eyeglasses and a rather pale complexion, made a satisfied noise as he came over from the window. He was wearing the kind of dark-grey suit that any lay visitor to the Anvil house might wear. Hubert looked about for the Pope, but his father had gone down on one knee and bowed his head, so he hastened to do the same. He kissed a plain ring with a gold cross on it, felt a hand laid on his own bowed head and heard some words in Latin spoken. They were not spoken clearly and he did not understand them all, but they calmed him.

'Ah, now, please make yourselves comfortable, the pair of you. You'll find that's a good chair, Master Anvil, and Hubert lad, you settle yourself down next to us. Our excuses for receiving you thus meanly apparelled: we're so often required to appear swaddled like a babe that we've come to take advantage of every private moment. Rome will be so hot in these months. Sometimes we feel we'd give our throne for a few breaths of a North Sea breeze. Well, tell us, what do you think of our city? You'll have been here before, no doubt, master.'

If challenged, Hubert would have said that of course he had known that Pope John XXIV was an Englishman, was a York-shireman; but knowledge was different from being faced with the fact. He willed himself to believe that this pleasant, homely-looking person was indeed God's representative on earth and also the most powerful man alive. His father was answering the question.

'A number of times, Your Holiness. It still fills me with extreme awe. So much to be aware of. Republican Rome, Imperial Rome, medieval Rome, modern Rome, and above all –'

'Ay, there is that. For us, there's almost too much. It's more than eight years since our coronation and we still couldn't truly say we knew the place. And it's not like home. Take our church, for instance.' The Pope moved his dark head to one side, presumably to indicate St Peter's. 'You must have remarked the outside of it on your way here, Hubert. How did it impress you?'

'We saw the inside of it too, Your Holiness,' said Hubert, surprised by how easy it was to sound natural. 'It impressed me very greatly.'

'So it should, lad, so it should, considering in whose sanctified name it stands. We meant in what way did it impress you as a piece of architecture. Did it match your expectations?'

'Not quite, Your Holiness.' Hubert heard his father inhale sharply. 'I thought it rather . . . bare.'

'Austere, as you might say? We agree. We and you look to St George's for a notion of a cathedral basilica, a place rich with holy images testifying to the glory of God, eh? That was what St Peter's was first designed to be, but old Martin wouldn't have it so. No, Germanian I was a very severe and sober kind of customer; God's first house on earth must not be a temple of luxury, he said. He tore up the plans at last and dismissed the Italian master-builders and masons. One of them was so mortified he committed the unforgivable sin – Boonarotty or some such name. A fair number of the others had the craft to go to Coverley and settle down to their trade. There were places for them in plenty, for old Martin had sent after English artificers along with men from Almaigne and the Netherlands to make St Peter's according to his will. Out of the common, that. But enough of lessons. Now you're settled, forgive us if we show you our little cloister. We're a mite proud of it, we're afraid.'

A moment later, the three stood on the tessellated pavement of an arcade that ran all the way round the open space, which occupied perhaps half an acre. The roof was supported by slender pillars, none seemingly like another in detail. In the centre, a fountain was playing; Hubert remembered that the one in the garden below had not been. Flowers, flowering shrubs and dwarf trees of species unknown to him grew in beds of exact geometrical shapes. Between them, the turf was no less level and smooth that would be seen at a premier club-ball field in England. Three gardeners in white overalls were hard at work under the strong sun.

'A beautiful sight, Your Holiness,' said Tobias as they moved slowly round the arcade, 'and a wonderful stroke of engineering.'

'It is that, master. There are we don't know how many thousands of tons of soil up here. You wouldn't credit that it was a Frenchie who began it, would you? Old Sylvan II back in the eighteenth century. And since then every Holy Father has added a shred of his own. We brought those roses, look. Now you'll be wanting to know, the pair of you, why we asked you to pay us a visit. Well, we see it like this. Rome is the centre of Christendom.' The Pope said this with some force and nodded his head several times, as if he had recently heard the point disputed. 'So Rome should be the greatest city in the world, with the foremost and the finest of everything and everybody, a city fit to make Byzantium look like a mill-town. Ee, we don't speak of mere temporal glory, magnificence for its own secular sake. To follow after that would be a sin, and if there's one thing we can't abide at any price it's sin. We think we can safely say that.' After a reflective pause, he added, 'Yes, we think we can safely say that. What we design is all in God's praise and in the adoration of His Holy Name.

'To this end, we fetch here the best architects, the best sculptors, the best inventors, the best physicians, the best furniture-makers, the best arborists, the best masons, the best tailors on earth, wherever they might have been born. And the best singers besides. Now, we ourselves can hold no view in this province, as we have the misfortune to be tone-deaf, but we have access to prime advice. Your voice has no equal in memory and your skill is pretty fine too is what we're told.' (By the two altered men at the Chapel, thought Hubert.) 'We called you to Rome, Hubert, on purpose to offer you a post as principal, uh, soprano in the choir of our church here. Do you consent?'

Tobias Anvil checked his stride. 'Your Holiness! What an honour! I'm overwhelmed – I can think of nothing more –'

'We thought you'd be pleased, master; we assumed so. We ask what Hubert has to say.'

'I can't tell you all I have to say, Your Holiness, because I never dreamed of such a thing before. But oh yes, of course, of course I consent. But I must live in Rome, I see I must, and everyone I know is in England. But . . .'

'Consider that London is merely seven hours away, and we hear it's soon to be five and a half. You'll often be at leisure, your family and friends may visit you – everybody comes to Rome at last, not always to pay homage to us. You won't be lonely.'

Hubert hesitated. He saw the Pope, who had turned slightly to face the room they had left, make a curious small signal with his forefinger, a motion like that of jerking or pushing aside. When he looked in that direction himself, there was nobody to be seen. He squared his shoulders and said,

'I humbly beg Your Holiness' leave to ask a question.'

'Ask away, lad; have no fear.'

'Your Holiness called me to Rome and has just invited me to take this post. But I'm only a child and you're . . . Your Holiness. All that was needed was to instruct me, or instruct my father to send me. So I . . .'

The Pope chuckled, shook his head to and fro, rested his hand on Hubert's shoulder and resumed progress round the arcade. 'Here's an acute one, eh, master? We can see we'll have to admit you both to our counsel. Mind this, now. We can indeed do as we please throughout Christendom. We are the Holy Father.' Again there was emphasis, almost enough to suggest the undisclosed existence of a rival claimant. 'But we're not omnipotent. We can't direct men's minds. Not that we wish to, or at any rate . . . But just here and there, there's been some – some reluctance to accede to our wishes. Folk of this nation or that have shown themselves obstinately and perversely wishful to keep their gifted sons at home. Last year – take a case – there was some stir over a Portuguee bridge-builder whom we required here in our city. The talk in Lisbon, and not only in Lisbon, said that his care was the Tagus, not the Tiber. We were obliged to take urgent steps to remind the laical rulers there of their duty to God. Now, that sort of thing doesn't conduce to right feeling among our flock. How much better if the lad had declared that he came here freely and joyfully. He did say so after a while, of course, but after a while wasn't soon enough for our liking. After a while made it sound as if words had been put into his mouth. We must avoid that this time. So we command your help, Master Anvil.'

'Anything in my power, Your Holiness. And in Hubert's.'

'A short predication from each of you affirming your delight and gratitude at the honour we do you by our offer.'

Tobias and Hubert avowed their willingness to provide what was asked for.

'Good enough. We'll have Berlinguer, who brought you to us, agree with you on a form of words, and then he'll put it in our paper. He's a serviceable lad, is Berlinguer. Oh, and there'll be a photogram besides, so that all shall see for themselves that you were here with us. But that's not yet.'

Clocks far and near began striking the quarter. The nearest of all, though Hubert had not noticed it till then, was in the cloister itself, a splendid twenty-four-hour piece with an ultramarine face and representations of the signs of the zodiac done in

113

gold around the dial. The Pope made the same pleased noise as when the Anvils had first arrived, and conducted them back to his parlour. Here, afternoon table was waiting: dropped scones, riddle bread, quince conserve, bloater-paste arundels.

'We fetch all our fare from England. Over these years our stomach still hasn't accustomed itself to the local muck. (Benedictus benedicat.) We mean, that's what it is. Our vicar at York is well situated to serve our taste, and he's kind enough to send us whatever we need. Shall we be mother?' The Pope picked up the teapot, an ample affair painted with very luxuriant white roses. 'Well, we're happy our business is settled. Now we and you can take our time. We don't mean to make you scramble, Hubert. You'll have concerns to settle in England before you return here to live; we don't expect you back in Rome before the end of next month, or later. Meanwhile you must be watchful you don't grow too flushed with your fame. Two accounts of you in our paper in two days, and no doubt the English ones will copy.'

Hubert's bewilderment, already considerable, sharpened a little. 'Two accounts . . . in your paper, Your Holiness?'

'Ay, lad, there was one this morning: we didn't want to keep your arrival a secret, did we? Just that today we were to receive in private audience a foremost chorister from England and his reputable father. That's what we told Berlinguer to say. Of course, we don't quite know how it came out in the lingo, but such was the drift. And then, tomorrow, your and your father's predications, as we and you agreed. Now, Master Anvil, it's all too seldom we chance to receive a lay visitor from England. These clerics are too set on the Church's concerns to pay much regard to any others. How is it in England now, master? – among the people as well as the gentry.'

Tobias spoke up and the Pope showed many signs of listening until Cardinal Berlinguer reappeared, when the three men conferred on the matter of the predications. This took only a very short time, because His Eminence had seemed to know in advance just what the two Anvils would have wanted to say: he had even brought with him documents already prepared. Next, a photographist was brought in. His part in the proceedings went on longer, even though all that was wanted was a picture of the Pope standing with his hand on Hubert's head and smiling down at him while he looked up at the Pope. It was the expression on Hubert's face that proved difficult to get right: 'look grateful, lad,' the Pope kept saying – 'look honoured.' When at last it was done to his satisfaction, some practical details were quickly settled, His Holiness conferred his benediction upon father and son, and the two were ceremoniously shown out, emerging into the piazza as the three-quarters began to sound. Immediately a swarthy young man with the dress and bearing of a servant came up to them.

'Salve, magister.'

'Salve, amice.'

'Maestro Anvil, per piacere? Ecco, signore.'

With great deference, the man handed over a sealed packet. Tobias broke it open and ran his eyes over the deckled sheet of paper it contained. He lowered his black eyebrows and said,

'Attend, Hubert. "Honoured Sir, – I had recently in Coverley the pleasure of becoming acquainted with your excellent son. I read today in *Observator Romanus* that your honoured self and he are to have an audience with His Holiness the Pope. I should estimate it a great favour if afterwards you and he would care to call upon me in my lodging. I send this by my valetto Giulio, who will conduct you to me if you are so minded. The distance is no more than a few minutes on foot. With the profound respects of your servant in God, honoured Sir ... Federicus ... Mirabilis." Well, my son?'

While Guilio, hands behind back, politely kept his eyes turned away, Hubert explained as much as he could explain. He was surprised at first when his father's frown was quickly displaced by a look of amiable tolerance, then reflected that good humour was to be expected in someone who, now that the Pope's wish had been revealed, must be feeling rather like a boy being given the largest slice of his favourite cake he had ever seen.

'What a pleasant and courteous offer. – Buono, andiamo.'

Giulio led them across a corner of the piazza and into a narrow street empty of vehicles but full of strolling foot-passengers and hung with artisans' and traders' signs. Hubert saw little of anybody or anything: he was too intent on the strange thought of living his life in this city. In time, he would own a house in it, furnish the place after his own wishes, keep servants, entertain friends, speak the language, visit England and no doubt many other places, but always return here as to his home; most likely this was where he would die and be buried. Yes, that was how it would be.

He did not start to notice his surroundings until he was crossing a cobbled yard and entering a squat marble portico. Inside, it was dark and cool, with a noise of water dripping into water. The valetto knocked at a door covered in green leather. A high-pitched voice sounded from within, and the two visitors were shown into a long narrow room with a balcony at the end of it. Polished tables on which silverwork was carefully arranged, cushioned couches, and screens covered with small pictures took up a great deal of space. There was an unfamiliar sweetish odour in the air. As Hubert had expected, the writer of the note, Mirabilis, had his friend with him. Both wore long, brightly-coloured silk gowns gathered by cords at the waist.

Mirabilis brought forward the other man, Viaventosa, who seemed in rather worse physical condition than before, his skin as well as his eyes and mouth exuding moisture. Bows were exchanged. Tobias declined refreshment but accepted a seat, though not quite fully, in the sense that he stayed on its edge. His answers to questions about the journey from England, his experience of Rome and so forth were brief, if civil. There was not much left now of the geniality with which he had agreed to come here. His glance moved round the room in restless jerks. After a little, Mirabilis turned to Hubert.

'You have seen the Holy Father, then, my dear. May I know his purpose? Such audiences are somewhat out of the common.'

'His Holiness invited me to join the choir of St Peter's, master.'

Mirabilis gave Viaventosa a slow nod. 'It's a great honour, Hubert, no? You must be so joyful. And your good father too.'

'Oh yes, master,' said Hubert after a brief pause. 'May I ask you something?'

'Surely.'

'It was you and the other master here who recommended the

Pope to send for me, wasn't it, sir?'

'In effect – yes.'

'Did you ... was it part of the reason you were in Coverley, to hear me sing in the Requiem?'

'Not part. The whole reason. Yes, Hubert, you're of great mark already for one of your years.'

'Master: when you came to the Chapel, did you confer on me with the Abbot?'

'Yes, and also with your other preceptors.'

'Did you tell them the Pope had sent you?'

'No. I wasn't asked.'

'I see.' Hubert hesitated again. 'What did you tell them?'

'That your voice and your musician's qualities were of the finest.'

'And therefore I must be altered.'

'That did not –'

Tobias had been fidgeting: rubbing his face and twisting his feet from the ankle. Now he broke in abruptly. 'What was your authority, sir?'

'I must be clear, Master Anvil. My lord the Abbot asked Viaventosa and me to tell our opinion of your son's gifts, and for that we had the authority of our experience. To what use his lordship puts our information is not in our control. Exactly the same holds for our commission from the Holy Father.'

'I understand.'

'Thank you, master. So: may I ask you? – your honoured self and Hubert will be kind enough to sup with us this evening? I ask now because my cook –'

'Thank you, but I regret that I'm tired and we depart early tomorrow.'

'Just an hour or so – there's so much to talk of, touching Hubert's future. We can arrange his –'

'I regret ...'

Viaventosa, who had followed the last few remarks with ease, pulled and pushed his bulk upright. 'Please, Master Anvil,' he squeaked, 'sup with us. It will be very good.'

Tobias stared at him for a second and jumped to his feet. 'I must go at once. Come, Hubert.'

'Also I must speak now.' Viaventosa had risen almost as quickly and was making snuffling noises. 'I say to you: no . . . Änderung, altering. No altering for Hubert. No no no. You see me, master, I'm altered. H'm, h'm. Not this for Hubert.'

'Sei ruhig, Wolfgang!'

Tobias, with Hubert's hand in his, was making for the door, but Viaventosa, waddling to and fro, impeded him. 'No altering, please, for your son.' His voice slid further up the scale. 'See me like this. Hear me speak, like a woman, like a child. No wife, no friend but another altered one. They see me and they hear me and they think, "Not a man, not a man." All, all, all. Always. Überall.' He went on, louder, weeping freely, as Mirabilis tried to pull him away. 'See my face. No hair.' He made a contemptuous wiping gesture across his fuzzy upper lip. 'They laugh. I don't see them but I know. They laugh or they . . .' He imitated the act of vomiting. 'Think you, master, your son will be like me. Not a man. Hubert must not be altered, for the love of God.'

The green-leather door slammed. Hubert saw that there was more in his father's expression than embarrassment or revulsion. He was about to ask him not to hold his hand so tightly when something amazing happened: in a yard outside a house in Rome, while hundreds of the people passed by and others in ones and twos stopped to watch, Master Tobias Anvil of the London Chamber of Merchandry knelt down on the cobbles in his thirty-shilling breeches and clasped his son in his arms.

'What is it, papa?'

'God aid me, God send my soul tranquillity. Pray for me, Hubert. Pray to Christ to take from my memory what I have seen and heard.'

'Yes, papa. It was rather displeasing.'

Tobias's embrace grew tighter. 'Oh Christ, I pray Thee to take away from this child, Thy child, that sight and those words. Oh Hubert, how should I bear it that you should become such a creature as that?'

'He's old, papa, and he's silly, and he was piling it up – surely you could see –, and he'd most likely have looked the same whether he'd been altered or not, or much the same. The other was very different, not only in his looks.'

Releasing his son, Tobias sat back on his heels. He made no move to stand up, heedless or even unaware of the small talkative crowd that had gathered a few yards off. He seemed calmer when he said, 'What can ever make me able to drive that voice from my ears? I must find a priest tonight to pray with me. Oh God, where am I now to find the strength to endure what will be done to this child of mine?'

'Will be done?'

'Because endure it I must.'

Hubert looked down at the top of his father's bowed head.

After supper that night, as arranged earlier, Sebastian Morley and Father Dilke attended Abbot Thynne in his parlour. He offered them brown sherry, which Morley accepted and Dilke declined, then picked up a strip of newspaper from the marble top of his writing-table. His face was grave.

'This comes to me from my old friend Ayer at New College. As Professor of Dogmatic Theology he must see the *Observator Romanus* daily: it reaches him every afternoon. My New Latin is not of the best, I admit to you, but the core of the matter is clear. His Holiness will receive – will by now have received – Hubert and his father on purpose to confer on Hubert's future.'

'And tomorrow we'll read that Hubert, with his father's more than willing sanction, is shortly to take up a high post in one of the choirs there, probably that of St Peter's.' Morley sounded unconcerned, almost bored. 'The Vicar of Christ is a diplomatist. This is his means of countering the complaint that he considers too little the wishes of those he calls to Rome. Nobody will be deceived, but the form's important.'

Dilke stood gazing towards the tapestry, his hands clasped in front of him. He said heavily, 'So Hubert is lost to us.'

'I'm sorry for you, Father,' said Morley in the same tone as before. 'But Hubert has been lost to us for some time.'

'Why must His Holiness do this?' The Abbot seemed not to have heard the last remark: he was as near anger as the other two had ever seen him. 'It's acknowledged that he has no ear for music, no . . .'

'He has an excellent ear for what folk tell him of the best

performers in any craft. Anvil's going to the Vatican was inevitable as soon as the Pope heard of him. I knew it was only a question of time, and when you told me, my lord, that Mirabilis and Viaventosa were to attend our late King's funeral, I knew the time was here. Why does an opera singer come from Rome to attend a requiem mass in England? Why does an elderly chapelmaster make his first visit to our country on the same occasion? And how is it that two such men, even though foremost in their function, gain entry to St George's among princes and spiritual lords? Because they do the Pope the same service as they do you, my lord.'

'Sebastian: you said nothing of this.'

'I feared I might have said too much when the two came here to sup, and had to plead melancholia. Oh, I was bitter then. But no more. I said nothing later because I could see no purpose in speaking.'

'Did you make the same surmise, Father?'

Dilke hesitated, blinking rapidly and avoiding Morley's eye. 'I was perplexed for a little, my lord, but then my attention was diverted to matters of more immediacy.'

'I suppose I must believe it,' said the Abbot after a pause. 'I thought ... Hearing that Mirabilis was in Coverley, I thought to renew an old friendship and at the same time grasp what appeared a heaven-sent opportunity to hear two such competent advisers. It grieves me that Fritz played such a part before me, before us all.'

Morley gave a short laugh. 'What would you have had him do, my lord? Tell us of his commission from the Pope, or refuse to answer your inquiry?'

'It might have been more honorable in him to decline my invitation.'

'And disappoint you, sir, and deny himself an evening in your company and at your table? For what good? Nothing would be changed. No, Mirabilis is no worse than most of us, and he has more wit than many. He sees that in our world a man does what he's told, goes where he's sent, answers what he's asked. And, after seeing that, one is free.'

There was a longer pause. A bell pealed; further off, a cow

lowed; in the courtyard, three or four voices, excited and yet under restraint, moved into hearing and died away in a distant corner. Morley refilled his sherry-glass and remained standing. As gently as he could, he said,

'At any rate, my lord, this removes one difficulty. Anvil's alteration is no longer any concern of yours.'

'How not so?'

'It attaches to the Pope now. Since he must have Anvil, let him have too the task of rendering him fit to carry out his duties. It would be a remarkable obstacle that His Holiness couldn't surmount.'

'He shall not have Anvil. I'll take steps to prevent him.'

'Steps? What steps, my lord?'

'I'll form a design. More of that later. However it may fall out, at least Hubert is not to be altered in Rome. It's not to be thought of.'

Morley said with some pity and more exasperation, 'My lord, the foremost surgeons alive are in Rome.'

'I don't doubt it, Sebastian; this isn't a question of surgeons but of Hubert's feeling. Consider that alteration is a . . .'

'My lord Abbot means,' said Father Dilke, stepping forward, his hands still clasped, 'that Hubert's a child, and in some proportion our child too. For him to be altered in a foreign land, among foreigners, however deft and considerate, would be intolerable. Both before and after the action he'll need his family round him, his friends and fellow-clerks, and all of us. It must take place in England, in the name of God's mercy.'

'Anvil's feeling was never mentioned before,' said Morley.

'Before, there was no occasion,' answered Dilke. 'Before, everything was to follow in due course.'

Morley nodded briefly, as one acknowledging a point of minor interest. There came a gentle tap at the door and the grey-clad figure of Lawrence entered the room. With the unobtrusiveness of a well-trained servant, he made up the fire and replaced a guttering candle while his betters continued to talk.

'Then that difficulty of yours remains, my lord,' said Morley. 'This chaplain to Master Anvil – this Father Lyall, who refused to put his name to the document permitting the boy's alteration. The last I heard, he still refuses.'

'Indeed he does, out of nothing more admirable than obstinacy and the enjoyment of some brief influence over matters beyond his proper scope.' The Abbot was close to anger again, though he spoke with all his usual deliberation. 'Father Lyall is puffed up with pride of the most dangerous sort; I mean the sort that works in heretics and apostates, and in mutineers too. It confounds me – I might go so far as to say it outrages my sense of the fitness of things that, for all I know, he's never yet run foul of those in authority; it confounds me hardly less that so zealous a Christian as Master Anvil should hold him in his employ. I've no power to command his obedience, but if I had I should remind him to his duty in the most forcible terms.'

'Forgive me, my lord,' said Lawrence, who had finished his tasks – 'do you require anything more of me?'

'No thank you, Lawrence. You may go to bed.'

Dilke turned solicitously to the Abbot. 'It'll all come right, I'm quite certain. At the worst, Master Anvil will simply eject Lyall and obtain someone less self-willed. As you say, my lord, Anvil is a zealous Christian and he knows what he's under obligation to do: he wouldn't let a wretch of that petty mark stand against him. If it goes so far. We have three clear days yet; I predict that Lyall will submit at the latest moment. And the action can after all be easily postponed. All will be well, my lord. Or rather, that much will be. Heed my forecast.'

Lawrence had long left the parlour, and he made a point of never listening at doors, so he heard nothing of this speech of Dilke's, nor of the Abbot's thanks for the reassurance it offered. He went straight to his room, which was small but perhaps surprisingly comfortable, brought out ink-stylus and paper and wrote a letter in a hand that was, again, better formed than might have been expected. After addressing the cover to The Lord Stansgate, The Holy Office, The Broad Arrow Tower, London, he sealed the packet, put on his hat, walked over to the stables, took out the horse that went with his position as the Abbot's principal servant, and rode through the moonlight across to Coverley railtrack station, arriving there in plenty of time to put his letter on the midnight rapid.

The next day was pleasantly mild, though thick clouds shut out the sun. Tobias Anvil returned home in the early afternoon, briefly divulged the news from Rome and, having eaten aboard the train, left again almost at once, in a hurry to reach his counting-house and set about undoing the errors that must have been made there in the day and a half of his absence. By that time, Hubert was three parts of the way back to Coverley, alone in the cabin he had shared with his father; the servant who had accompanied them to Rome sat at the rear of the baruch, ready to escort him to St Cecilia's. Anthony, at his hospital, was attending to instruction on the use of opiates in the treatment of cholera. Margaret Anvil and Father Matthew Lyall moved slowly round the garden at Tyburn Road. They were two or three yards apart, far enough to prevent them from falling into each other's arms without thought.

Margaret looked at the flowers and shrubs, and Lyall looked at Margaret. She seemed to him more beautiful than ever before, whether because his feeling for her had induced him to see her differently, or because her happiness had made her indeed more beautiful, or the two together, he neither knew nor cared. He studied her hands and arms, her healthy skin and straight mouth, thinking he would never tire of the sight. Recent memories, intense yet vague, ran through his mind. The question of what was to become of him and her suddenly raised itself and he shut his eyes. Though he made no other movement and no sound, she turned her head in one of her quick glances.

'Such a night it was, dearest Matthew. How many times have I said that?'

'Perhaps a hundred. A long way short of enough.'

'Will there ever be another?'

'There must be. I don't know how, but there must be.'

'When Tobias dismisses you, as he will very soon, I know it, I saw it in his eye in the few minutes he was here today – when he dismisses you, where will you go?'

'Not far. No further than I must.'

'I wish you could take me with you.'

'If I did, you'd never see Hubert again.'

'Ah, I'd forgotten poor Hubert for it must have been three minutes. What's to become of him now that he's to go to Rome? Do they mean to alter him there or . . .? I don't understand.'

'Nor I, in full. But, for the moment, if you saw what you thought you saw in Tobias then, it would look as if the original design is being held to; he would have no reason to dismiss me otherwise. And the Pope must prefer the action to be in England. Our overlords enjoy the appearance of humanity, so long as their ease isn't hurt. Yes, perhaps I can hold them off a little longer.'

'The three of us must escape together.'

'Escape? The ends of the earth are too near for that.'

'Nearer yet, Matthew. Only to New England.'

'That you've said more often than enough. Fine incomers we should be there: a Romish priest and his woman and her son. Oh, their discipline isn't ours, but it's strict enough. And how should we ever gain an exeat? And to try to leave without one would be lunatic. We'd be taken and shut away for ever. At best. Now please walk on. Even the pantry-boy, seeing us like this, would know that you and I are not a lady and her spiritual counsellor. Which puts me in mind. When will you visit Father Raymond?'

'Never, that I can think of. Why should I go? He'll call on me to repent and to cease from sinning. I can't repent and I won't cease from sinning. Finis.'

'Finis too to your expectation of heaven, Margaret. Like mine, your soul is in mortal danger.'

'Twaddle – I don't mean to die until the century's out. I'll repent at leisure. Of which I'm apt to have all I need. And when were you last confessed?'

'That's of no import. You must go to Father Raymond and try to obtain absolution. You must try to repent, at least.' Something lifeless had entered Lyall's tone. 'The pleasure you take in sinning is an index of the gravity of the sin. The more irresistible the repetition of the offence, the more certainly we know that we are doing Satan's work. The act of repentance . . .'

He stopped speaking as if he could not go on. Her sudden

look into his eyes held curiosity and a shade of horror.

'Matthew: you believe in God and His Son and Our Lady and all the saints and the blessed martyrs? And the authority of the Holy Father and the –'

'Of course. Of course I do.'

'Will you swear?'

Now the priest's gaze grew lifeless. 'No,' he said at length.

'Then you don't believe after all?'

'No. I used to, quite unquestioningly and unheedingly, until the other day.'

'What happened the other day?'

'I found I'd begun to love you as you love me. The Church holds without the slightest equivocation that everything you and I do together is a sin. I know that to be false. Therefore . . .'

'Oh, Matthew, I've taken your faith from you.'

'I have you instead of it. It's a fair exchange. But that won't do for you, dearest Margaret. I may be in error, and although I'll face the consequences to myself I can't permit you to come within a million miles of damnation. If there's anything to be safe from, save yourself. Go to Father Raymond.'

There was silence, apart from birdsong and the hum of bees. Whatever vehicles might have been passing along Tyburn Road, their sound did not carry to the two in the garden. Margaret reached forward and lightly grasped a red rose. Then she said,

'Love works changes, doesn't it? When they first let me know Hubert was to be altered, I was no more than a doting mother anxious to protect her child from anything that might possibly cause him the least distress. Now I mean all that I said before.'

'I know, and I understand, and my feeling is the same as yours.'

She looked at him, not in passing as she usually did, but steadily. Her breathing quickened. 'Matthew.'

'No, Margaret.'

'Yes. Nothing would bring Tobias back early from his counting-house after being away from it yesterday and this morning. Go to your room. I'll tell the steward I visit my milliner. I'll come to you in five minutes. Go now.'

Lyall went to his room. As he stood motionless by the bed,

his body was filled with an excitement that was also the deepest calm he had ever known. After a minute, there was a knock at the door. He was mildly surprised.

'Come.'

Two strangers entered. They were men in their thirties dressed in black jacket and breeches, both garments piped in scarlet. The left sleeve of each carried the scarlet, black and white bracciata of the Secular Arm.

'Father Lyall?' The speaker wore eyeglasses and had a cultivated accent. His tone and manner were cold without being in the least discourteous.

'I am he, master,' said the priest, squaring his shoulders. 'How can I serve you?'

'Officer. Officer, not master. I am Officer Foot. My colleague here is Officer Redgrave.' There were appreciable, regular pauses between the sentences. 'How can you serve us? Very simply. There's a document that requires your signature. You refuse to affix it. Tell us why.'

'How can that be your concern? Officer.' As soon as the words were out, Lyall cursed his own foolishness. Bewilderment at this irruption, simple fright, and agitated speculation about who it could be that had informed the Tower of his recalcitrance (surely not Anvil?) had between them caused him to play for time when time was what he had least of: Margaret must arrive at any moment and he had, he realized, no idea how she would respond to unforeseen danger – for danger it was. If either of them were to let fall a hint of the terms they were on, both would be vulnerable to a charge of SU (Suspicion of Unchastity), which, having been close to attachment on such a charge more than once in the past, he knew carried a standard penalty of eight years' purification.

With just a hint of weariness, Redgrave had said, 'Where were you hatched, Father? Surely you must know that everything is our concern. Now do as Officer Foot tells you, and if you've any craft you'll do so at once, on the spot, rather than a little later, down at the Tower.'

The interval gave Lyall time to steady himself and to start thinking. 'Your indulgence, officers: I was surprised to see you. I expected Dame Anvil, my master's wife, whose confession I'm to hear.'

'In this room of yours?' asked Foot flatly.

'Of course. The luxury of the house doesn't conduce to the spirit of devotion that's needful.'

'I see. Answer my first question. You refuse to sign the document I spoke of. Why?'

Here Lyall was given another breathing space, though not one he would have chosen. A light step was heard on the stairs. At once, without reference to each other, the two officers moved over to the corner of the room by the chest-of-drawers, where they were out of sight from the doorway. Lyall bit at the inside of his cheek: if Margaret was going to do as she usually did, she would hurry up to him immediately the door was open, saying things that nobody should ever say to a priest. The door opened and she appeared. Although she had for the moment no ordinary way of knowing that there were others in the room (certainly not from any intended move by Lyall himself, who was under the careful gaze of both officers), she responded as fast as she had in the garden ten minutes before, stood her ground and uttered not a word. He said mildly,

'Dame Anvil, I'm well aware that I'm in your honoured husband's service, but these are my quarters, and I'd be greatly favoured if you'd knock before entering them. However, please come in. These are two gentlemen from the Tower.'

She gave them a distant nod as she walked forward, her mouth set. 'I, Father Lyall, should be greatly favoured if you'd refrain from admonishing me in the hearing of strangers. That's no way for anybody, high or low, to conduct himself.'

'My excuses, dame, I . . .'

'Perhaps you'll attend me in my sitting-room when your business here is done. Good-day, gentlemen.'

The door shut behind her. Redgrave looked sidelong at Foot, who shut his eyes briefly in negation. The pair approached Lyall again. He almost groaned aloud with the effort of not showing the smallest sign of relief at Margaret's successful departure, which he had done his best to round off with a shrug and a shake of the head. Officer Foot came and stood, legs apart, hands behind back, a yard from him. After staring him in the eyes for some seconds, he said as deliberately as ever,

'I ask you for the third time. You refuse your signature. Why?'

Lyall was no longer frightened. Relief still had hold of him, accompanied by a sense of triumph and, more than either, love. Until just now, he had supposed it impossible that his feeling for Margaret could grow, but in that moment it had, and this woman loved him. He was possessed by elation, though he had room also for the thought that here in front of him was about as good a representative as he would find of everything he most disliked in the world he had been born into. The priest had come to a very dangerous mood. Trying to match the other's tone, he said,

'I choose to. No more than that.'

'I must have more than that. Your reason for so choosing.'

'I choose not to give it.'

'Give it here and now, or elsewhere later.'

'Your indulgence, officer, but I can't take you seriously. How in the name of St Peter can *why* I act as I do be of import?'

'If it was on the orders of certain unlawful –' said Redgrave before Foot interrupted him.

'It's only my first question, Father.'

'Still one too many. Now I'll make a compact with you. You give me your reason for wanting to know my reason, and I'll consider giving you my reason.'

Redgrave sighed noisily. 'We don't make compacts, Father. Have you learned so little in your life?'

'Then I've nothing to tell you.'

'You first defy the wishes of your superiors, the Lord Abbot of St Cecilia's Chapel and Master Anvil, and now you defy the Holy Office,' said Foot.

'If you say so.'

'Don't be a nitwit, Father,' said Redgrave, screwing up his face. 'You ask to go to the Tower.'

Lyall had not even reached the point of dismissing this

threat as idle: he simply disregarded it. 'Fuck a fox, the pair of you,' he said without warmth. 'You're mean of spirit – none who was not would lower himself to do your tasks, even so slight a one as this present errand. You're false, claiming to serve a just and merciful God and at the same time proud to wear the colour of blood on your dress. And you're dull and dismal, you're enemies of all wit. Hope at best to be laughed at, officers, with your pretty armlets like some gewgaw from a boy's motley-box. Now take yourselves back to your beloved Tower and leave me to my work.'

Foot had listened to this with close attention and total impassivity, restraining his companion's several attempts to interrupt, one of them physical. 'Is there more?' he asked.

'You may have more.'

'No, we have enough.'

'Enough to attach you,' shouted Redgrave.

'Upon what inculpation?' Foot betrayed very slight surprise. 'It's an offence to cast a servant of the State or the Church into obloquy and disrepute, and, uttered in public, a tenth part of what we've heard would surely fetch an inculpation. But all this was in private.'

'But his gross defiance – his refusal to . . .'

'Our commission was only to ask questions, not to compel replies.'

'But the type outfaces our threat to remove him!'

A silent message passed from Foot to Redgrave; the latter at once stopped protesting. Foot addressed Lyall.

'Your conduct has been noted. That concludes our dealings.'

Trying to hide his puzzlement, Lyall said, 'For the moment.'

'The Holy Office has no more to say to you on this count.'

The two moved off without a word of farewell, though Redgrave looked over his shoulder with something like contempt as he reached the door. Lyall groaned and rubbed his forehead, then turned to the long narrow window that faced Tyburn Road. At the edge of the footway stood a black express, its varnished panels trimmed out in scarlet. In ones and twos, a dozen or more of the people had gathered near it, on the chance of seeing some offender, perhaps with the marks of a beating on him, flung inside and carried away. Foot and Redgrave came into Lyall's view walking down the drive from the express-house. Already, the bystanders had seen that they were unaccompanied and begun to disperse, but by degrees, staring dully up at the house as if it could tell them what man it was that had attracted the notice of the Secular Arm, whether to give orders or supply information. The driver of the vehicle came round from his place and, first jostling an old woman out of his path, opened the rear door. Redgrave got in at once; Foot paused and looked straight in the direction of Lyall, who drew back a pace even as he told himself that he could not possibly have been seen. Then the door shut after Foot, the driver took his seat and the express pulled out, causing an omnibus to brake sharply.

Lyall left the window. Could it be so easy to have beaten them off? The Tower was known to be most punctilious in adhering to the letter of its own statutes: no doubt the officers were on their way to sift its archives for material that might provide them with a firmer grip upon him. But would they not have done that before visiting him in the first place? Perhaps. Who had been the author of the citation against him? He was more than ever certain that it had not been Tobias Anvil, who had a much simpler means of overcoming him, one that could never be said, even by the most ingenious enemy, to comprehend trouble with the authorities. The Abbot? There was little enough to be said for that dignitary, except that this sort of work seemed not to be in his style. Collam Flackerty (from whom nothing had been heard since their interview)? Not at all impossible – but why?

There was no more time for questions when Margaret came back into the room. They stood with their arms round each other and did not move.

'I saw them go.'

'Outraged dignity. Like Winifred the Queen-Mother herself.'

'What did they want?'

'Blessed are the keen of apprehension, for they shall arouse desire. They – those, those two – they tried to cow me and I remained uncowed.'

'Will they return?'

'Not in the next hour. Not for long enough, if ever.'

'They made me afraid.'

'I'll take your fear away. I promise to. I can take no other fear away, but this I can, and only I.'

CHAPTER FIVE

In the dormitory at St Cecilia's, Hubert finished folding a coloured shirt and tucked it carefully away in his valigia, watched by Thomas and Mark. Thomas said in the customary after-dowse-lights undertone,

'You should go to the woods. You could find a hollow, wrap yourself in a blanket and not be cold. We'd bring you food.'

Hubert shook his head firmly. 'You'd be missed, then seen, then followed. I won't have you suffer penance for me. My way's best.'

'Tell us where you do mean to go.'

'As before, Tom, I won't have you lie or be held sinfully obstinate on my account.'

'Then – why do you go at last? After not going at first? Because of . . . fucking? Say, Hubert.'

'No, because of something Master Morley told me about myself just before I was summoned to Rome. That's as much as I'll say.'

'But weren't you tempted at all by what the Pope offered you?'

'Oh yes, greatly, but not enough, and so my mind was made up. If something of that mark didn't signify, nothing would.'

'I beg you not to defy the will of the Holy Father, which is also God's will.' This was Mark. 'In the name of your saint. In Our Lady's name. In Christ's name.'

Without speaking, Hubert again shook his head.

'You think you can continue as runaway for ever?'

'A few months will be enough, Mark. Perhaps only a few weeks. Until I'm too old to be altered and save my voice.'

'Fool! Apostate!'

'Silence, Mark,' said Thomas in a hiss. Then he turned and reached under his pillow. 'Before you fasten those straps . . . I don't know if you'll have time to do much reading.'

Hubert glanced at the almost intact cover of the book. '*Galliard*. Keith Roberts.'

'It's CW. What would have happened if the Schismatics' attempt to abduct Elizabeth Tudor had succeeded and they'd reared her as one of themselves.'

'Flying machines?'

'No, but electricity.'

'Wonderful. Thank you, Tom.'

'Now you must be away.'

Thomas carefully opened the door, listened, and nodded to Hubert, who picked up his valigia.

'Stay a moment.' Mark took from round his neck a thin chain bearing a plain silver cross and transferred it to Hubert. 'God give you His protection wherever you go.'

'Thank you, Mark,' said Hubert, and paused. He wanted to kiss Thomas, and would not have drawn back from kissing Mark as he would then have been obliged to, but he did not dare, and shook hands with them instead. 'I'll see you both again – that I know. Good-bye.'

'Be lucky,' said Thomas.

Hubert went out; the door shut silently behind him. There was almost no light in the corridor, but the positions of the windows along it showed well enough to give him his bearings. With his fingertips brushing the inner wall he moved along to the stairhead, his feet in rubber-soled shoes making no sound on the tiles. The handrail guided him down to the hall and he found the outer door after only a few moments' groping; it was unlocked, as he had been told it would be. Closing it on the far side, he unguardedly let the latch fall with a loud clink and stood rigid. Nothing happened. He turned his head and there was the central statue of St Cecilia, showing as a dark shape partly edged with pale silver under the moon, a candle or two burning inside the buttery, the window of the Abbot's parlour defined by an oil-lamp. It was in that direction that he now made his way, then through the arch into the completely unlit rear yard, past the carp-pond and towards the left-hand cluster of farm buildings. From among these, an affronted barking suddenly burst out; it died down again as suddenly when Hubert, kneeling by Smart's kennel, passed over the chunk of boiled beef he had taken out of supper for the purpose. He added some strokes and pats which brought tail-thumps in return, perhaps in recognition, and whispered a farewell.

The going was more difficult after that, up a slanting slope broken by tussocks of long grass. After stumbling twice in a dozen yards, he halted and collected himself: he must not turn an ankle now. As he stood there, something like a joined pair of fists butted him in the small of the back, not hard enough to knock him down, though, twisting aside half in alarm, half in an attempt to strike out at whatever it was that had shoved him, he did fall on to hands and knees. There was a grunt, a quick footfall or two, and a snapping of stems, but, by the time he was up again, nothing to be seen. Just then he heard a faint whistle from under a clump of small trees, and went there as fast as he safely could.

'So, master runaway,' said Decuman's voice. 'Have a piss before you set off. There's six hours at least till full light, so wherever you mean to go you needn't scramble. If a constable questions you, you act like a noodle. 'The priest . . . send . . . for me,' and if he asks where, point the way you go. He'll soon tire of you. Get your food at stalls and pattie-shops, never at an eating-house, however low. Journey by night, except through towns, and sleep in the open by day.'

'You told me all this before.'

'I tell you again. Now come and stand by me. There's the road. Left to Coverley and London, right to Oxford and the North. You see? Good. Mount, then. Give me your foot.'

Hubert was quickly settled astride the pony that had been waiting almost in silence near by. It looked black, but then so would most horses in such deep shade.

'This is old Joan,' continued Decuman. 'She's well-behaved – just let her carry you. Now in here there's cheese, bread and apples. Water. And . . .' He reached for Hubert's hand and put some coins into it.

'You give me too much,' said Hubert, stowing the money away in his pocket: he did not care to count it in front of Decuman, but he could feel the milled edges of a half-crown and a shilling. 'Too much of everything. How can I ever thank you?'

'By staying free.'

'You put yourself in serious danger, stealing a horse.'

'I didn't steal her – you did.'

'The Abbot will know different.'

'The Abbot never acts without proof. And that puts me in mind : try not to be caught with Joan. You're less than twelve, therefore they can't send you to gaol, but they can give you infants' purification. I hear that's best avoided.'

'No doubt. Why do you do all this for me, Decuman?'

'Because I'm safe and you're not. I'll always be safe from whatever they may try against me – I'm too crafty for them. Not you. You've plenty of wit, more than I have, but you're not crafty. And you entered my dormitory.'

'That wasn't your choice or mine : I was allotted.'

'You entered just the same.'

Joan, impatient for the journey, tossed her head and blew gently down her nostrils. Hubert said,

'If I'm not crafty, how can I hope to stay free?'

'By following what I told you, and by luck, and by their stupidity : they're well practised in the catching of felons and apostates, but where are they to look for you if not at your father's house – and you don't mean to go there, I hope?'

'No.'

'By God's grace too. There must be such a thing. Good-bye, Hubert.'

'Decuman, I wish I had a hogshead of ale and a pretty young miss to give you.'

'So do I, my dear, so do I. Now go carefully.'

Catching the note of farewell, the pony had already started to move; the merest touch of Hubert's knee brought her round the small distance necessary to set her straight downhill. She stepped as carefully as Decuman could have wished, but without fuss or hesitation, and Hubert looked forward to an easy ride. Everything was in place : the provision-bag, the water-flask, his valiga with its carrying-strap handily looped over the pommel in front of him. He took a deep, slow breath, and all that he had left behind him faded from his thoughts. Even the Chapel itself to his left, a dark pointed bulk touched with light here and there, served only to give him his bearings. He reached the road and turned Joan towards Coverley and London.

It was neither a warm nor a cool night: when the breeze touched his cheek, it felt to be of exactly the same temperature as himself. Patches of shadow passed briefly over him and slid away down the road ahead. He looked into the sky and saw thin rags of cloud twisting about over the face of the moon with a speed and violence whose soundlessness seemed the more unnatural for the multitude of sounds, soft but clear, that came from close by: the groan of leather, the regular thud of hoofs, Joan's occasional snorts, the scurrying of some small creature through the grasses near the road, the indignant shriek of an Athene's owl, with, further off, the notes of a bell in Coverley, the muffled beat of a manufactory machine and, rapidly approaching from behind, the unmistakable noise of a vehicle engine.

Before he thought, Hubert had urged Joan into a canter; when he did think, it was to reason that pursuit could not be on its way so soon, then, as the noise grew nearer and lamplight began to illuminate his surroundings, to reason further that he must have been seen by now and had better behave like someone with no cause for fear. He pulled the pony back to a walk and a moment later halted her against the hedge, patting her neck and telling her gently that she was not a green young filly who would shy at anything a little out of the way. As it happened, she had been to market scores of times, felt perfectly indifferent towards all forms of transport, and did nothing more than toss her head when the express, as it proved to be, came drumming past. As before, the head-tossing showed impatience, but when Hubert indicated that they should move on again she stood her ground for some seconds, evidently to mark her disapproval of the abrupt and unjust ending of an enjoyable scamper.

By the time the rear lamps of the express had disappeared, other lights, fixed ones, were in clear view, and it was not long before boy and horse made an upward turn on to the stone facing of the street that led to the centre of the capital. It was bright with gasoliers on poles and gantries; Hubert held off the impulse to wheel aside into the protective darkness of one alley or another. He had calculated earlier, and now told himself again, that to do so would be the act of a nitwit. The side thoroughfares were long since under curfew and patrolled by the constabulary; anyone found in them without a valid transeat (which even Decuman's resources could not have secured) would be attached at once. Far better to stay in the light with the honest folk. Hubert pulled down the peak of his cap, tried to look as tall as he could in the saddle, and quietly rehearsed the rumbling bass voice he would use if accosted.

There seemed no likelihood of that for the moment. Publics and expresses passed to and fro; an overnight express-omnibus thundered by on its way from London to the North. From the ristorantes and caffès, still brightly lit and resounding with music, the last guests were coming out on to the footway in their many-coloured silks and velvets, laughing and talking loudly. None of them had any eyes for Hubert. Somebody who did was a young constable with whiskers, readily identifiable by his spiked helmet, but before anything was done or said an ill-clad man of the people rushed across his path out of an alley, followed by another holding aloft some sort of club, and there was no attention to spare for a nondescript figure on a quietly plodding horse. Hubert took a further deep breath.

Soon, it seemed within a few yards, the character of the street changed. The overhead lights continued, but the buildings were mostly dark and silent: shops, theatres, extravaganza-houses, concert-halls. Only the churches were illuminated, though dimly – the churches and the doorways and curtained windows of establishments Hubert did not at once identify: he had seldom visited this part of the city, and never at night. Then he saw one of the comparatively few foot-passengers, a middle-aged man, respectably dressed, pause at such a doorway, pull the bell, and at once move apart as if to peer into the unlit front of an adjacent bottega. Just as Hubert drew level, someone answered the bell, and the man, head lowered and hand over face, hurried inside. At the same time, there drifted across a snatch of music, not of the sort heard earlier. It came to a cadence and was followed by applause and by shouts of approval that had a curious growling undertone to them. Hubert understood, and said to himself that he must tell ... But he hoped never to see Decuman again.

Here was the turning; Hubert leaned to his left and Joan followed or went with the movement. Two hundred yards away was safety, and shelter too: small drops of rain had begun to touch his face and swirl slowly under the gaslight. There was nobody to be seen, and no sound came from any of the houses he passed, none either from the house whose courtyard he entered, but a lamp was burning over the doorway. Halted close by, he took the water-flask and drained it; he was not thirsty, but he must use what it had cost Decuman trouble and risk to get for him. The same reasoning led him to transfer to his valigia the provisions, wrapped in coarse paper. This done, he dismounted, tied the pony's reins to the hitching-rail beside the steps, and wielded the door-knocker.

In not much over a minute, there came the sound of bolts being withdrawn and, with a squeak and a rattle, the door opened. The man who had once before opened it to Hubert stood on the threshold. He wore a red nightgown and carried a lighted candle.

'Yes?'

'Are you Samuel?'

'No, I'm Domingo.' The man held the candle-flame forward and his puzzled expression gave way to a smile, though his eyes were still alert. 'I know you, young master. You come here before. To afternoon table. And you sung after.'

'Yes, Domingo. I give you my humblest excuses for disturbing you at this hour, but I'm in danger. I come to ask for the protection of the Ambassador.'

'His Excellence is not here.'

'Where is he?'

'His Excellence is at his embassy in London. He stays there two weeks more.'

'But I must see him,' said Hubert helplessly.

'His Excellence is in London,' said Domingo, and started to close the door.

'I have nowhere to go and nowhere to sleep, and if I'm caught I'll be locked up. Please let me in.'

'No permission, no permission.'

'Would you see your son driven from his friend's door? When Master van den Haag hears of it, he'll –'

'I don't have no son.' After a moment, Domingo smiled again, with all his face this time, and pulled the door wide open. 'But I do have nephews, and it'll rain more soon. Please to come in, young master.'

Hubert followed him across the spacious hall, in which the candle gave vague glimpses of paintings, flower-baskets, a looking-glass in a heavy frame, and down a passage into what must be the kitchen. Here Domingo lit a gas-lamp above the long wooden table and considered Hubert again. He looked sad when he was not smiling.

'You want to eat?' he asked.

'Yes. Yes, please.' Hubert had taken care to sup well that evening, but policy as well as inclination required acceptance of any offer of food.

Very soon, Domingo had set in front of him salame, dark bread, a kind of sweet cake with chopped nuts, and a mug of milk. 'I come back quick,' said the man, and left him.

As he ate and drank, Hubert's spirits declined. He told himself he should have taken account of what he had known perfectly well: that Coverley was the capital of the land, but London the seat of its government, and that ambassadors might be expected to spend less of their time in the one than in the other. All he had gained by coming to this house was a respite, a brief interval before he must mount Joan again and set off on a journey of almost sixty miles through rain and darkness – some of it through darkness, rather, for it would be broad day long before he could even hope to reach London. What was his chance of finding van den Haag there before he himself was found by the constables? Small: at least it felt small.

When Domingo returned he had with him the other Indian, Samuel. The two had clearly been conferring on Hubert and what was to happen to him.

'Please to tell Samuel and me why you come here,' said Domingo.

'They – the Abbot at the Chapel, and the priests – they mean to have me altered and I want to escape, and Master van den Haag is the only –'

'Altered? How altered?'

'Act on me so that I can never be a man. Take from me what makes a man.'

Samuel was the first to understand. He said in a horrified voice, 'What you done, little boy?'

'Nothing. Nothing except sing. They mean me to continue to sing with a boy's voice after I should be a man.'

'In New England, they don't do that to children, they . . .'

Abruptly, Samuel stopped and looked at his companion. There was a short silent conversation carried on with facial movements and strange gestures. It ended with an exchange of nods, then turned into talk, a kind of talk that reminded Hubert of what Hilda had said when she talked like the people in New England (so she had remembered well). He followed the earlier part without much trouble: Samuel suggested that the boy should stay here while a message was sent to London, Domingo objected and mentioned some disagreeable person called the Secretary, and Samuel took his point. Thereafter intelligibility lapsed, but agreement was soon reached. Domingo turned to Hubert.

'Do you have money?'

Hubert brought out Decuman's gift and what had been in his own purse and counted. 'Six shillings and three farthings.'

'Enough. Now Samuel take you in the express to the rail-track station. You go on the late rapid to London. Then you go to the Embassy. You tell Citizen van den Haag how you come.'

'Where is the Embassy?'

'On St Edmund Street.'

'Where's that?'

'By St Giles's.' Domingo hesitated. 'I . . . stay here; I don't go there.'

Hubert took his meaning, that his knowledge of London was poor. 'No matter, I'll find it.'

'Good. You go now.'

'My horse!' said Hubert, remembering. 'I left her outside.'

'Your horse, yes?'

'Please would you shelter her and feed her, and take her home tomorrow? You needn't deliver her – if you set her free within half a mile of the Chapel, she'll find her way home.'

Domingo considered, then nodded his head. 'It'll be done. Go with Samuel now or you miss the rapid.'

'Thank you, Domingo.'

'It's nothing, young master.'

'But it isn't nothing. You've been good to me out of no need. I'll pray for you.'

To Hubert's surprise, the man looked stern for a moment, even angry. When this passed, he gave another nod and a faint smile, murmured something and went out by the door that led to the hall. Samuel, now holding a lighted lantern, signed that Hubert was to follow and moved away in the other direction, through a still-room where shelves of preserves and cordials were fleetingly to be seen, and at last into the open. The rain was blowing more strongly, but seemed no thicker. Samuel locked up after them and set off again along the side of the building to what proved to be the express-house. Hubert looked on in wonder when Samuel pulled down a lever set in the wall and, with a hiss of escaping compressed air, a long door swung slowly upwards and outwards. When it had come to rest in a horizontal position, the Indian motioned towards the express, the same that had carried Hubert the previous week, or its twin.

'May I sit by you, Samuel?'

'Surely.'

Hubert watched while the man lit the lamps at front and rear, then, having climbed in beside him, started the engine with the clockwork motor, shifted the gear-arm and let in the gland. The express moved slowly into a short lane that brought it to the street, where it gathered speed. Raindrops whirled against the windguard and, although the swabbers were in action, Hubert found it hard to see out and soon lost his bearings.

'Will it disturb you if I talk?'

'No.'

'What did I do that offended Domingo?'

'Not offended.'

'There was something that didn't please him.'

'Ah now, see, little boy, we think a man saying his prayers, that's his own matter. We don't love him to talk about it. We, I mean we at home in New England. But you don't go and think you offended that Domingo. He knew in a minute you was just thankful to see him. See, it's all right.'

'You are kind, Samuel. And Domingo too. Please tell me – the boys at the Chapel helped me, but they're my friends, they must be, but you and Domingo have met me only once before, he hardly saw me, and yet you're both so kind, out of no need, as I said. Why?'

'Same idea. Religion. Hear this between you and me: we at home, we hate your Pope and your monks and your priests. Domingo parts from Mexico and comes to New England, the Archbishop of El Paso, he says Domingo isn't a Christian no more, what is it he done?'

'Excommunicated him?'

'Say so. He wants Domingo to go to hell. That don't make Domingo go to hell, but that Archbishop, he don't know that. Goddam popeling. So you come to hide from the priests, we help you. And, see, at home, anybody runs away any time, we help him.'

'Do many folks run away in New England?'

'Indians, they do. Now, pardon, this piece of road, I go mighty careful.'

Hubert took the hint and said no more on the subject. Somewhere in the distance he noticed an irregular patch of light that might have been the station. He half-listened to the hammering of the engine and the swish of the rubber tires through the rain. His curiosity was again at work, but it was a full two minutes before he yielded to it.

'Samuel, whom do they alter in New England?'

'Uh?'

'When I told you the priests meant to alter me, you said they didn't do it to children there. That shows they do it to some others.'

'I don't remember, young master.'

Stealthily, Hubert turned his head and scanned the exotic, handsome profile beside him. He could not make out much detail, and his experience of reading characters from faces had been necessarily brief, but he thought he could read a firm self-respect, some obstinacy, and a distinct trace of the sadness he had noticed in Domingo, a look of long-remembered disappointment. But there was humour too. Hubert said abruptly,

'I won't let the Secretary know anything.'

Samuel gave a faint smile, but his voice was not merry when he spoke. 'A man sins too much with women, they alter him. A man sins in other ways, ways of not being pure, they alter him.'

'A man? Surely not any man. Surely a priest.'

'A pastor. No, any man. Like my brother. Now I take you to the train.'

The station was crowded with travellers taking advantage of the cheap fares payable late at night: Hubert's half-price journey-tab cost him ten minutes' wait in a line and threepence-farthing. Most of the folk were pilgrims in bands of fifty or a hundred, bound for Rome, for Jerusalem (a destination unattainable for over thirty years before the Sultan-Calif, as part of his policy of detensione, had re-opened it to Christians in 1967), for the tomb of St James of Compostella in Spain, for the shrine of St Thomas Becket in Canterbury, the richest in northern Europe.

With Samuel at his side, Hubert walked up the pavement beside the train, past the mail vans being filled with the familiar grey sacks, past the loaded cargo vans to the passenger baruches. Samuel found Hubert a passage seat in a people's baruch opposite a friendly-looking old woman who carried on her lap a closed basket of chirping and rustling small birds. He asked her please to tend to this young stable-lad on his way to visit his sick mother in London. Then he looked hard at Hubert and said in his strange accent,

'Good-bye, little boy. I hope your God take care of you.'

He was gone before Hubert could reply. After a time, a shrill bell rang, doors slammed, the baruch shuddered gently and the journey started. The man next to Hubert, a hireling by the look of him, curled himself up on the wooden bench and began to snore almost at once. Dirty children ran up and down the passage, a game of dice on the bench behind aroused increasing emotions; somewhere further back, a blurred voice sang very slowly and unsteadily (and with copious ornamentation) a song from an extravaganza of the Thirties. But despite all these and other distractions, despite having meant to share his provisions with the old woman and to encourage her to talk about her family, he fell asleep almost as soon as the train was out of the station. He dreamed he was on Joan's back again and the ground under her feet was so soft, or her gait so smooth, that the saddle did not move at all, except forwards in a straight line. In the end she stopped; he woke to find that it was the train that had stopped, and half the other passengers were already on their feet. The old woman asked him if he needed help in making his way to where his mother lived. Her speech was uncouth, but her meaning was as plain as her good intentions. He thanked her and told her he would have no difficulty.

Nor would he, he was confident. Instead of taking an express-omnibus to the St Giles's neighbourhood and searching for St Edmund Street on foot, an exercise he had not been looking forward to, he would do what had been in his mind when he woke and be carried straight to the Embassy by public. (The drivers of London publics were famous all over Christendom for knowing their city down to its remotest alley; each had to pass the Civil Constabulary's rigorous probation in such knowledge before being granted his charter.) This obvious course had not occurred to Hubert earlier because travelling in this fashion was not expected in an unaccompanied child, even a child of the higher degree.

Beside the long arcade on the east side of the station stood a long file of publics, showing as well as their road-lamps the green light indicating that they were vacant. Instinct, and a touch of chill in the air, kept Hubert in the shelter of the arcade while the couple of dozen folk waiting at the head of the file were accommodated and driven away. Then, after a quick glance to and fro, he hurried across to the vehicle that stood at the front. The driver turned and saw him, but instead of opening his window on its pivot to hear instructions, as would have been customary, the man scowled fiercely and jerked his thumb and first two fingers downwards in the 'go to hell' gesture. Hubert understood at once. His cap, trousers and corduroy jerkin effectively disguised him as one of the people, an advantage at most points in his travels, not so here: he had of course been taken for a beggar or a tout. He reached in his pocket, found a shilling and held it up. The publicman's expression showed surprise, then thought. After a moment he swung the pain of glass aside.

'Ay, well?'

'Take me to the New Englander Embassy in St Edmund Street,' said Hubert authoritatively.

More thought. 'What you want there, then?'

'The Ambassador requires me to visit him.'

'Ah, does he so? That'll do, young master. One shilling.'

It was scandalous overcharging, but Hubert had no choice. 'I accept.'

'I take you,' said the driver, thus sealing the contract, and doused his green light.

Very soon, the public had entered Tyburn Road and was passing the Anvil house. It was in darkness, as was nearly every other building. The gasoliers still burned, illuminating stretches of empty footway. An express, moving slowly and in a series of irregular swerves, was the only vehicle Hubert saw. Then, to his surprise, the public turned left into Apostle Andrew Street; he knew that St Giles's lay in the opposite direction.

'Why do we go here, driver?'

'Excuses, young master, I must get me more fuel. Only a minute to it.'

As he spoke, the driver took them left again, away from the gaslight down a narrow alley which, after more turns, ended in a small cobbled yard. The roadlamps showed soot-stained brick walls, two pairs of wooden doors, a shed with a broken window.

'Is this the place?' asked Hubert doubtfully.

'Oh yes,' said the driver, cutting off his engine. 'I got to wake him now. Not more nor a minute to it.'

The man leaned forward and opened some compartment in front of him; there followed a rustling noise, as of thin paper. Hubert sat and peered without success and wondered: he knew nothing of the kind of place where publics took in their fuel, but this one seemed rather remote. At last the driver left his seat and walked across to one of the sets of doors. Instead of knocking, he put his hand to his chest, swayed, and called hoarsely,

'Young master! I'm that sick! Give me your arm, for Mary's sake!'

Hubert jumped down on to the cobbles. He noticed that the moon was shining again and that a dog was barking somewhere on the far side of the yard. He reached the driver, who at once straightened himself, seized him, and slapped over his mouth and nose a piece of damp cloth with a smell like that of flowers that had been cut too long. It made his body begin to feel light and empty. There was a humming or droning sound, and the skin on his cheeks and the back of his neck first tingled, then slackened, then went numb. He remembered that he had never asked the old woman in the train what birds she carried in her basket.

'Hear him speak, Jacob, you see I'm right.'

'I hope you are. And I hope I shall hear him speak soon. A lad that size needs no more than a whiff.'

'I gave him no more.'

'I hope not.'

The man the public-driver had called Jacob pronounced his

words in an odd way, as if he had difficulty with his tongue and teeth. The air was warm and permeated with the smell of wood-smoke and damp, also with sharper, less identifiable smells. Hubert found himself lying under a blanket on a lumpy divan or day-bed. He opened his eyes a little to discover something of his surroundings while still supposedly unconscious, but could not make out much more than streaks and shadows, so he abandoned subterfuge and raised his head. Apart from severe thirst, all he felt was a dull puzzlement.

The two men left their chairs by the rusty iron fireplace and came over to him. The driver, now seen clearly for the first time, had nothing but an uncommonly loose, moist pair of lips to distinguish him from countless others of his degree. His companion – Jacob – was tall and round-backed, with a long shawl of some kind thrown over his shoulders and gathered at his breast by a curious fermaglio, so that the rest of his garments were vague; after the same fashion, a full grey beard and whiskers allowed little more of his face to be seen than a high-bridged nose and a pair of deep brown eyes. He wore a black skull-cap. After a moment, he said in his lisping voice, 'Speak, boy. Be good enough to let us know your name.'

Hubert sat up straight on the edge of the day-bed. His father's training made him say as imperatively as he could, 'I'll let you know nothing until you bring me a glass of water.'

'Eh, eh! Won't you so? Very well, very well. Jack, do as the young master requires.'

The driver hurried off into what was evidently a scullery. Aware of the scrutiny of Jacob's eyes, but ignoring it as far as he could, Hubert looked about. He was sitting in a narrow kitchen with a low ceiling and a single tiny window near a door that must lead to the front of the dwelling. The only light came from the fire and a couple of bare candles stuck on the shelf above it, though near by he noticed an elaborate candle-stick with seven empty sockets. There was something curious about the walls, more than that they were discoloured with damp in places and smeared with grime: no pictures hung on them.

Soon, Jack returned with a large earthenware mug. The

water in it had a stale taste, but Hubert drained it.

'You wish for more, young master?' asked Jacob, his long hands clasped in front of him.

'No thank you. Not now.'

'So ... Ah, Jack, my boy, I give you my excuses for doubting you. You are right. The Embassy might have been a story, the dress is of the people, but now I hear him speak ...'

'So – my drink, Jacob?'

'Of course, of course. You know where to find it.'

Jack nodded eagerly, reached into a cupboard or other receptacle on the further side of the chair he had sat in, and brought out a tin mug and a bottle labelled *Fine English Brandy: Cordone Blu*. Dreamily, Hubert remembered the blazing brandy that had crowned the family pudding the previous St Lucy's Day, its flames symbolizing (so his father had said) the baptism of fire prophesied for the earliest followers of Our Lord. But Jacob was speaking again.

'Now, young master, you merit an explanation. It's all very simple. My good friend Jack here and I are in commerce together. Every time he goes out at night and takes up in his public some likely one of the gentry – an old person, a sick person, or this time a very young person, sir – he gives him that opiate of his and brings him to me. Then we send to the person's family and we ask for quite a small sum, maybe twenty pounds, maybe more, in return for the person's being set free unharmed. We hold to our word. If the money comes, well and good. If it doesn't, the person is harmed and set free, but that's rare indeed, rare indeed. Isn't it very simple, sir?'

'Too much so.' Hubert tried to maintain his air of superiority. 'How simple is it when the constables come looking?'

'About the same, yes. The constables in these parts, we see to it that they like us a great deal, so they don't look too closely. If the person himself and his family come looking, they never find this place: do you know just where you are, sir? – no. And if they did find it, we wouldn't be here. Everybody in these parts likes us a great deal, you see. And so on and so forth. It's all simple. Now, I'm sure your father will have the wit to pay the money as soon as he can. And don't think to scream or call for help now, young master. Some folk might hear you, but they won't come to Jacob's house for that, and if you continue, then I'll hurt you, I'm afraid.'

'But you don't know who my father is or where he lives.'

'No no, sir, but you'll tell me when I ask you.'

'You will that, no error,' said Jack, draining his mug and refilling it. He went on genially, 'No more nor two ways it can happen – he asks you the once and you tells him quick, or he asks you and asks you and asks you till you tell him. M'm, simple it is indeed. There's that iron in the fire there. You wouldn't much care to –'

Jacob raised his hand in a solemn gesture like a priest's. 'Enough, Jack. Leave your drink and take that public of yours to the garage. It's in the way, you see. The constables don't like that. Go, my boy.'

Hurriedly again, Jack reached over his chair and put his mug down on the cupboard, then went out of the room by the further door. To his great surprise, Hubert at once felt a faint but unmistakable sense of affinity with Jacob, a much reduced version of what he would have felt when Mark left him alone with Thomas, a sense that the time had come for any confidences or confessions. Perhaps Jacob felt the same: at any rate, his glance now was directly questioning. Hubert began at the one obvious point.

'Don't you wonder that I dress like a child of the people?'

'It's no interest of mine, young master.'

'Attend, Jacob, I'm a runaway from – my school and from the priests. From my father too. If you send me back to him he'll punish me severely and hand me over to the priests and they'll punish me more and lock me up.'

'Eh, eh, what have you done?'

'Been disobedient and now run away. A sin and a crime. I'm at risk of infants' purification. Please keep me here. I'll work for you.'

'Such a pity. Sinner and criminal. Disfavoured by both Church and State. Such a pity.'

Jacob's stoop-shouldered figure moved slowly up the room in the direction of the little window. Under this and along the adjacent half-wall there ran (Hubert noticed for the first time) a narrow ledge on which lay a row of small objects. Some of them – a painted paper fan, a balance and set of weights, some finger-rings and necklaces, a china doll, a silver stylus-holder – were easy enough to identify; others were not, or were containers with no certain contents. Jacob touched or momentarily picked up each one, muttering gently to himself or to them, or both, like a man on some rural task, a farmhand feeding hens, a shepherd greeting as well as numbering his flock. Hubert sank back on the day-bed: nothing painful or frightening or of any importance could happen until Jack returned.

Whatever Jacob had been doing came to an end. He turned aside to a battered press of unvarnished wood and took from it a small box, from which in turn he took a rough russet-coloured cylinder five or six inches long. Putting one end of this in his mouth, he struck a phosphorus and held it to the other. When a thin cloud of greyish smoke appeared, one of the unfamiliar smells in the room was explained. Hubert felt a mild instinctive disgust: tobacco-smoking was the practice of New Englanders and other low persons. A gentleman would as soon think of indulging in it as of eating with his fingers or appearing drunk at Mass; a thought to keep to oneself.

Puffing smoke with signs of satisfaction, Jacob walked back, stood above Hubert and gazed down at him. After a pause, he drew his shawl away from his left sleeve, revealing a small yellow star sewn to it. He said quietly,

'You know what this is, young master?'

'Yes.'

'Yes, you know what it is. And you know what it means?'

'Yes.'

'No, you don't know what it means. Oh, maybe you know it must be there by law. Maybe you know it means I may not own land or fight the devilish Turk or serve the King or any of his ministers. Maybe. But to know all of what it means you must have led my life or the life of one of my tribe. You understand that, sir?'

Jacob was not talking quietly now. It could never be said,

thought Hubert, that a man's eyes could blaze, or said only by writers of TR, who need have no care for truth; all that could be said with truth was that eyes could be bright in colour, and bright because there was enough moisture on their surface to reflect everything else that was bright, and prominent because that was how they were, and prominent because the skin round them was stretched – but, however true, that fell short.

'Ask yourself, ask yourself where goes the money that comes from the families. Not into any part of my house, that you can tell. Ah, when I began, when I got my first hundred and then my second and my third, I had brave ideas, you see. The money would go to the people, not to my tribe but to all the people, I mean all those who'd dare to do what I'd dare to do and rebel against Church and State. I'd begin – and I could only begin – to lead them out of captivity into a land where the Pope and the King could never reach them. But – at first I couldn't believe it – they preferred to stay. They preferred to be poor and hopeless and full of sin and crime, because they were afraid not to be. No no, because they'd come to need to be as they were. I was four hundred and fifty years too late. So now what do I do, what do I do with the money? I give it to my tribe, for food and medicines, and for schooling for those with wit, you see. I've led a few from the captivity of the spirit – ah, but how few.'

Out of an obscure feeling that it would be best for him if Jacob continued to talk, Hubert said, 'But what made you a rebel at first? Had you wanted to fight the Turk or serve the King?'

Jacob did not answer, or not immediately. He put his cigar down in a chipped saucer on the shelf above the fireplace; then, in another of his priest-like movements, he gripped the upper edges of his shawl each side of the fermaglio. He seemed to be inwardly rehearsing some harangue or recitation, and when he spoke his voice carried that quality.

'Have we not eyes? Have we not hands, organs, proportions, senses, affections, passions? fed with the same meat, slaked with the same draughts, subject to the same diseases, healed with the same physic, warmed and cooled by the same summer

151

and winter, as you are? If you prick us, do we not bleed? if you tickle us, do we not laugh? if you envenom us, do we not die, and if you wrong us, shall we not revenge? If we are like you . . .'

Hubert said into renewed silence, 'I still don't see –'

'You know those words? You know who wrote those words?'

'No.'

'No. Your priests burnt his playhouse and his books, and would have burnt him besides but for the King, whom he'd once made to laugh.'

'Laugh? What was his name?'

'So instead, you know what they did, those priests? They attached his goods and excommunicated him and transported him to New England. There, you may see his plays.'

'In New England.'

'Yes, in New England. So, then?'

Hubert shook his head without speaking.

A log clattered out of the fire, which had sunk low. Cigar in mouth, Jacob put the log back with a pair of tongs and added others from a basket beside the grate. Then, settling his shawl about him, he squatted down on his heels, picked up a pair of bellows and went to work with them, his attention evidently concentrated on the task. The bellows sounded cracked, but the wood must have been dry; anyway, quite soon a flame appeared and grew. Hubert wondered what time of night it was, where he was to sleep, what was to come. He sat forward and drew a shivering breath.

'I'm cold – may I move nearer the fire?'

'Yes, yes, child.'

Settled in the chair Jack had occupied, Hubert said, 'Just now you talked of captivity. What of my captivity here?'

'What of it indeed?'

'According to yourself, you began with brave ideas: you'd save not only your tribe but other folk too. Have you quite forgotten those ideas?'

'Long ago, long ago.'

'You'd send me into captivity of the body to help others out of captivity of the spirit?'

The fire in front of Jacob had become a blaze. 'Why not?'

'God forgive me.'

'For what, young master?'

Hubert's right hand darted out and shoved at the back of Jacob's neck; with his left, he threw the contents of Jack's mug, about a gill of strong spirits, into the heart of the flames. There was a puffing, roaring noise and a bright flash as the brandy ignited. Jacob screamed. Within three seconds, Hubert was in the scullery. He found the outside door at once, drew the bolts, turned the key and kept it in his hand. While he was doing this, he heard slow, heavy irregular footfalls from the kitchen and smelt a terrible odour. He opened the door, slammed it after him, turned the key the other way, threw it over his shoulder and was off into the darkness.

Anthony Anvil lay asleep in his bed. Something seemed to him to be chipping at his sleep, like a knife-blade at an eggshell. It gave; he awoke and, with no memory of the chipping, heard instead a tapping, a steady tapping at his window. Too puzzled to be alarmed, he struck a phosphorus and was lighting the candle on his night-table when a voice he knew quietly called his name. Anthony hurried over with the candle and helped his brother across the sill.

'Hubert! What do you do here? You look —'

'I've run away. May I sit down?'

'Oh, my dear . . . You've climbed the wistaria.'

'I must have done, mustn't I? I've run away so as not to be altered. I came to London on the rapid. I was taken by two men called Jacob and Jack. Jack went off and I . . . eluded Jacob and escaped and I didn't know where I was till I saw I was almost at Edgware Road. They took my valigia with Decuman's food in it and Thomas's book, but I still have Mark's cross. Not valuable enough for them to . . .'

'I can't hear you.'

'Eh? I must go to Master van den Haag, but not now. May I sleep in your bed, Anthony? Or on the floor?'

'Wait a little.' Anthony considered. There were a dozen questions he would have liked to know the answer to, but for the time being he asked only one. 'Who is Master van den Haag?'

Hubert yawned like a small animal. 'Master van den Haag . . . is the New Englander Ambassador. He's my friend. He heard me sing and I went to his house in Coverley and sang to them. His Embassy is in St Giles's. In St Edmund Street. I shall be safe there. Tomorrow. Later. Where may I sleep?'

'When you call this van den Haag your friend, it isn't a tale or a dream? And he is the Ambassador? Say, Hubert.'

'It's all true, every word,' said Hubert with bemused indignation.

'Very well.' Anthony went to his night-table, poured a glass of water from the caraffa there and handed it to his brother. 'What will you ask him to do?'

'Keep me. Hide me. Take me away. Send me to New England.'

'But you're a runaway – to hide you is illegal, and to convey you out of the country must be . . .'

'He can at least hide me safely. They wouldn't think to search for me at his Embassy, and even if they did they couldn't enter there, because it doesn't belong to England – it's part of New England. Everybody knows that.'

'You forget what they are: they'd have means of persuading him to give you up . . . Hubert, my dear, why should van den Haag do as you ask?'

'He's my friend. No, I can't tell, but who else is there to ask?'

'No one, but that's not enough.'

'He's kind. He loves music. He doesn't like to be called my lord. He's proud of New England and pleased he's not English. I think . . .'

'Yes?'

'I think he doesn't like the Pope.'

'I see. So. Drink that up.'

'. . . No more, thank you.'

'Yes, more. Drink it and stay awake. You have a journey to finish.'

'Oh, Anthony – tomorrow. In the morning.'

'Attend, Hubert, it must be now. Before long, the first servants will be stirring. Then it'll be light. No question but that you'll be seen and fetched to papa, and that'll be the end of your escape. You can go only while it's still dark. I'll take you.' Anthony was dressing as he spoke. 'I can leave this house without making a sound: I've had practice enough coming the other way. Follow me and put your feet where I put mine and you'll be as silent as I am. We'll be in St Edmund Street within an hour.'

In the event, they were there much sooner than that, thanks to a vacant public that drove out of Apostle Andrew Street and turned west as they approached – Hubert stayed clear until he was quite certain that it was not Jack at the wheel. Soon they were passing the elegant and extraordinary structure that housed the Japanese Embassy, like Nagasaki Cathedral the product of the mature genius of Yamamoto, and recognized with it as the culmination of Oriental achievement in modern ecclesiastical architecture. Both in size and in splendour the rest of the street was outdone, not least the modest two-storey brick building proclaimed by a blue-and-white sign to be the Embassy of the Republic of New England.

Anthony ordered the publicman to wait and, with Hubert at his side, approached the entrance where, between a pair of lamps on brick pillars, a gate of tall iron railings shut off access to a paved yard and, beyond it, the Embassy itself. Reaching out, Anthony shook the gate. Within a few seconds there appeared a sentry in red-and-blue uniform with white facings, fusil at the shoulder.

'Good morning, sir. May I help you?'

'Good morning. Yes, you may. I have important business. Please fetch me your officer.'

It was after an almost imperceptible hesitation that the man turned and walked back the way he had come, and less than a minute before he reappeared accompanied by a tall, thin figure in a similar but more opulent uniform. The newcomer held himself stiffly upright and wore a fierce mustach, but he could not have been more than a year or two older than Anthony.

'Good morning, sir. I am Subaltern Reichesberg. I am let know that you have important business here. Kindly state it, sir.'

'I am Anthony Anvil and this is my brother Hubert. We are the children of Master Tobias Anvil, merchantman, of Tyburn Road and Bishopsgate. Your master, His Excellency van den Haag, has employed my brother to obtain for him some information of the highest confidence. He now has that information and is here to deliver it in person, as instructed.'

Anthony thought to himself that this speech had not run very well when he rehearsed it in the public, and sounded no better when delivered. The subaltern seemed to take the same general view, but he did glance for a moment at the sentry before replying: a hopeful sign.

'Why should His Excellency send a child on such an errand? And an English child too?'

'I don't know. A child can obviously find his way to places closed to his elders.'

'Such places as ...?'

'I mean of course that folk will speak freely in his presence when they would not before an adult.'

'Ah. Of what import is this supposed information, sir?'

'Considerable, I suppose, given these circumstances. It must touch nothing less than the well-being of your country.'

'Have you no documents at all?'

Anthony had foreseen this question. He answered with well-simulated surprise, 'Naturally not, in a matter of such confidence.'

Reichesberg sighed and raised a white-gloved hand towards his mustach, but lowered it again. 'May I ask you to return at a more suitable hour?'

'That would be to run counter to the boy's instructions. He was told to present himself directly he got the information, at whatever time.'

'Why was I not told to expect you?' asked Reichesberg in a pleading tone.

'To promote safety?' Anthony shrugged his shoulders. 'But I warn you, Subaltern: unless you admit my brother without further delay, you must answer to His Excellency.'

Reichesberg looked hard at Anthony, then at Hubert. 'You, boy – you have every look of a child of the people in that rig. Account for yourself now.'

'I assumed this disguise, sir,' said Hubert at his most gentlemanlike, 'in order to penetrate the disreputable circles where my mission lay.'

There was a pause. The sentry shuffled his feet on the pavement, rolled his eyes a little and drew his index finger to and fro under his nose. Anthony raised his head and looked at the top of the lofty staff from which, its colours indistinguishable, the flag of New England fluttered.

'Goddamn,' said Reichesberg without much emotion. 'Open up, Paddy.'

So Hubert stepped on to the soil of the only nation in Christendom into which the Pope's servants could not enter at will and of right. There was delay while the subaltern aroused a succession of household functionaries, each of whom had to go through his own cycle of disbelief followed by grudging acceptance, but before very long Hubert's arrival had been officially recognized; as much to the point, a bed-chamber was put at his disposal pending his introduction to the Ambassador at a later stage. The brothers kissed and took their leave of each other. Reichesberg escorted Anthony to the street.

'Well, have you fooled me, sir? I can't undo now what I've done.'

'Some particulars are not as stated, but His Excellency will surely approve your decision, so your professional honour is safe.'

'That was never at risk; I'm concerned only with my powers of judgement. Thank you, sir. Good day.'

It was indeed almost day when Anthony, back in Tyburn Road, paid off his public and approached the house, not frontally but, to avoid inquisitive eyes, up the express-house drive in the first place. He had reached the corner of the building when he heard a loud but muffled groan from indoors, from the express-house itself. A few seconds later, he was bending over a man who lay in a very uncomfortable attitude at the foot of the staircase. Anthony did not at once recognize him, because the lower half of his face was covered with a large gag secured by tapes, but well before this had been removed he could see that it was Father Lyall who lay there, lay there in pints of his own blood, his hands fastened behind his back, his left leg broken. It was later established that he had been attacked in his room and had fallen while trying to get down the stair in search of help, but for the moment there were more important questions to be answered. The main source of the bleeding appeared to be somewhere about the lower abdomen; Anthony lifted the hem of the nightshirt. What he saw made him turn his head violently aside and drive his fists hard against his cheekbones. Then he remembered his duty and his training, felt the pulse, listened for the heart-beat. There was almost none of either. The priest's eyes were shut and his breathing was imperceptible; the flow of blood seemed to have stopped. Anthony was as sure as he could be that death was unavoidable and imminent, but training had something to say about that too. He ran at his best speed to the Cistercian hospice across Edgware Road, where a surgeon was known to be always on call. From there he was able to inform the authorities. Not till then did he set about rousing his father.

Half an hour afterwards, Tobias Anvil sat in his library giving information to two members of the constabulary, a proctor and a serjeant. Anthony was in attendance.

The proctor, a heavy man with a massive head and neck, said slowly, as he slowly made a note, 'Very good, master. You never once inferred that he was given to offences against chastity.'

'Certainly not.' True enough: Tobias had gone to some trouble to avoid finding himself compelled to infer such a thing. 'If I had, I should have dismissed him from his post in my household.'

'Your servants brought no word of that sort.'

'No. Why do you pursue this line of inquiry, Proctor?'

'I must first pursue the obvious, master. The crime declares itself as an act of jealousy and revenge on the part of a rival, perhaps a husband, as witness the mutilations.'

Over the past nights, Margaret Anvil had slept better than at any time since she was a young girl. She had not stirred when her husband, sent for by Anthony, left her side. It was no more than a minute since she had suddenly awoken and at the same time become aware of some unusual and untoward agitation in the house. Immediately filled with fear, she had put on a breakfast-gown and gone to find her maid, who told her that Father Lyall had suffered an accident and could or would tell her nothing more. Hearing voices from the library, she entered it without knocking for the first time in her life, at just the right moment to catch the whole of the proctor's last sentence.

'What mutilations?' she asked in a steady, unexcited voice.

'There has been a terrible mishap, my dear.' Tobias had left his seat in concern. 'Father Lyall is dead. These men are –'

'What mutilations?'

The proctor was not only a slow speaker, he was also slow to adapt himself to the unexpected or unfamiliar. So he said, as he would have said to a superior, to a State official, to a magistrate, 'Certain organs were removed.'

'What organs?'

Nobody spoke. Anthony hurried over to his mother, not knowing why he did so.

Margaret screamed. Soon she was weeping too, but she continued to scream at intervals. Her hands moved in the air and over her head and body to no purpose. Someone – Anthony – put his arm round her, caught her hands and gripped them. The constabulary serjeant said an urgent word or two to the proctor and half bundled him from the room. Margaret did not take in their going nor, when at last she looked up, the fact that they had gone. This was understandable, if only because, a couple of seconds after she did look up, Tobias hit her across the side of the face with an open hand but a stiff arm, so that she lurched and fell to the floor, her head missing a corner of the oak desk by about an inch.

'Harlot,' he said in his clear tones. 'Designing adulteress. Hell and all its flames receive you.'

Anthony made the Sign of the Cross. 'The sword of Michael

stand between my mother and any harm.' His mouth was now as straight and composed as hers had ever been. 'If you touch her again, father, you touch me too. Be warned.'

'I'll have her attached for unchastity, I'll see her purified, I'll . . .'

'Twaddle,' said Anthony, helping Margaret to her feet. 'You'll do nothing. Firstly because there are no facts. Secondly because you're a man of mark, and wherever you go – to St Mary Bourne, to Bishopsgate, to your gaming-rooms – you prize your dignity. And thirdly because you'll never allow yourself to become involved in any disturbance that touches the Church in the smallest degree. – Let me take you to your room, mama.'

'I'll turn her out of doors. It's my right.'

'Then, as before, you turn me out too.'

'Hubert will stay with me.'

'Hubert is . . . Hubert would go with his mother if he had the choice.'

For the first time that morning, Tobias looked Anthony straight in the eye. 'Is there nothing to be said in my favour? Nothing at all?'

'Of course there's something, papa, though less than you think. For instance, it's not in your favour that what hurts you most is damaged pride. But we'll talk later.'

The first thing Hubert saw when he woke up looked rather like a small brass lantern, but all there seemed to be inside the case was two white squares of bone or china with black numbers on them: 2 44. In an instant, and without a sound, 44 became 45. He stared, then smiled as a clock not far away struck the three-quarters. Glancing round the spacious, airy room, he remembered the previous night, or most of it: Joan and the ride, Domingo and Samuel, the train, the public, Jacob and Jack, Anthony, the sentry and the officer, himself and Anthony entering the shadowy hall, but after that came a confusion of footsteps and voices. He recognized the bed he lay in, the striped outer cover and the smooth sheets that smelt faintly and cleanly of some herb he did not know, the vividly-coloured rugs, the slender furniture, but he had never consciously seen before the great sweep of wallpaper on three sides of him, vivid as it was with its designs of birds, animals and fish in rounded square or rhomboid medallions on a green-and-grey lattice background. But he had little time for it even now, in view of the loaded tray on the night-table beside him. At the mere notion of food, hunger overwhelmed him.

Under a starched cloth were rusks, paninos, blackcurrant conserve, butterscotch squares with almonds, lime juice, milk, cheese and a bowl of soft fruit. There was also a card with a red-and-blue border and an image of the American lion, the New Englander national emblem. On it was a print-written message with a final sentence and initials added in stylus. Already eating fast, Hubert read:

If you prefer cooked food, please ring. Rest as long as you wish. The bath and commodation are through the door to your left. When you are quite ready, come down to the hallway. Anyone you find there will fetch you to me.

We all welcome you to our house.

C. v.d. H.

Hubert stretched out for the silver hand-bell, with the idea of calling for cooked food as well as rather than instead of uncooked, then changed his mind. The cooking would take time, and his desire to see van den Haag and tell him his story was urgent, urgent enough to overcome even greed.

In five minutes, he had cleared the tray of everything but the cheese (how queer to offer it for breakfast), got out of bed to look for his clothes, failed to find them and found instead, laid out on a linen-chest, a complete set of new garments: underdress, drawers, stockings, a shirt of pale yellow silk, a darker yellow stock, black velvet jacket and breeches, black shoes with cut-steel clasps, and, not least, a pocket-napkin edged with yellow lace: whoever had done this was acute as well as kind. He went into the next room and used the commodation, a grand affair with a seat of dark foreign wood – hickory? Next, he drew a hot bath, came across, at the basin, a tooth-cleaner still in its transparent paper, used that, and took off the blue cotton nightshirt that an unknown benefactor – a servant-lad, probably – had supplied. Lying in the warm water, he felt for a moment completely refreshed and safe, safe for the first time since deciding to run away, safe not for ever, but for the small distance he could see into the future. No agent of what he had run away from could reach him here; he had a friend who could and would absolutely prevent it. The returning thought of that friend brought him to his feet and out of the bath. He dried himself on a towel big enough to dry a horse and was soon dressed. As he had come to expect by now, there was a new hair-brush and comb on the toilet-table in the bedchamber. Before leaving he knelt by the bed and prayed, with special mention of Decuman, Thomas, Mark, Domingo, Samuel and Anthony, and plea to St Hubert to intercede for him in the matter of Jacob. He also begged pardon for involuntary remiss-ness in attendance at services of the Church.

The hall, though not large, was full of marble: floor, columns portrait busts, and urns containing sheaves of the tall grass he had noticed on his first visit to the house in Coverley. He had barely reached the foot of the stairs when an elderly Indian in livery came up and took him to a small room somewhere at the rear of the building. Here he settled down to wait for some time, but in fact it was not two minutes before the heavy white door opened and van den Haag came in, preceded by his wife.

Hubert had not expected to see her, or not at this stage, but even if he had he most likely would not have been able to do otherwise than he did, which was to hold his hands up to her and burst into tears. At once she went down on her knees, put her arms round him and stroked his head. She made soothing noises, and van den Haag told him over and over again that everything was in order and there was no cause to be troubled. He had no idea how long this went on, but when it was over he was sitting in a splendid chair of gold-painted wood and the man and woman were close to him on each side.

'My excuses,' he said, and blew his nose into the pocket-napkin, blessing again whoever had fetched it. 'I should never have had to do it if you weren't so good.'

Dame van den Haag was holding his hand. 'No excuses, Hubert dear. Something must be very wrong, we know that.'

'Yes, I think something is.'

'You have a tale to tell, haven't you? We want to hear, but you're not to tell it before you're quite ready. We'll wait.'

'Thank you, dame, but I can tell it now.'

Hubert told it. When he had finished, he saw with slight astonishment that van den Haag's blue eyes were full of tears, some of them starting to overflow down his cheeks.

'The pigs,' he said several times.

'Ach, there are pigs everywhere, Cornelius. Forget them and determine what can be done for Hubert.'

'Yes. Yes. He's safe here for a time, perhaps for a few days. No longer. A servant or a soldier will let fall at the inn that a young English boy stays with us here, and someone will attend and pass the word. Then ... a mannerly threat from the Papal Cure that, unless Hubert is given up at once, a man of ours will be attached for meddling in the affairs of Church or State, and may well be condemned. I couldn't handle that.'

'All this over a truant child?'

'Dearest Anna, you haven't had to learn the ways of these Romanists as I have. To them, Hubert will be something far more and far worse than a truant child. He defies authority, he rebels against the will of God, and that mustn't be tolerated in anyone, young or old, gentry or people, layman or cleric. The only ...'

Van den Haag stopped speaking and began to stare without curiosity at an elaborate flower-holder in white-painted wrought iron from which leafy stems trailed. Hubert noticed that he was wearing some kind of formal costume, including a high-necked blue tunic frogged in red and with multi-coloured decorations: a reminder of his status and his function.

'Sir,' – Hubert remembered in time his friend's preferred style of address – 'please don't let me distract you from your affairs.'

'No no,' said van den Haag, absently adjusting at his breast the miniature gold likeness of some heraldic bird; 'a reception

163

at four and a half o'clock. The Australian High Commission. I may be late if I wish.' He nodded his head slowly, as if disposing of parts of a problem in succession; some others appeared still unresolved. 'Anna . . .'

'Cornelius?'

'Anna . . . kindly take Hubert up to your sitting-room and give him tea, show him photograms. Hilda's studies will be finished shortly and she'll come along to you. Tell her Hubert stays with us while his parents visit whoever you will. There are matters that require my attention.'

Hubert clearly saw pass between the pair a short series of unvoiced messages such as his mother and father never exchanged: an offer to do whatever else might be needed, a gentle negative coupled with an assurance that explanations would be furnished in due time, an acknowledgement that added a promise of support. Thereupon the three left the room; the Ambassador went off towards the hallway, his footsteps sounding sharply; his wife took Hubert in the other direction, and they were soon comfortably settled near an upstairs window that gave a distant view of Whitehall Palace, the King's London residence.

'Where are the photograms?'

'Do you truly want to see them?'

'Are there some of New England?'

'Yes, a great many.'

'Those I should love to see.'

So a handsome portfolio was produced, full of pictured wonders both natural and man-made: the Zachary Taylor bridge linking Manhattan Island with the Waldensia shore; the National Museum of Art in New Wittenberg; a great grassy plain overshadowed by what looked like a rain-cloud, but what was in fact (Anna van den Haag explained) million upon million of passenger pigeons; the Benedict Arnold Memorial in the city which had taken its name from his; the Hussville Opera House; a vividly beautiful autumnal scene in the woods of eastern Cranmeria – the last in particular was well captured by the new Westinghouse colour process. Then, as he turned over the pages, Hubert came upon a large photogram of a mountain crest, not a particularly high one, to judge from the presence of trees and tall bushes, but hung with curling strips of mist. The light was pale, casting long dim shadows.

'This looks a strange place,' he said.

'It is. They say that however bright the sun may shine just a mile off, it never touches the summit of Mount Gibson. The Indians call the spot Dawn Daughter's Leap, and they tell a tale of it. Would you like to hear?'

'Oh yes, please.'

Dame van den Haag had opened a tall quilted box beside her chair and taken from it a tray on which there were a number of small pots of different colours, some pointed sticks and a coffee-bowl of white-coated earthenware with a pattern of fruits drawn on it and partly filled in. As she talked, she used the sticks to coat other parts with green, red and malva, working slowly and accurately. 'Well, Dawn Daughter was betrothed to a chief, but she loved a young warrior named White Fox. On the night before the marriage, White Fox came to Dawn Daughter and took her up on his horse, and off they went together. But the moon was bright that night, and they were seen escaping, and the chief gave chase with all his men. Now White Fox's horse was the biggest and the strongest of all the tribe had, but with the two on his back he began to grow tired, and the chief's men began to draw near. So White Fox called to the Spirit the tribe worshipped, and asked him to send another horse. The Spirit heard him, and suddenly there was another horse running beside them, a wondrous horse with eyes that shone in the dark. He came so close that Dawn Daughter was able to climb on to his back.' There was a short pause while a fresh stick was prepared. 'They rode on together for an extent, and the chief's men fell behind, but then the Spirit's horse galloped faster and faster, and White Fox couldn't stay with him. He saw him come to the mountain and start to climb it, and he followed at the best speed he could ... Pardon me a moment, Hubert.'

Hilda had entered the room, was already approaching, coming straight towards him. Her green frock was not the one she had worn when they first met, but it reminded him of it.

He stood up and they shook hands; hers was warm and dry, as before. By the window, Dame van den Haag had begun to talk in low tones to a middle-aged person with eyeglasses, most likely a preceptress of some sort, who must have come in with Hilda, though he had not seen her do so. He smiled at Hilda, hoping that she could tell from that how pleased he was to see her; she smiled back, at least. She showed not the slightest surprise or curiosity at his presence: he guessed that embassy life taught one to expect what others would find unexpected.

'Your honoured mother was showing me the photograms.'

She reached down to the sofa and turned the open portfolio round towards her. 'Oh yes – Dawn Daughter's Leap,' she said in her hoarse voice – how could he have forgotten that voice? She went down on her bare knees with something of a bump and, while still looking closely at the photogram of the mountain top, lifted the corner of the page as if about to turn on.

Hubert quickly knelt beside her. 'How does the tale end? The tale of Dawn Daughter and White Fox. I heard only part.'

'My mother will finish it for you. She knows it best.'

'Your mother's occupied,' he said, hoping she would continue to be. He could not have told why he so much wanted to hear the rest of the story from Hilda.

'How much did you hear yet?'

'They had just reached the foot of the mountain.'

'Oh, now . . .' She put her elbows on the edge of the sofa, clasped her hands and looked down at the portfolio. 'Well, they went on up. I suppose a god's horse can go anywhere, but the real horse must have found it tough. I was there that time, the time paps made the photogram. Yes, when White Fox was almost at the top a mist came down and hid the moon, so he couldn't find his way. That was the god's work. White Fox had to wait for daylight before he could do anything.'

'Where was the chief and his men?'

'I don't know. So: White Fox went right to the top and found there was a cliff below him. Just here.' She pointed. 'It doesn't show in the photogram it's a cliff, but it is. At the edge of the cliff were four hoof-marks in the rock. They don't show either in this, but they're there: I saw them.'

'Real hoof-marks? In rock?'

'Well – they surely looked real,' she said with reluctant conviction, then hurried on in the businesslike tone she had been using earlier. 'The horse had taken a leap into the sky, where the god was waiting for Dawn Daughter. He'd seen her and loved her when he sent the horse. And when she came to him he was so mightily glad he forgot to take the mist away, so it's still there.'

'What did White Fox do?'

'I don't know. White Fox. Isn't that a fool name? Dawn Daughter too.'

Hubert did not speak. To him, those were not fool names.

'What I think,' said Hilda, abruptly standing up, 'some old Indian just fancied the whole tale to explain the mist and the marks in the rock.'

'It doesn't quite explain the mist. But you said the marks looked real.'

Her manner changed again. 'Yes, they did.'

'Where is Mount Gibson?'

He had not wanted to know, only to continue the conversation. As soon as the words were out, he knew he had made a mistake, and from the way she looked past him and muttered her reply (which he failed to take in) he knew just what he should have said: that, whatever she thought, he believed the tale of Dawn Daughter and White Fox. It would have been too late now even if, having finished her conversation with the preceptress, Dame van den Haag had not been on her way to join them. But there would be another time: there must be.

The next morning, Abbot Peter Thynne sat in his parlour over a breakfast he had hardly touched. Normally he ate this meal in the refectory; he found it a useful occasion for meeting those in his charge before the day's work began and offering any necessary words of encouragement and advice. But in his present mood, the mood that had fallen upon him more than twenty-four hours earlier, when the news had been brought of Hubert's disappearance the notion of company was distasteful to him. Within his reach lay two books delivered not long before from Blackwell's bookshop in Oxford: a new commentary on the *De Existentiae Natura* of Monsignor Jean-Paul Sartre, the French Jesuit, and an analysis of Count William Walton's church music. The Abbot had eagerly looked forward to the arrival of both volumes; as yet he had not had the heart to open either.

There was a knock at the door. 'Yes?' he said rather sharply.

Father Dilke came in, bowed, and said, 'Good morning, my lord. I trust your lordship slept well?'

'No. Of course not. What is it, Father?'

'I have a little news, my lord.'

At once the Abbot's demeanour altered. 'Sit down, Father. Forgive me for speaking as I did. What news?'

'The ostler advises that the mare Joan is returned.'

'At what hour?'

'Some time in the night, my lord. She was grazing near the stable when he made his early round. He further advises that she hadn't been ridden far and had been fed and watered yesterday afternoon or evening.'

'Where, I wonder? In Coverley, one would think. By whom? That's more difficult. Or it should be. I can't get free of the idea that that New Englander type is involved. Who else in Coverley has acquaintance with Hubert, pattie-shop men and such excluded?'

'But at his second visit the proctor was positive that the Ambassador is in London and that his Secretary here denies all possibility of a visit from Hubert. And surely . . .'

The Abbot sighed. 'Where then did the mare carry him?'

'To a train or omnibus.'

'Which might have carried him anywhere in the land.'

'But most likely to London.'

'And the New Englander Embassy, into which our constabulary can't enter.'

'I hardly think the Ambassador would shelter an English runaway, my lord. The diplomatic consequences –'

'The fellow's a New Englander, confound him,' said the Abbot, rubbing his eyes wearily and sighing again. 'I should never have allowed him across this threshold. See the proctor here is let know of the mare's return and of the other advice.'

'Yes, my lord.'

'Should we talk again to Decuman and his party?'

'I find no advantage in it, sir. They told the truth, as I think, when they denied knowledge of Hubert's goal.'

'Yes, yes. It was Decuman who took the mare at first.'

'Oh yes, my lord, and he knows we know it, but . . .'

'Yes.'

The Abbot was silent for a long time, but gave no signal that he wanted to end the interview. The skin over his cheekbones was stretched and shiny, and his shoulders had lost their habitual squareness. When he spoke again, it was in a thin tone Dilke had never heard him use before.

'Father, I want your help.'

'Anything, my lord.'

'I'm frightened, Father. This atrocity we learned of yesterday: the murder of Father Lyall. He was a proud and rebellious man and an unworthy priest, but no human creature deserves an end like that. Who could have done such a thing? And why?'

'Some beastly quarrel, my lord. Spiritual impropriety must show its counterpart in behaviour. There'll be a woman or a gaming-debt at the back of it. Or it might be some brush with agents of the law – they can be savage if they're provoked. I remember your lordship saying in this very room that you were surprised he'd never collided with those in authority. Well, perhaps now he has, once and for all.'

'Do you mean a constable would take a knife to a man who'd crossed him?' asked the Abbot disbelievingly and with a hint of distaste.

'Oh yes, my lord.' Dilke smiled for an instant. 'A constable or other officer. It's not probable in this case, which was, as you say, atrocious. A disfiguring slash would not be so unusual.'

'Who tells you such stuff?'

'I have some children of the people among my charges, my lord.'

'Don't listen when they feed you thieves' cackle.'

'No, my lord. I beg your lordship's forgiveness for the diversion.'

The Abbot gestured with the back of his hand. After a moment, he went on with evident difficulty, 'And yet there's the terrible fact that Lyall was killed by having worked on him the very same ... deed as that resisted by him in Hubert's case. I know there was a further mutilation, but ... It's as if someone said, "Obstinately and rebelliously resist alteration in another and suffer it yourself for your pains." Not revenge or quarrel. Chastisement.'

'Someone? Who, sir?'

'I dare not think.'

Dilk said gravely, 'When I told you just now, my lord, of private violence against the citizenry, I spoke indeed of constables, of the minor agents of the law, of petty authority. Such acts would meet – I'm sure they do meet – the sternest possible rebuke from those of substantial power. That Father Lyall should have died through any sort of sentence or warrant of theirs is not to be dreamed of. Our policy is imperfect, but not evil. And besides, who knew of Lyall's resistance other than ourselves here and Master Anvil – not one to proclaim differences with an ecclesiastic? No, my lord, dreadful as it is, this is a concurrence. There can be no connection. Do I relieve your mind?'

'No. That's to say no more than partly, though I thank you for it. See you, Father, it was to the purpose, all too much to the purpose, that you recalled a moment ago what I said of poor Lyall within these walls. That's what has discomposed me far more. That and what I thought of him. I wanted him removed. I prayed for his removal. But I didn't intend this kind of removal,' said the Abbot, swallowing hard.

'Oh, my lord, of course not. No one could suppose such a thing.'

'My fear is that God has taken this enormous means of rebuking my pertinacity and self-will and desire for worldly acclaim in pressing for the alteration of Hubert. Until yesterday morning, I could lay that fear aside as a sick fancy. But now that Hubert is gone, become a runaway, it returns, redoubled. I take his departure as a sign, an unmistakable sign of God's displeasure.'

Father Dilke had gone down on his knees in front of the Abbot and taken his hands between his own. 'My lord, you were not pertinacious or self-willed in what you did: you showed nothing but a proper resolve in pursuing what you took to be right. And your design was not worldly acclaim but the renown of this Chapel, Hubert's welfare and the greater glory of God. Believe me, my lord; I know you and I speak out of that knowledge.'

The Abbot gave another sigh, but this one had no impatience or fatigue in it. 'Thank you, David. You're a good friend.'

'Your lordship honours me.'

'I tell you the truth. Will you pray with me, Father?'

Unable to speak for the moment, Dilke nodded. The two knelt down side by side on the Abbot's Beauvais carpet. Together they made the Sign of the Cross.

'In nomine Patris et Filii et Spiritus Sancti, amen,' said the Abbot.

'Most loving and merciful God,' said Dilke a little unsteadily, 'hear Thou the voice of Thy servant.'

'O God, I humbly petition Thee to remit Thy justified wrath at my sins and to forgive me and to send me comfort if in my thoughts or prayers I betrayed peevishness or animosity at what in all good faith I took to be the stubbornness of that Father Lyall whom Thou hast lately taken to Thyself. And I crave Thee most reverently that Thou have mercy on his soul and at the Last Day number him among Thine own.'

'Amen.'

'And I further humbly petition Thee to take Thy most especial care of the temporal and spiritual well-being of Thy child Hubert Anvil, wherever he may be and wherever he may go. Enter into his heart and mind, O Lord, and send him the desire to return here among those who care for him. Or, if that is not Thy purpose, bring it about in Thine own way that he forsake the path of rebellion and outlawry and be brought at last to serve Thy will.'

'Amen.'

'Give ear, I beseech Thee, O Lord . . .'

Just then, Lawrence arrived outside the parlour door on his way to remove the Abbot's breakfast dishes. He had already raised his hand to knock when he caught from within the familiar sound of a voice in prayer. To stay and listen would, in such a case, have been not only a breach of established procedure but also an act of profanation, and Lawrence was a very devout man. In addition, he had a warm personal attachment to his master. So he went back the way he had come, mounted to his bedroom and himself knelt down. He prayed to God to answer whatever petition the honoured and pious Abbot might have put forward, then supplicated for the personal intervention of St James the Apostle in his behalf.

His Honour Joshua Pellew, Archpresbyter of Arnoldstown, came out of the main entrance of the New Englander Embassy and moved at a dignified pace between two lines of guards standing with presented fusils. With him were his chaplain, Pastor Alan Williams, his Indian servant Abraham, the Ambassador and Ambassadress, a couple of senior diplomatic officials, and, somewhere near the middle of the party, a small brown-complexioned figure burdened with baggage, evidently a page of some sort. The group passed through the opened gates and, with due deliberation, boarded a pair of expresses drawn up beside the footway.

The man who had for some hours been sweeping that part of the street ran his eyes over those outside the gates and went on sweeping, having been told to keep watch for a child of the English gentry and not having seen one. He was a very stupid man, selected for this duty because his superior, always short of non-stupid subordinates, had considered it most unlikely that a boy of ten could have made his way so far without assistance, more unlikely still that if he had he would have been allowed in, and unlikeliest of all that, once in, he would come out by the front door. (The back of the building was being watched by a slightly less stupid man.)

One after the other, the expresses pulled out and travelled at a moderate speed towards the Palace, in front of which they turned right, then, after a quarter of a mile, they turned left into St Osyth Street and were soon moving over Westminster Bridge. This, though extensively repaired and rebuilt in 1853, was still in all essentials Labelye's caisson-founded structure of a century earlier, and one of the sights of London. The vehicles on it this afternoon were as many as ever, since all cross-river traffic not using London Bridge had to go this way: the new Temple Bridge would not be open till 1978. On the south bank of the Thames, it was only a short run to Dahnang Station, named to commemorate the victory over the French in 1815 whereby the whole of Indio-China had passed under the English Crown. But, before entering the station yard, the two expresses drew in and stopped for nearly ten minutes. Accurate timing was of great importance in what was to follow.

At exactly the prearranged moment, the party halted at the outer side of a post of inspection which allowed (or withheld) access to the tracks. There were other such posts for the use of persons of lower degrees; this one, as had been calculated, offered immediate attention. On one side, two blue-uniformed recorders sat at a baize-covered table; on the other stood a railtrack constable and a man in grey who, to an educated eye, looked not quite unlike the man who had been sweeping St Edmund Street. Pastor Williams handed the nearer recorder a sheaf of documents and waited. The Ambassador and the Archpresbyter exchanged some rather weighty remarks while the others remained silent. After half a minute, the recorder conferred briefly with his colleague, then turned to Williams and said politely,

'My excuses, Father, but there's a paper lacking. It concerns your master's page ... Elisha Jones. I have his sanction here, which is –'

Pastor Williams said in his gentle but resonant voice, 'The original was lost, as is explained by the temporary replacement you have, which was produced by our Embassy here in London, and is valid.'

'Yes, sir, that's entirely valid – it's the lad's moretur that's lacking.'

Every visitor to England, as to any other land in the Pope's dominions, required a moretur, a certificate of permission to stay for a prescribed period, supplied on arrival and to be shown at all posts of inspection. Since it was ultimately the Lord Intendant of the Exterior Office at Westminster who gave out these documents, even van den Haag's ingenuity had not sufficed to acquire one. He had known of the illegal trade in lost or stolen moreturs, flourishing because of their value to runaways and despite the heavy penalties attached to it, but this source had likewise failed him.

'It was missed at the same time as the sanction,' Williams told the recorder.

'No doubt, Father; for all that, it is lacking.'

'What do you suggest? That it might have been sold or given away? Of what use could it be to anyone but a ten-year-old Indian?'

'I suggest nothing, Father. I simply have plain orders that all exterior travellers passing this post are bound to lay before me a moretur.'

At an eye-blink from van den Haag, Joshua Pellew intervened. He spoke without overt impatience. 'What is this delay? Our train departs at any moment. I am the Archpresbyter of Arnoldstown, RNE, visiting England at the personal invitation of His Majesty the King. My affairs make it imperative that no check be placed on my progress.'

'My humble excuses, my lord. I . . .'

The man in grey had moved over to the recorders' table. He was quite intelligent and observant enough to have uncovered the deception being attempted if he had known of its possibility, but his superior had considered it not merely most unlikely but too unlikely to be regarded, and had spared him the burden of having yet one more would-be fugitive from London to keep an eye open for. After a long look round the waiting group, designed to do little more or less than emphasize his own true mark and their lack of it, the man in grey gave the recorder a tiny nod. At once stamps thudded into ink-pads and on to papers, brief stylus entries were made in prescribed places, the documents were bundled together and handed back to Pastor Williams, the travellers were wished a fair journey, the diplomatic contingent showed their passes, and in a few seconds the post of inspection was behind them all.

Van den Haag betrayed relief at not having had to intervene himself: if needed, ambassadorial authority might have swung matters in the party's favour, but, men like the man in grey being what they were, it was almost as likely, exercised on behalf of someone as insignificant as an Indian page, to have excited suspicion. 'Good work, Your Honour,' he said. 'It was your reasonable address that did it.'

'Thank you, Cornelius. I hope there'll be no further such ordeal. I'm not sure I could suffer it.'

'Most unlikely, sir, as I told you. The rest should be a formality.'

No more conversation was possible for the time being. They had emerged into the main hall of the station. Here, under the soaring dome of glass and steel, the noise of an arriving train could barely be heard through the noise of humanity – vendors of food, drink or ricordos crying their wares, balladiers rattling their coin-bowls as they sang, touts offering a full range of services, beggars who declared their Englishness by displaying insolence rather than abasement. There were plenty of the last-mentioned to be found on the inner side of the post reserved for the passage of the rich and exalted. Pellew had the bulk and the weight to shove aside even the most importunate, but he would have been at some trouble to hold his party together without the assistance of the railtrack constable and the staff he wielded. At last the struggle was over, the last huckster – a one-eyed woman putting up gaudy china replicas of Whitehall Palace – pushed out of the way, the journey-tabs slotted, and the group admitted to the pavement beside the train.

Departure-bells were already being rung. Abraham went aboard at once to see that the heavy baggage, sent ahead from the Embassy, was all in its place – though nobody had considered what to do if it were not. The others gathered round the steps of the baruch for what would have to be brief farewells. Van den Haag shook hands with Pellew and Williams, then turned to their small companion. Even here and now he dared not behave as he wanted to. All he did was say quietly,

'Good luck, Elisha. I'll let your mother know tonight. We'll meet again – perhaps sooner than you think.'

Almost as he spoke, bells pealed on a higher note than before and the train seemed to shudder all over. The three passengers climbed the steps. The wheels began to turn.

When he could no longer see the van den Haags on the pavement, Joshua Pellew made his way to the cabin and settled heavily in a padded chair by the window. He gave a yawn that ended in a long sigh. For the next hour or more, nothing could happen: no hurry, no anxiety, no decisions. Abraham appeared momentarily and reported that the baggage was complete and safe. The Archpresbyter let his eyes fall shut.

His tour of western Europe had been undertaken at the personal instance of the First Citizen of the Republic, who had excellent reasons for wanting to strengthen the still-precarious ties between their nation and the more powerful of those under the sway of Rome. It had been an arduous enterprise for a man nearing seventy, but an enjoyable and apparently successful one. The funeral of King Stephen III had been a natural and convenient starting-point; a two-day visit to the Prince-Bishop of Durham, the richest man in England and virtually a sovereign ruler within her shores, would have provided a comfortable conclusion. But Pellew had found waiting for him on his arrival at the Principal-Episcopal Palace a tachygram that summoned him urgently to the New Englander Embassy in London. Although no reason was given, he had considered his duty and set off as soon as politeness allowed. His annoyance at being asked, even more urgently, to cut short his stay and smuggle home to safety a runaway English boy, however deserving he might be, had been over-taken by astonishment: was this not excessive even for van den Haag, known as he was in Arnoldstown to be no strict observer of diplomatic nicety? Whether it was or was not, Pellew had found at the end of a few minutes' talk that he had agreed in principle to do as asked; a reference to his numerous grandchildren had turned the scale, he was not quite sure how. His only objection had concerned the parents involved, or rather not involved. When the boy had said that he knew his mother would want for him what was proposed, that he would swear to it on her own head, Pellew had believed him, and the matter was settled. Since then he had suffered some anxiety, but counted himself compensated in full by the agreeable sensation of helping to give the Romanists a sore nose.

What they had intended to do to little Hubert Anvil was shocking without being surprising, considered Pellew. All their temporal over-magnificence, all their pharisaism, all their equivocation, all their ruthlessness came from one source: the celibacy of their priesthood. This made it impossible for their hierarchy to understand the family, that most directly God-ordained of all human institutions. It was of no help that that celibacy was always and everywhere broken: a mistress was not a wife and an illegitimate child brought no notion of real fatherhood. And the hierarchy's blindness meant the laity's spiritual and moral deprivation. If the Holy Family meant anything . . .

'We're about to arrive, Your Honour,' said Pastor Williams's gentle voice. 'Three minutes to Cholderton.'

Soon afterwards, Archpresbyter Pellew and his three companions had reached the centre of what was, the two major cities excepted, the largest mass of buildings and installations in the land. The place was an anchorage, a dockyard, a vast manufactory, a testing-tract, a fuel store, a military headquarters and a considerable market-town rolled into one. No vessel was more prominent there than the RNEA *Edgar Allan Poe*, the pride of her nation and a worthy memorial to the brilliant young general who had perished at the moment of his victory over the combined invading forces of Louisiana and Mexico in the war of 1848–50. She and her sister ship, the *James McNeill Whistler*, were the two crack liners on the transatlantic run. They were also the largest vessels ever to have used the anchorage – each was over a thousand feet long – and some controversy had been caused when, at their coming into service in 1973, special berths were erected, even though the New Englander government had agreed to provide most of the money.

Pastor Williams looked up at the great silvery length of *Edgar Allan Poe* and almost caught his breath. He had travelled in her on the outward journey, but it seemed to him that a thousand crossings in such a craft would not abate his wonder. When his turn came he climbed the gangway and, once past the rail, was possessed by a new sensation, a joyful relief at being home again. The very plainness of the furnishings was a refreshment after all the mannered elaboration he had seen in the previous fortnight; the crew's voices, careless, almost rough, sounded like a favourite song to one who had had his fill of the clipped, over-precise English accent. When the purser, a solid-looking Calvinan with a windburnt complexion, welcomed the group aboard, Williams astonished him slightly with a spirited handshake.

The sleeping quarters, reserved by tachygram, were more than adequate: a double apartment for the Archpresbyter alone, another, communicating with it, for Williams and Hubert. Abraham and an anchorage porter brought in the baggage and made their exits. The pastor crossed to the porthole and looked out. Passengers were still coming up the gangway, at the foot of which stood an English soldier with fixed baionetta and a blue-clad recorder. Neither showed the least interest in the documents proffered them, merely waving their owners on, just as they had done when the Archpresbyter's party presented themselves.

Williams turned from the porthole. 'Well, Hubert, we're safe now.'

'Altogether safe?'

'Surely. We stand on New Englander soil. The English or Papal authorities may no more board this aircraft than a ship of ours at sea.' Williams brought out his pocket-watch, which was a miniature version of the clock Hubert had seen at the Embassy: the squares showed 5 33. 'We rise off at six o'clock. The time set for our descent at Arnoldstown Port is two to-morrow afternoon, but winds can advance or retard us.'

After a pause, Hubert said, 'That's very quick.' He was sitting on the cot assigned to him with his knees drawn up.

'The craft can touch 160 miles an hour through the air. But

soon, quite soon, that'll be nothing. Would you like to learn a secret?'

'Yes, Father.'

'Pastor. I think I may safely tell you this, since we've intrinsically left England. Three years ago, at a place in our State of Waldensia, two scientists, the Smith brothers, launched a flying machine, one that lifts itself by means of wings, not gas.'

'I understand, Pastor.'

'It carried only one man and barely touched 90 miles an hour, but that was no more than a beginning. By 1980 a speed of 200 is promised, and more later, much more. Air travel will be transformed.'

This information did not arouse the wonder or enthusiasm Williams had expected. It was in a seemingly listless tone that Hubert said, 'Where's Abraham?'

'About his affairs, I reckon. Why do you ask?'

'Oh . . . no reason, Pastor. He seems a good man. A very kind man.'

'Indeed he is a good man and a kind man, for an Indian.'

'Your indulgence – I don't understand.'

'We expect less from him,' said Pastor Williams, settling his compact, middle-sized frame on his own cot. 'You see, Hubert, God created the Indians and ourselves for two different purposes and in two different ways, and he proclaimed this by making them a different colour from us. This is something everyone must accept. When you come to New England, you must accept it, so let me expound it now.' He paused and put the tips of his fingers together. 'Consider that I speak out of my proper knowledge. The Indian . . . is a child in many ways, very often a virtuous child, but still a child. His mind is less capable to be developed than yours or mine, because his brain is smaller, as our scientists have proved. To mingle with him truly is impossible, and no good can come of trying to. That's why, under God's guidance, we in New England have a design we call separateness: each kind keeps to itself as far as possible, which isn't always easy, because the fairer Indian will constantly try to pass as one of us – they're not all as dark

179

as the colour you wear. Oh, by the by, we'll have that walnut-juice off your face any time. His Honour will open to the Captain that you . . .'

Williams's melodious voice died away. What he had just been saying had led him to do more than merely glance in Hubert's direction, and what he saw made him hurry across the apartment and look more closely. There were streaks of damp among the dye on the forehead and upper lip, and the mouth was clenched tight.

'What is it, child?'

'Please fetch . . . Samuel here.' Hubert spoke as if the muscles of his throat were strained.

'Samuel?'

'I mean Abraham. Please fetch him to me.'

'Hubert, what is it?'

'Oh, Father – Pastor, I've such a pain, such a dismal pain.'

'What pain? Where?'

'I think it started while we prepared at the Embassy. It's in my . . . there,' gasped Hubert, gesturing at the base of his abdomen.

'Let me take a look.'

'No, Pastor, you shouldn't, it's not your . . .'

'My dear, I'm a minister of Jesus and I have children of my own. Lie down straight. Yes, my son has eleven years, more than you, and he's a little taller, but he doesn't talk as well as you do. Raise yourself. I don't think children in New England are as well instructed as they are in your country. Not all our preceptors are . . . Well, Hubert, you cover yourself now and try to rest while I go to the dispensary and fetch you an opiate.'

Pastor Williams walked at a measured pace across the thick carpet to the door that led to the Archpresbyter's apartment. When there was no reply to his knock, he went in and slid the door shut behind him. The dark, heavily-panelled room, its walls hung with excellent coloured photograms of urban and rural New England, was empty. So was the small cubicle, enclosed with fogged glass, that held the sluice and commodation. Williams went out into the passage and broke into a run. The main hall at the head of the gangway was crowded with late arrivals and departing baggage-men. The Archpresbyter was not there, nor, as it proved, in the conversazione-room, the gallery or any other public place on that deck. At last Williams remembered, chided himself for his slowness of wit and hurried to the elevator. Soon a steel cage was carrying him and others up a steel tube that ran between the massive tanks of helium to the top of the envelope. Here was the observation-lounge, its curved ceiling made of a single sheet of glass by a process unknown, or never practised, outside New England. For the amusement and possible edification of passengers, two fair-sized and several smaller telescopes were available, together with star-maps, appropriate chairs, and curtaining-systems to exclude unwanted interior light. On the voyage out, Archpresbyter Pellew had spent most of the hours of darkness gazing at the heavens, and had more than once returned to the room when, as now, there was nothing to be seen from it but day-time sky. It was under this roof that he heard Williams's stammered report.

Within three minutes, they and the ship's surgeon, a fair-haired young man with a slow Cranmerian voice and quick eyes, were standing round the cot where Hubert lay. While left alone he had managed to wipe off most of the dye from his face and hands. He was sweating freely now. The surgeon inspected the reddened swelling with its hard and soft regions, asked a couple of questions, spoke some words of reassurance, and took the two clergymen off with him into the next-door apartment, where he immediately pulled the bell and motioned to the others to sit down.

'We have fourteen minutes before rise-off, which should be quite enough,' said the surgeon, writing on a tablet as he talked. 'The boy must leave the ship and be taken to a hospital aground here. I'll see to it. He needs an action I haven't the skill to perform. One of his testicles has become turned over and its blood-provision thereby cut off. Maybe both are affected – I can't tell for sure. This occurs now and then among those of his age, it seems by chance, or as if by chance. And suddenly, as in thise case. Enter.' The uniformed man who had been told to do so did so, was given two leaves of manuscript

181

and some spoken instructions, and withdrew. 'Someone with the necessary deftness must try to reverse what has happened and restore the blood-provision. Otherwise the organ, or organs, will die.'

'And that would mean . . .' said Joshua Pellew.

'Possible removal.'

'What are the chances?'

'I can't tell.'

'Can't we delay till we reach Arnoldstown?'

'No, Your Honour,' said the surgeon.

'We shall be there in twenty hours.'

'One hour may be too long, sir. To save the organ, at any rate.'

'Surgeon, there are reasons of great import why the boy should remain aboard. Diplomatic reasons.'

'I'm sorry, Your Honour, but I can't be persuaded by any other reasons than surgical ones, and those are quite plain. Hubert, isn't it? Well, Hubert's health is in serious danger, maybe his life. For all I know, infection is possible. But my predictions can't be expert. Any more than my deftness. Whatever the event, Hubert must go aground immediately.'

The Archpresbyter looked at his chaplain, who had been thinking hard, and who now said,

'Your Honour: go to the Captain and tell him we have a stowaway here whom of course neither of us has ever seen before. Tell him the truth if you wish, but that must be the public tale. When the stowaway goes aground to have his sickness relieved, I go with him, out of simple Christian charity, to be of comfort. I'll join you by the next aircraft, or as soon as I can.'

'I mustn't let you do it, Al. The English constabulary will attach you.'

'On what inculpation? Once Hubert's sanction from the Embassy is destroyed, there's no link between him and any of us, none they can prove. And he'll be back in their hands – their task will be done. Now you must give me leave, sir. I have to get myself and my baggage out of this ship.'

As Williams spoke, motors fore and aft set up their deep

throbbing, bells were rung and voices began to be heard repeating, 'All visitors aground.' Hubert was given an opiate by the surgeon, taken from the aircraft on a litter, put into a hospital express that had been standing by for casual needs, and driven off with Williams beside him. Before the vehicle had gone more than a hundred yards, *Edgar Allan Poe* was slowly standing up from her berth, and, by the time the hospital had been reached, she was already distant, half a mile above the western edge of Salisbury Plain and still ascending and accelerating. Williams watched her, his eyes screwed up against the sun, till her course brought her more directly between it and him, and he could no longer see her at all. Then he turned and followed the attendants who were carrying Hubert into the contingency department of the hospital.

CHAPTER SIX

Four days later, though he himself was not at all clear about how long it had been, Hubert awoke from a vague dream of disappointment, of having failed to meet somebody because of a mistake about the place or time. It was the latest of several or many of the same sort, hard to distinguish now from equally vague recollections of comings and goings at his bedside, of being taken from where he was and brought back, of finding himself in another room where bright lights were reflected off metal. But other things were less obscure. Two officials had wanted him to tell them how he had come to be aboard the aircraft, putting their questions in soft voices but over and over again; as Pastor Williams had instructed him before the opiate was administered, Hubert had answered that he had made his way on his own with assistance from a succession of strangers, and that he could remember very little more. Very little? How much? Nothing. How much? Nothing. Father Dilke's curiosity about such points had been easier to satisfy, or to silence, and their talk had shifted to the state of affairs at the Chapel, including the prosperity of Decuman and the others that persisted despite certain understood considerations. Anthony would of course be told the truth in full (or rather that part of it he did not already know at first hand) as soon as possible, but the opportunity had yet to arise, because so far Hubert had seen him only in the company of their parents, and they must not hear any of the truth, not until these events were finished and done with, if then.

At the news that Hubert must be considered a runaway, and on the instruction that any clue to his whereabouts must be reported, Tobias Anvil had done nothing. At the further news, the next evening, that Hubert was lying ill of an unspecified malady in Cholderton Hospital, Tobias had shared it with his wife, to whom he had not addressed a word since the previous morning, that of Lyall's death. He had proposed that the two of them put aside their own difficulties for the time being, and she had agreed at once. On arriving at the hospital, they had been introduced to a surgeon, who had nothing to tell them except that Hubert was receiving attention and that no danger to his life was foreseen as things stood, and to a priest from New England, who had not been very communicative either. It seemed that the latter had insisted on interrupting his journey home, in case Hubert, with whom he had only the most recent and accidental connection, should feel the need of spiritual or other comfort. Even now, when he might have departed with perfect propriety, and indeed with an English transatlantic aircraft near the point of rise-off, he refused to move until he should know the issue of the boy's illness, of the nature of which he said he was altogether ignorant.

They had not had very long to wait. The surgeon had come back, a small paper in his hand; on seeing his face, Pastor Williams had turned and left without a word or a look. The Anvils had started to learn about what had afflicted their son, but after the opening phrases Margaret had collapsed, and Tobias had had to hear the rest of the story alone.

'The name of it is torsion, master, in this case bilateral, which is somewhat unusual. I penetrated the scrotum and tried to untwist the cords, but with no success in the result. The swelling has increased, and one testicle begins to be necrosed, to die. The other must follow. That process would spread unless checked. I must be ready to remove them both.'

'Is there anything different to be done?'

'Believe me, master, I'd do it if there were.'

'Very well.'

'Would you sign this document, sir? It authorizes the action.'

Tobias had taken out his pocket-stylus. 'You'll need a priest's signature besides,' he had said in a voice that made the surgeon look at him suddenly.

'No, this is a casualty, master. Thank you. My deep regrets. However, with God's help your son's health will soon be fully restored.'

'Amen.'

Hubert had not been told every detail of this, but, as on a

previous occasion, his father had seen to it that he understood the essentials. Once again he went over them listlessly in his mind. The division where he lay was neither crowded nor noisy, but there was enough to distract him from his thoughts: the neat rapid movements of the nursing nuns, the shuffling progress of an aged vendor of eggs and fruit, the bell and shaken bowl of a mendicant friar. Then, through the double doors at the further end of the division, Anthony appeared. Hubert felt pleased. They greeted each other, and Anthony asked after Hubert's condition, a shade perfunctorily: it seemed he had a point to come to and, explaining that he could not stay long, he soon came to it.

'There's something I must let you know.' He looked rather grim.

'About me?'

'No, my dear, not about you. About mama. When she came to you here with papa and me, did you see anything you found curious or unaccustomed?'

'Yes,' said Hubert promptly. 'She was sad at what had had to be done to me, but there was more, more in her mind than me. And papa looked at her constantly, but she wouldn't look at him.'

'Yes. This isn't agreeable, but you must hear it. If you don't, you'll be doubtful and distressed, and you may cause hurt.'

'Oh, Anthony, say, for Jesus' sake.'

Anthony took his brother's hand and brought his face close. 'Mama and Father Lyall ... mated together. Then Father Lyall was murdered – I found him dying when I came home after taking you to the Embassy.'

'Oh, Mother of God.'

'As you say. When papa tells you of it, as he'll have to at last, be sure to seem to hear something altogether new.'

'Yes, Anthony.'

'There's more,' said Anthony, tightening his grip. 'Father Lyall wasn't only murdered. He'd been altered besides. That was the more that mama thought of when she was here.'

'What a dreadful concurrence.' Hubert was mildly surprised at how flat the words sounded. 'Her ... and then her son.'

'Not a concurrence – not merely coincident. He tried to obstruct your alteration; perhaps mama persuaded him. That ran him foul of Church and State. So the pigs murdered him by altering him and ... and seeing to it that he bled to death, as a piece of instruction and purification. I had no doubt they were vile, but I thought that the law at least –'

'How do you know, Anthony?'

'I know. I know without having to be let know. But the rest I saw. When mama was told of what had been done, she screamed and wept – she confessed by her actions that ... about herself and Father Lyall. Papa saw it too, and abused her. So, when she was here, she wouldn't look at him, and he looked at her because he was –'

'Yes, I see. How could mama do that with Father Lyall?'

'You'll understand when you – when you've considered it. You mustn't hate her, Hubert.'

'I don't; I grieve for her.'

Neither spoke for a time. Irritably, Anthony tossed a farthing into the friar's bowl and hushed his blessing. Then Hubert said,

'What will papa do? Will he turn her out of doors?'

'No. Our father isn't a bad man, simply one too much given to self-love. This may even improve him. Well, now you see why I had to let you know.'

'Yes, I do. Thank you.'

'Are you troubled? Greatly troubled?'

'No, not greatly.'

'You must consider everything, Hubert.'

Hubert promised he would and, after Anthony had gone, tried to do so, to consider everything. That began with his mother. She had suffered what anyone could have recognized as a cruel loss, and it was no more than the truth that he grieved for her; but, as he lay there, he found that the thought of that loss was being pushed aside – not for ever, not for long – by other thoughts, ones that would not go away.

He believed, he would have had to say he believed, that his mother had had done to her what Ned had done to his girl in the woods, or she could never have borne two children, and that to have had it done to her by Father Lyall had somehow been wonderful enough to make her betray herself to her husband on learning that that would never happen again. He believed those things, but not in the way he believed her words to him in the bower concerning the love of man and woman; from them, he could imagine how she felt, even though he now knew that she had been founding them on a love in every way forbidden; he could reconcile that with all the many things he knew about her, her smile, her step, her handling of a needle or a bowl of tea. To believe both in the same way, to be able to consider both at once, was as difficult as it would be to understand how the same part of a man's mind or body could make Ned talk and behave as he had in the brewery and make de Kooning paint his picture of Eve.

He, Hubert, was going to find that too much for him: he would never fit the pieces together, just as he would never decide what he really felt about having been altered. He saw for a moment that he would never have to do either: the sight of two lovers kissing, news of a friend's marriage, a successful performance in church or opera-house, the smile of a pretty woman, contemptuous stares and whispers as he passed, going among children, praise from an admired colleague, clumsy or malicious inquiries about what it was like to be as he was, suddenly-aroused memories of St Cecilia's, of the night of his escape, of any part of the time when he had been as others were – such small events would bring up one question or the other for a time, leave unaltered his state of confusion or apathy on the point, and then be forgotten as he went on with his life. Perhaps that was how everyone found themselves going about matters, nothing ever measured or settled or understood, not even when they came to die. After all, mankind was in a state of sin.

But what about God? It must be His will that things had turned out as they had, indeed more obviously so than seemed common. That meant that He must be praised for having put an end to all rebellion on the part of His child. The grave young monk who had twice at least visited Hubert's bedside had been positive that it was not required of the sick to pray on their knees, that prayers offered, when possible, in a pious attitude – face to the ceiling, legs extended and together, hands joined – were fully valid. Hubert turned on to his back and made the Sign of the Cross under the covers. In silence, barely moving his lips, he praised God for a time and thanked Him for His favour; then he turned to others. He petitioned that God should show his mother mercy and send her comfort, that He should soften his father's heart towards her, that He should not be angry with those who had helped him when he was a runaway: he ran through the list. What now? Perhaps, though he had ceased to rebel in action, there were still scraps of rebellion in his heart. He prayed for their removal and, after that, for resignation. Let him be patient whatever might befall; let him be not cast down nor puffed up; let him . . .

Hubert realized suddenly that he had stopped praying for some seconds or minutes. Instead, he had been putting his mind into the undirected state in which music, music that must be his because it was nobody else's, might be found there. There was none, which was unexpected after so long an interval: he had not thought of music in this way since before his journey to Rome. This might be a result of the action: the surgeon had warned him not to hope to be altogether well at once. To exercise his abilities, then, he would hear through the Prometheus Variations. This went well enough for a few minutes, but at about the half-way point, immediately before the section in triple time, he was forced to stop, because he could not remember how to go on; the harmonic sequence stayed in his head as firmly as ever, but the flow of the notes had been checked.

At this vexatious moment, one of the nuns, little Sister Ho from Indo-China, came bustling up, all smiles as usual, and presented him with a letter-packet. On the front, his name, nothing more, was written in a hand he thought he recognized; on the red-and-blue bordered card inside, the same hand had written,

My wife and I are below. We know your true state. Hilda is with us. She believes you to be recovering from a stomach ailment. May any or all of us come to visit you for a few minutes?

C. v.d. H.

Hubert could not decide at once. He wanted very much to see his friends, but was afraid that doing so might cause him to feel sad. The thought that they had come nearly a hundred miles to visit him made up his mind. He sent Sister Ho to fetch the three and put the card out of sight. Very soon they were with him. Dame van den Haag kissed him on the cheek, and squeezed his shoulder to show that she would have embraced him more warmly in private. The Ambassador gave him a steady glance and a firm handshake. Hilda stayed near the end of his bed, but smiled and nodded cheerfully. She was dressed for travelling, in a coat of some short reddish-brown fur and a pointed hat of the same material.

'How do you do, Hubert?' asked van den Haag.

'Very well, sir. They tell me I may go home at the week's end.'

'Good . . . I was grieved to hear of your sickness.'

'Yes, it came at an unfortunate time.'

'When I think of the immensity of the chance that brought it about, I'm reduced to silence. Just then. And just that. It's as if . . . I don't know. Maybe a man shouldn't speculate. Well, that's an end of the matter.'

'Yes, sir. I'm heartily grateful for all you did and all the risks you ran.'

'It's nothing, Hubert.'

Van den Haag, by the look in his eyes and the way he spoke, had been trying to tell Hubert of his sorrow at what had happened. Now bitterness had entered his tone for a moment, but he quickly roused himself and asked about the hospital, the nuns, the food. His wife had questions too. Hilda was silent, gripping the bed-rail, leaning back and pulling herself upright after a fashion Hubert had seen before, but she still smiled at him now and then. Quite soon, van den Haag took out his watch and said they must think of going.

'But, sir, it's only a minute since you arrived, and to have come so far for so little . . .'

'We have another reason. We'd still have come without it, but we have an aircraft to take. To New England.'

'How long will you stay, sir?'

'For a long time, I think. I'll be back here next month for a few days, but my office is ended. Our First Citizen has displaced me.'

'Not for what you did on my behalf?' asked Hubert in two sorts of distress.

'No, no. Well, only partly. I'd offended the English authorities a couple of times before. This was just the finale. They knew of your visit to me in Coverley, you were discovered in the aircraft apartment of a New Englander just come from my Embassy, and, although it seems they've learned nothing of the process that took you from one place to the other, that was enough. Yes, the suspect and the guilty are the same to a Romanist – my excuses, Hubert.'

'I should never have asked you . . . I should never have allowed you . . .'

Dame van den Haag laid her hand on Hubert's head. 'Peace, Hubert. We're honoured that you trusted us and asked our help. It was only an evil dispensation that exposed us. And – in private – my husband was never a happy ambassador. For that, a man has to love ceremony, and he doesn't.'

'But to be displaced . . .'

'He's talked already of resigning – no, Cornelius? And we miss our country.'

'But isn't your First Citizen angry?'

'Maybe, maybe,' said van den Haag, smiling. 'He may swell up with rage till he bursts, for me. Oh, it's quite true, I'm altogether too much a Schismatic for this function. So are most of my countrymen. It amounts to a national weakness.'

Half Hubert's distress had been half relieved. 'What function will you take to, sir?'

'I'll build a concert-hall and you shall come and sing in it. We must go, Anna. Yes, Hubert, I will and you shall. I'll write to you at St Cecilia's. Well, I reckon even in England a father can kiss his son, so . . .'

He bent and kissed Hubert and his wife did the same.

'Good-bye, my dear. The Lord protect you.' He turned to Hilda and said severely, 'Two minutes, maid.'

'Ya ya, paps.'

When they were alone, Hubert said awkwardly, 'Your father and mother are very gracious folk.'

Hilda came a little nearer and leaned her hip against the side of the bed. She spoke not fast but with great determination, as if she had taken a wager to finish what she had to say however it was received. 'We have a farm in Latimeria with two hundred Indians on it. Sometimes in the evening we go to their huts and see them dance and play. There are cows and pigs and hens – paps has me help in the dairy. And horses – I have one to myself, named Springer. I mean when I'm there he's mine. He's all black but for a white stocking on his far hind. Some of the tracks in the hills are rough, but he never stumbles, not Springer. It's good that we're done with England and Naples : we can be at the farm much more. Do you love horses?'

'Yes.'

'But maybe you love cities more than farms.' She looked at him, frowning, then said, businesslike as before, 'Would you come to our farm?'

'Yes, but –'

'The sun shines all day long and we swim in the lake. We bring fruit and cookies to eat there, and we light a fire and make hot chocolate, because the water's all melted ice and snow from the mountain. I give you this.'

With hasty movements, she took from the pocket of her coat and passed to him a plain cross enamelled blue, not the same blue as her eyes, but blue.

'Oh, Hilda, how pretty. You must have paid shillings for it.'

'No, nothing. It was mine.'

'Thank you,' said Hubert, closing his hand round the object. 'I wish I had something to give you in return.' (He could not give her, or anyone, the cross Mark had given him.)

She smiled and shook her head, looking at him very directly. 'No need, no need. So . . .'

'What was that word you said in the garden that afternoon? It began with a C or a K. You said it was an Indian word.'

'Kisahkihitin?'

'Yes. What does it mean?'

'Oh, now . . . Well: it means "I love thee." It's Indian. It's truly what they say to each other, the Indians. But other folk say it too. Sometimes. Good-bye till we meet.'

She pointed towards the window, but it must be New England she was pointing at. Before he could speak or make any movement, she had kissed her hand to him, turning away as she did so, and was running off down the aisle of the division.

Hubert realized at once that he had failed to wish Hilda, and her parents too, any kind of divine blessing on departure, and, more slowly and dimly, that that failure had not sprung from any fear of offending Schismatic susceptibilities as he had Domingo's. He would pray to God that the omission might be remedied, but he would not do that for the moment. He could not: he could think only of how it was impossible that he should go to New England before he was twenty-one years old, because his father must by law either go too or send an accredited proxy, and his father would do neither. And after he was twenty-one, indeed much sooner, the design was even more impossible, because he could never be with Hilda after it was obvious that he had been altered. What had Master van den Haag meant by his talk of a concert-hall and singing?

Here, the reasoning part of Hubert's mind shut down. He turned on to his side and pulled the covers up almost over his head, so that only a little light came through. With the blue cross still in his fist, he pretended that he and Hilda were riding horses, side by side. Then he found he could pretend that her horse was running faster and faster, but that his horse did the same, and, even when the ground began to slope upwards and the track become rough, they stayed near each other.

Pope John XXIV was nearly at the end of his day's business in the cabinet of his summer quarter: the documents on the porphyry work-table had been reduced to three, and only three persons remained in attendance. These were Count Paolo Maserati, Inventor-General to the Papacy, Father Gregory Satterthwaite, SJ, the privy secretary who had served His Holiness since eight years before his coronation, and Cardinal Berlinguer. Curtains of Swedish ermine kept out the late-afternoon sun and moved now and then in the slight breeze. At this hour, the plain, the City still scorched in the heat, but it was no more than pleasantly warm two and a half thousand feet up among the Alban hills, and, thanks to clever siting and careful building, the air seemed always fresh in the spacious apartments of the Castel Alto.

The one who evidently found it not quite fresh enough at the moment was Count Maserati. Despite the thinness of his biscotto-coloured woodman style suit, he was sweating a little. He said now in careful English, the mode and language in which the present Pope greatly preferred to be addressed,

'The size of the assay was determined by the Chamber after due process, Your Holiness.'

'On your advice, Count.' The Pope stared heavily through his eyeglasses. 'And, as we and you have just been let know, it was too small.'

'But no assay can ever be large enough to guarantee –'

'We're struck dumb by you. We don't know what to say, we're sure. There's no lack of subjects, after all. Over a hundred and fifty thousand without having to look outside Italy. And what are they? Heretics, apostates, runaways, New Englander spies, Turkish spies – grievous sinners every mother's son. They mean to defy our authority, Count. Do you understand? They're – they're bad folk.'

'Yes, Your Holiness,' said Maserati with conviction.

'And what do you do? You take two hundred of them, a measly two hundred, and have them fornicate their heads off in between doses of Crick's Conductor. Ee, what a shocking fate! What do they care if they do lose their fertility? – they're inside again at the year's end, and they'll never need it there. Why did you not take two thousand? Four thousand? Then the deformities must have appeared, would have been ten or twenty times more likely to appear. Eh?'

'Our facilities would not have allowed so many, Your Holiness.' Maserati spoke with less conviction than before.

'Fuck your facilities! If they lack anything it's your blame and you know it. You are the Inventor-General, we believe.'

There was silence but for the faint sound of cicadas. Frowning, the Pope stared at the nearest wall. It was fifty feet away and, like those adjacent to it, was hung from top to bottom with olive-green velvet. The purpose of this was to rest the eye and to conceal from it the beautiful travertine stone of which the room was built. The ceiling, painted with an awe-inspiring Creation by Tiepolo, was likewise hidden by an immense sheet of white linen. No object was visible, not even a clock or a candlestick, that might show signs of more than the absolute minimum in the way of craftsmanship: not an inch of floor showed between the plain rugs, the table bore a thin but opaque cloth and the chairs were of some black-painted wood with tied-on cushions covered in white silk. It was not (so he often said) that John XXIV disliked art, simply that he saw enough of it at other times to make its absence refreshing when he was at work. Throughout the rest of the building, as throughout the Vatican palaces except for the various cabinets there, art flourished unchecked, indeed perceptibly added to in one room and another by the reigning Pope himself, who knew that this was one ready method of furthering his very settled ambition to be remembered with exceptional vividness as long as the Papacy should last.

The Vicar of Christ let Maserati wait for it a few moments longer, then said with some curiosity, 'How old are you, Count?'

'Fifty-seven, Your Holiness.' Maserati spoke as if the fact singled him out for special and favourable notice, which was what he always tried to do when the Pope asked him this question.

'Well, that's not truly old as men go today. Some reach the zenith of their powers at such an age.' (The Pope was fifty-four.) 'And then again some ... begin ... to decline. Do you feel that you begin to decline?'

'No, Your Holiness.'

'Another error of half this proportion and out go you. Further than that door into the bargain.'

'Yes, Your Holiness,' said Maserati, trying this time to hide his relief.

Here, Cardinal Berlinguer broke in. His English was not nearly as good as the Count's, but then it did not need to be: he had got his red hat two years earlier than the Pope and was second only to him in power. 'May I speak?'

'Oh, we suppose so,' said the Pope impatiently. 'There are two matters still to be conferred upon.'

'I will be short. Consider these numbers. The children we expect in the year is eight thousand and some more. The children who are born is six thousand and some more. This is just the ... denatalità ...'

'Fall in the birth-rate,' supplied the Jesuit.

'Yes, which we want, exact. The deformed children is one per centum and some more. This is almost seventy. Corsica is three thousand three hundred ... square miles and some more. This is one deformed child in forty-seven square miles and some more. This is nearly the same as the English island of Jersey. This morning I study it. Is this ... so bad?'

The Jesuit, a pale, thin-lipped man of fifty, said without expression, 'The design was to run at first for ten years. What do you say to ten deformed children in Jersey, Your Eminence? And some more.'

'It is not so good,' agreed Berlinguer, nodding seriously. 'But I ask is it so bad.'

'We'll be buggered!' The Pope sounded incredulous. 'Here you are, two grown men, and you talk of Jersey, where all they do is farm or idle. We and you don't intend to work our design only in such parts, leave alone dirty little savage places like Corsica. Consider not the square miles but the number of folk. There are almost twelve hundred thousand in London. If Crick's Conductor goes into the drinking-water there, in ten years we have ...' The point of his stylus moved quickly over the tablet in front of him. 'We have almost three thousand children with this particular deformity, and in all England ... over a hundred thousand.'

Cardinal Berlinguer spread his hands. 'But –'

'Yes, it is so bad! There'd be ill feeling among our flock, and if there's one thing we can't abide it's that. There'd be talk of divine displeasure, special pilgrimages to us and all manner of nuisance. And don't forget the matter of safety. Ay, that's what we said – safety. Do you think that no one in Corsica, even in Corsica, has remarked or will ever remark that the year of deformities was also the year when officers were uncommonly interested in records touching births, and when the births themselves were uncommonly few?'

'Shoot them,' said Berlinguer.

'Why, you ... You go too fast, our lad. We're all for a bit of shooting when it's needed, but to shoot the guilty folk means finding them, and finding them means questioning, and questioning means a further threat to safety. We won't have it, do you hear? Crick's Conductor must not be applied again as it now stands.' The Pope turned to Father Satterthwaite. 'Have London let Crick know and order him to continue his trials. No, fetch him here to us ... Now, as to our plague,' he went on, with a glance at the second remaining document, 'we need say very little to you. Our Inventor-General was right at first and at last, as he so often is.'

None of the other three showed the smallest surprise at this change of tenor, certainly not Maserati, who knew quite well that the last phrases were intended to harrow his companions for talking of Jersey, not to mollify him in the least.

'Yes, the indications were plain enough after the provings at East Runton and, uh, that Frenchie spot. The principle was too deadly to be transmitted. By which we mean' – the Pope gave a series of weighty nods at this point – 'that the bastards awoke to life immortal before they could pass it on to their neighbours. The Sitges proving wasn't really needed, but we like to be on the safe side, as you know. We're afraid you'll just have to bear with us. We know we can rely on you to do that. Well, that's nearly four hundred souls the fewer, anyhow. And at least they didn't die in vain. To be reminded that the wrath of God can be strange and terrible and sudden does folk a power of good.

Cease all trials of deadly principles,' he added abruptly to the Jesuit.

'All?' asked Berlinguer.

'Ay, all.' His Holiness gave a long sigh. 'Safety again. See, if we were a canny sod in a village on the coast and we learned of these incidents, do you know what we'd do? We'd conduct a design of night sentinels to watch for strangers, for anything out of the common coming by sea or land. That's what we'd do. And then . . .'

'I said we were wrong to publish these things.'

'Worse to let rumour do its work. Now, we graciously thank the honoured Inventor-General for his attendance and give him our blessing.'

There was more silence when Maserati had taken his leave.

The Pope, neatly-brushed head lowered, gazed at the final paper on the tablecloth before him. His expression was very grim indeed. Berlinguer and Satterthwaite exchanged looks of foreboding.

'It's all too slow,' said the Pope finally. 'Try this, try that, try the other damned thing, give it time and it'll sort itself out. But time's what we and you are short of. Time runs out. We blame these medical inventors. For ever on the go saving life, extending life, protecting life and we don't know what all. Are you aware, Father Satterthwaite,' he demanded with an air of challenge, 'that at this pace there'll be eighty million folk in England by the year of Our Lord 2000?'

'Yes, Your Holiness,' said the Jesuit, who was well enough aware, having himself supplied the figure to his master. 'Too many to feed.'

'Too many to rule,' said Berlinguer.

'There's nought else for it,' said the Pope.

'War,' said Berlinguer.

'If we could only have it our way, it'd be simplicity itself. The English clobbering the bloody Frenchies, that's how it ought to go. But it can't be done. We'd have to intervene, quickly and decisively, else our authority would be weakened, and to our way of thinking that's out of the question. Ah well. Fetch us the Secretary of the War Chamber, the Captain-

General, the High Admiral, the Superintendent of Aircraft and the commandantes in the Active Sphere. By the week's end, Father. Eh, it'll be a right cordial to give old Abdul a sore nose. We're afraid we don't take kindly to Mahometans. All those wives. *And* disputing our authority as the Almighty's vice-regent. He wouldn't much care to have Bulgaria pinched off him, wouldn't our Abdul. Not but what he won't live to thank us at last. After all, he has an excess of folk himself, or will have inside a generation. But we must admit we'd as soon there was some other way.'

This theme was resumed when, Berlinguer having departed to his own castello down the valley, the Pope and his secretary stood on the long terrace that overlooked the plain and, in the furthest distance, the Tyrrhenian Sea. Only a little nearer, it seemed from here, lay Rome, still bright in the declining sun with tints of honey, pale rose, sienna and terracotta; by comparison, the two men were no more than a step from the ruins of the Castel Gandolfo, a Papal abode from early in the seventeenth century until the fatal night in 1853 on which a certain Percy Shelley, excommunicate English runaway and minor versifier, had set fire to it before perishing by his own hand. And the vineyard of the Castel Alto ran up almost to its walls, the source of a wine highly esteemed all over Latium but altogether disregarded by its proprietor, who now clutched a pewter mug of the Yorkshire stingo he regularly imported in bottle by aircraft.

'It's a cruel shame, Greg, truly it is,' said the Pope, munching his lips together as he drank. 'All those men doomed to die. In the cause of Christ, we know. It's the wrong way on, look. The folk to go for are the females. What we mean – a hundred females and one male, suppositional limit to pregnancies in any given stretch of time, one hundred; a hundred males and one female, suppositional limit, one. Our word, if only we could put the women in the field, like in that book of Burgess's. Interesting lad, Burgess. It's a mortal pity he had to go and . . . Well, as we said, we do what we must do. But if we could just go about it differently . . .'

'Aside from artificial regulation.' Only Satterthwaite was on such terms with the Pope as to be able to utter this phrase in his presence.

'That bugger Innocent XVII. We'd give him innocent. A Switzer, he was, and you can't whack them for contrariness. As soon as folk start to really believe – we're not talking about perishing inventors and suchlike, but sensible folk like us and you – as soon as they start to believe that the birth-rate desperately needs control, they go and put it to Innocent that he must sanction artificial regulation in some form. And what does he do? He ups and publishes a Bull declaring any such practice to be murder and its perpetrators to be subject to immediate excommunication. Do you follow us, Greg?'

'Oh yes, Your Holiness,' said the Jesuit, understating the case, in the sense that after all these years he was ahead of the Pope as well.

'Good. Now you see where that lands us and all the Supreme Pontiffs between us and Innocent. To revoke a Bull of an import like that, even to moot it, would lay any Holy Father open to a charge of heresy; at the very best, he must abdicate. Well, we say any: we mean any who's not so powerful that he hasn't a single enemy or rival in the whole Sacred College. In other words, more powerful than us, which we flatter ourselves is saying something. Yes, friend Berlinguer and his merry men would be at us like a pack of wolves and we'd have a Council on our hands before we knew where we were. We've not the slightest intention of landing up like our unfortunate predecessor and namesake in fourteen-whatever-it-was, thank you very much. That's that. And, as you may have heard us mention before, the only other design, to tacitly condone artificial regulation, to turn a blind eye, like Nelson at Lipari – that would be just as fatal. Mortal sin flourishing unrebuked by the Vicar of Christ? Don't make us laugh. See, it's already flourishing as much as we dare permit from Iceland to Cape Town.'

The Pope lifted his mug and a manservant hurried forward to pour a fresh bottle of stingo. Father Satterthwaite declined an offer of more white wine.

'Well, Greg, we and you mustn't take on. There are bright

spots. One comes up tonight, when young Hubertus Incus commences in Rome. A notable occasion.'

'I'd thought that music wasn't among Your Holiness's keenest pleasures.'

'You know bloody well it isn't, but appearing in the character of the foremost of all lovers of art is. You know that too. And this time there'll be a mite added. Now and then our thoughts will turn to Abbot Thynne, once the lad's principal. He's a right gowk, is Thynne. Someone lets him know – he'd never have guessed it himself – that we require Hubertus in our city. And what does he do? He goes and petitions his Cardinal Archbishop to intercede for him with the King. We ask you! What could the King have done, a mere babe, new to the post, not yet crowned even? His father might have made a good show, but' – the Pope shook his head slowly – 'no more than a show. As it is, of course, young William hears not a word of the matter, and . . . How does Thynne suppose a man's given Canterbury under an English Pope? As we said, he's a gowk. Well, we trust he soon settles down nicely in Madras. It's a fine city, we hear, though a touch hot in summer.'

The great bells began to sound in the tower above their heads.

'We say, is it that already? We must go and make ourselves beautiful for our guest. And you, Greg, hop to the transmitter and forewarn the Captain-General and the others of our design. No time like the present – that's our motto.'

Over fifteen years afterwards, in the first week of December, a new production of Valeriani's *L'Arlecchinata* was put on at the Teatro Nuovo dell' Opera. The recent alterations and additions to the building, designed to fit it for performances of works using the largest forces, such as the present one, Wagner's *Kreuz* and the Butterworth trilogy, had been the occasion of an impressive architectural feat. The opera-house now dominated the southern side of the Piazza Venezia, but by far the greater part of the medieval and ancient structures at the site had been preserved: in particular, the remnants of the tomb of Publius Bibulus, a landmark dating back to the first century BC, had been skilfully incorporated into the eastern end of the ridotto. To stand at that spot was to feel the continuance of all the centuries of Roman history as a living thing; so, at least, Pope John XXIV, now in the twenty-fifth year of his reign, had declared in a public letter to the principal mason.

On a great chord, sounded by seventy voices and more than a hundred and fifty instruments, including two piano-fortes and organ, the first of the two acts ended. A couple of minutes later, Hubertus Incus was stretched on a silk-covered day-bed in his private green-room, eyes closed and body relaxed. His wig and outer costume hung near by; letters and tachygrams, flowers, fruit and confectionery covered a large marquetry table-top and overflowed on to the floor. Now and then, he sipped at the glass of still mineral water which, by invariable custom, was to be his only refreshment until after the performance. There came a tap at the door and his dresser answered it. A liveried usher handed over two name-cards, turning his head aside and raising his eyes to heaven in a way that told of much pressure or reward. The dresser gave a shrug and approached his master.

'No, Ettore, nessuno.'

'Ma è dui gentiluomi inglesi, maestro – ecco.'

'Madre de Dio! By St George's sacred ... Well. Si si, Ettore, subito.'

Very soon the usher had admitted two well-attired young men in their later twenties. The shorter of them was an ordinary-looking priest in clerical black and grey, the taller a handsome dark-haired fellow in slashed velvet with pink lace at throat and wrists. What followed was an interval of happy shouts, embraces and hand-wringings.

'Hubert, my dear! It's truly you, then!'

'Thomas! Mark! After so long!'

'You look not a day older, Hubert,' said Mark. 'Quite unchanged.'

'Oh, taller,' said Thomas. 'Grander. And far richer!'

Upon that came more laughter and an offer of wine, which both visitors accepted readily.

'You surprise me, Mark – I remember you as one likely to grow into a famous abstinent.'

'Oh, Hubert, was I so dismal? Tom and Decuman must have improved me after you left us.'

'Do you hear of Decuman? Where is he now?'

Thomas grinned. 'At this moment, most likely in the parlour or bedchamber of some Bulgarian miss. He serves in the troops of occupancy there. Before, he was at the taking of Adrianople and won a cordon for valour.'

'I can well believe it. By St Peter, what a war that was.'

'Thirty million Christians dead, men, women and children.'

'Well, at least we won,' said Thomas, trying to restore a light tone. 'When the Turk entered Brussels I thought we were done for, and then ... Strange that he should come so far and be dislodged so fast. Enough. Hubert, your voice is a miracle still. Mark and I have been in raptures.'

'Thank you both, I'm pleased.'

'What a career you've had,' said Mark. 'It must be a great satisfaction to you – the practising of the art, I mean.'

'What do you do in Rome, the pair of you? You didn't come all these miles to hear me sing.'

'Wrong,' said Thomas. 'In my case, wrong. I am here on just that purpose. Oh, for the rest of the presentation too, and the state of the theatre. Let me explain. I have a post with a weekly journal called the *Onlooker*. They sent me to write of this occasion and of you especially.'

'I knew you'd be a writer of some kind.'

Mark said with a smile, 'He's a writer of another kind as well, though he's too modest to let you know himself. Of a most particular kind.'

'Not TR?'

'Certainly TR,' said Thomas. 'Oh yes, it's grown respectable since the war, some say because of the war. Even Mark will read it quite openly.'

'I never see it now. By the look of you, it must reward you well enough.'

'Nothing ever seems enough to a man with a wife and a child and another on the way.'

'I can imagine. You're in Rome about Church affairs, Mark?'

'Like Tom, to hear you. Or not altogether like Tom: I needed to make a pilgrimage, and I wanted to see the Vatican, but it wasn't till I found he was to come that I needed and wanted pressingly. And you've justified me, Hubert. Such music. Such a prodigious work.'

'Yes.'

'You speak as if you could do better,' said Thomas jocularly.

'Not now.'

'Do you still compose? Old Master Morley asked me, if ever I saw you, to ask you that.'

'No. Tell him he was right: there's never time. Oh, don't mistake me – of course this is a prodigious work, but some of that is in its size. Too much. Valeriani couldn't or wouldn't see that what he must do was simply abandon the whole system of . . .'

'We'll leave you now, my dear,' said Thomas, breaking the silence. 'Will you sup with us later?'

'Yes! Wonderful! But I must be host. Come back here afterwards and we'll go in my express.'

When the time came, Hubertus Incus moved in front of the long glass to be dressed. His eye fell on the reflection of the two crosses he wore round his neck. One of them was Mark's gift; he would produce it at supper and tell of all that had happened from when he received it till his capture aboard the *Edgar Allan Poe* – to talk of it as a simple capture was easiest and best. The other cross, the blue one, would probably excite inquiry; he would say as usual that it was his mother's gift. That too was easiest and best.

His wig was fitted; his paint was freshened; he was ready. Soon he stood in the wings, about to launch 'Che è migliore?', by common consent the aria of Valeriani's that made the heaviest demands on skill and musicianship. The double-basses began their pedal and he advanced on to the stage.

Two corpulent old men sat in the second row of the royal tier. Neither moved so much as a finger until the voice had ceased and the great auditory was filled with applause that quite blotted out the orchestral postlude. Then they turned to each other. Tears covered the face of the older of the two, who nodded his head slowly.

'Deo gratia,' said Viaventosa.

'Amen,' said Mirabilis.

ENDING UP	60p ☐
THE RIVERSIDE VILLAS MURDER	95p ☐
I LIKE IT HERE	50p ☐
THAT UNCERTAIN FEELING	50p ☐
GIRL 20	40p ☐
I WANT IT NOW	60p ☐
THE GREEN MAN	95p ☐
WHAT BECAME OF JANE AUSTEN?	
AND OTHER QUESTIONS	50p ☐
ON DRINK	60p ☐

All these books are available at your local bookshop or newsagent, or can be ordered direct from the publisher. Just tick the titles you want and fill in the form below.

Name ....

Address ....

   ....

Write to Panther Cash Sales, PO Box 11, Falmouth, Cornwall TR10 9EN

Please enclose remittance to the value of the cover price plus:

UK: 22p for the first book plus 10p per copy for each additional book ordered to a maximum charge of 82p.

BFPO and EIRE: 22p for the first book plus 10p per copy for the next 6 books, thereafter 3p per book.

OVERSEAS: 30p for the first book and 10p for each additional book.

Granada Publishing reserve the right to show new retail prices on covers which may differ from those previously advertised in the text or elsewhere.